P9-BHY-801

The Other Side
of the River

The Other Side of the River

Douglass Wallop

W · W · NORTON & COMPANY

NEW YORK · LONDON

First Edition

The text of this book is composed in Janson, with display type set in Janson Italic. Composition and manufacturing by The Haddon Craftsmen, Inc.

Library of Congress Cataloging in Publication Data

Wallop, Douglass, 1920–
    The other side of the river.

    I. Title.
PS3573.A44O8   1984   813'.54   83-23729

ISBN 0-393-01864-4

W.W. Norton & Company, Inc.
500 Fifth Avenue, New York, N.Y. 10110
W.W. Norton & Company Ltd.
37 Great Russell Street, London WC1B 3NU

1 2 3 4 5 6 7 8 9 0

Contents

Acknowledgments

For THEIR INVALUABLE HELP and advice, the author wishes to extend gratitude to Circuit Court Judge Harry E. Clark; to Dr. Leonard Ainsworth and Mrs. Elizabeth Ainsworth; to Richard H. Sothoron, Jr., and Jane Tolar O'Connor; and to Ben Forrest and Mrs. Norma Forrest.

Part I

Prologue . . .

One

SLIPPING INTO A WINDOW SEAT in the nonsmoking
section, she placed a slim black case on her lap and leafed
through its contents. Once the plane was in the air, she
latched the case, glanced briefly at the sunlit Manhattan
skyline, let her head fall back, and closed her eyes.

At thirty-two, Anne Ellis was a senior editor at Castle
Press, a highly successful publishing house on lower Park
Avenue. She was flying to Washington for a meeting with
a man named Hamilton Carver. A meeting with Carver had
been sought for years by every sizable publishing house in
New York. Financier, developer, womanizer, surrounded
by a battery of lawyers and a cadre of bodyguards, Carver
in the years since 1960 had played as large a part as any one
man could in changing the face of the eastern seaboard of
the United States. Little was known of his personal life.
What little had been published was fragmentary and specu-
lative, and there was every reason to believe that an "as-
told-to" story of his life or an unvarnished biography would
gross big money for the publishing house lucky enough to
land the contract.

Castle Press had been seeking an interview for almost a
year. Finally one of Carver's lawyers called to say that
Carver had agreed to a meeting, and several days later the
date and time had been set by a woman identifying herself
as Carver's appointment secretary. When she asked who
would be coming, she was told there would be two: Robert
Kendall and Anne Ellis. Bob Kendall was Castle's executive
vice-president and editorial director. Anne was one of several editors with whom he worked most closely. The
woman made careful note of the names, asking the spelling
of each. Three days later she called back to say that Carver

would see Anne alone and that Kendall's presence would be unnecessary.

When Kendall phoned to ask why, he was told politely but firmly that unless the meeting was held precisely on Carver's terms there would be no meeting. The woman then asked Kendall if he would be good enough to tell Anne that the shuttle leaving La Guardia at three o'clock Friday afternoon would be met at National Airport by a car and driver.

Anne had chosen her costume that morning carefully. With polished brown leather boots, she wore a flared gray skirt and a black turtleneck. Over her arm she carried a plaid cape. Shortly after four o'clock, as she filed out with the debarking passengers, she was greeted by a uniformed chauffeur, who seemed to have no trouble recognizing her. Tipping his visored cap, he introduced himself as Thomas. The car was a black Cadillac drawn up near the main terminal in the parking area normally reserved for members of Congress and justices of the United States Supreme Court. The driver opened the door for her, and soon they were moving along the Potomac and across the Fourteenth Street Bridge into Washington.

Twenty minutes later Anne was ushered into the living room of a house in Georgetown and asked to wait. As she waited she inspected the room with admiration. The walls were covered with vertical strips of pine paneling. In the intervals between the panels stood bookcases filled with expensively bound volumes so ornate and of such beautiful leather that one might have guessed the books had been chosen solely for the uniformity and beauty of their bindings. In one corner of the room stood a mammoth concert grand piano, a Bechstein, a renowned German make used by Wagner and Debussy and other notable composers—a make that by 1982 was bringing as much as twenty-five thousand dollars in elite New York auction houses.

The door opened and softly closed. As it did so, the telephone rang. Anne turned. The man who had entered was looking at her without expression. Circling behind the piano, he picked up the phone, said, "Yes," and stood listening, his back to his guest. "Yes," he said again, hung up, and turned.

Anne, seated in a yellow leather chair, cape over her arm, her long legs crossed, confronted Hamilton Carver. Already she was finding him a man of arrogance bordering upon rudeness. He seemed totally humorless. Lean and wiry, tall for his generation, he had the body of a gymnast. A tan suede shirt, buttoned at the neck, molded his upper torso as tightly as if it had been a layer of rawhide. A horseshoe of bristling gray hair outlined an expanse of baldness, and with it went a beard as closely cropped as his hair. The beard seemed to intensify the glitter of his dark eyes, as did the deep walnut tan he had taken from wherever it was that he had chosen to spend the winter and early spring.

There was something about his appearance that she found deeply disturbing. She summoned a bright smile. "Mr. Carver . . . I'm Anne Ellis. I love your house. It's just beautiful."

"It's not mine." His voice was deep and resonant. He was seated now on the piano bench facing the keyboard. "It belongs to a friend. I just borrowed it for the occasion."

Offering no food, drink, or amenities of any kind, still seated at the piano, eyes boring into hers, he came straight to the point. "What I have in mind is this. I'll find someone of my choice to do the writing. 'By Hamilton Carver,' in other words, 'as told to so-and-so.' Is that the way it's normally worded?"

"Yes . . . it could be done that way."

"The financial terms are of no great importance to me," Carver went on. "What I do insist upon is that you agree to publish the manuscript exactly as I hand it to you. Not a word is to be changed."

Anne frowned. With her long, slim fingers she pushed back her tumbling mass of auburn hair.

"Your part will simply be to publish it as written and

thereby make what I'm sure will be a considerable sum of money." Carver touched a piano key. "Your company will perform as functionary."

Anne recrossed her legs and cleared her throat. "Mr. Carver, I'm not at all sure that's possible. I'm not sure it would be possible at *any* reputable house."

She was trying to keep her composure, trying to control the fear that already was beginning.

Carver shrugged. "It's up to you."

"Mr. Carver, may I explain something? We are—"

Carver started to interrupt, then thought better of it. He smiled. "Go ahead, Mrs. Ellis."

"We are a commercial house. We will have a big stake in this book and for us to surrender all—discretionary authority would be, I think, out of the question. After all, we're not a vanity press."

For the first time in the three years since she had stopped smoking, Anne found herself longing for a cigarette. After a moment she went on. "I will, of course, carry back your terms to the company—but as tempting as it would be to publish a book about you, I think I know what their reaction will be. There's simply no way we could serve as your functionary, as you call it. The instrumentality of your published self-portrait."

Carver was looking at her without expression.

"Your writer, whoever he or she is, would be subject to the same editorial suggestions—editorial constraints—as our other writers. We simply couldn't write a blank check."

Carver was looking down at the keyboard, as if he had not heard her, as if his thoughts were far away.

"In addition to all the other factors, if the book should contain anything libelous—"

Carver wasn't listening. "Regardless?" he asked softly.

"I beg your pardon?"

"Suppose, let us say . . ."—he was looking into her eyes again—"the editor assigned to this particular book should be—yourself. And suppose, let us say . . ."—he shrugged and touched a piano key—"that a sum of money should be

14

deposited in your name. . . ."

"Mr. Carver, it simply doesn't work that way."

"At no price?"

Anne's eyes were pained, her brows knit. "I'm not sure I believe what I'm hearing," she said. "I think maybe this has been a terrible mistake, Mr. Carver. I think I should go now."

She looked away, then looked once again into his eyes, which had not left hers. He was smiling faintly. "Please don't go yet," he said.

"I see absolutely no point. . . ."

"Please don't go yet," he said again.

As she got to her feet, he at last rose from the piano and moved across the room. Although Anne was a tall young woman, he was a head taller. Again he was looking directly into her eyes. His were unlike any she had ever known. He touched her arm and something shot through her body. "You're a very pretty girl," he said.

"I'd like to go now," she said.

He circled to the telephone and pressed a button. "I'm sorry you came all the way down here for nothing," he said as he returned to her side. "But—maybe it hasn't been for nothing."

For long moments their eyes held. There were two taps at the door. Carver swung it open. At the threshold stood the chauffeur.

"Mrs. Ellis is ready to return to New York now," Carver said.

Anne was back at La Guardia by seven and home by eight. She lived with her husband in a three-room flat just off Washington Square. Too upset to eat supper, she sat in the dark at the bedroom window, sipping wine and looking out at the lights of the square.

Bob Kendall lived in Darien, Connecticut, with his wife and two boys. Toward nine, she called him and told him what had happened.

"Well the arrogant, pompous son of a bitch!" Kendall

said. "Okay, that's the end of that. Let's just forget it. I'd love to oblige the son of a bitch, but there's no way we can contract to print a manuscript exactly as he wants it before we even know what's in it. Sorry you had such a wasted trip."

"It's okay," she said.

"Have you told Charlie about it?"

"He's not home yet."

"I'm sorry, Anne."

"It's okay. . . ."

She hung up and looked down at the square, at the people passing in ones and twos beneath the lights.

She sat at the window for a long while.

Two weeks later, Carver's secretary would call her at the office and say that Mr. Carver wanted her to have drinks and dinner with him. A car would pick her up promptly at five. Could she make it? She said yes.

Two

IN AN ELEGANTLY RURAL setting on the Eastern Shore of Maryland, perhaps three months after Anne Ellis's meeting with Hamilton Carver, the day had been bright and sunny. Out over the cove, fluffs of cloud sailing before the mild breeze made drifting shadows on the bright blue water. The cove described nearly a full circle, with a big sweep to the east and its wide mouth to the west. Facing southwest across the mouth of the cove was a rambling gray-shingled house owned by a middle-aged couple, Warren and Martha Donaldson. On the opposite point stood a brick house of Norman architecture, surrounded by trees that had been allowed to spill their boughs over the slopes and turrets of the slate roof, so that it looked like a house in a forest in the chateau country of France. That summer it was being lived in by a young woman named Daisy King.

Daisy had spent the day very much as she spent most of her days. For an hour in the early afternoon she talked with her doctor. When he was gone she lay down in her room for a while and now toward evening went outdoors. Slim and delicate in blue jeans and a frilly white blouse, she sat across from the Donaldson house and watched the light begin to fade. Two mallard ducks lay nearby and it soothed her to look at them. She had love for wild things, love for light and dark and for the jagged silhouettes made by the tall, sharp blades of marsh grass bunched along the shore at the foot of the yard.

Silently, ritualistically, the ducks got up and waddled off in the twilight. She followed them with her eyes to the foot of the yard where, as she knew they would, each in turn jumped from the lawn up to the dock. The interval was only an inch or so, but nevertheless they jumped, and she loved them for the ungainly way they did it, and for all the ungainly things they did. A moment later, although she could no longer see them, she heard the abrupt, sustained flapping that meant they had flown off to spend the night somewhere on the water. By day they slept in the yard; by night on the water.

For Daisy, now in the second year of elegant imprisonment, nature could be a vast sufficiency. When there was a void, nature could rush in and fill the emptiness to overflowing. During these terrible years, she had taken refuge in nature and in observing the precise way things looked. She liked to feel herself dissolving into nothing, drowning in a job, or a higher thing—something more powerful than herself. Sometimes the tiniest thing could do it: a sprig of wildflower, the shape of a cloud, the way one twig branched from another. At other times nothing would do, and she would give in to the acute depression that made her life so miserable.

In the soft light her face glowed with fresh sunburn

from being out in the sailboat that morning. Her wispy flaxen hair was gathered in back with a white ribbon. She had a small face dominated by high cheekbones. Her eyes were deep, dark pools of sadness.

She continued to watch as the light deepened toward purple. Presently across the river at the Donaldsons' house, headlights flashed on. Watching, she saw the car turn and then leave, its headlight beams bouncing and then disappearing down behind the trees that lined the Donaldsons' driveway.

When the car was gone, she walked to the end of the dock and got into the boat that was tied alongside, the mainsail still draped over the boom, just as she had left it that morning.

She hoisted the mainsail, then the jib, and soon the boat was gliding through the water. Its bow sent back darts of light, and from the stern there was another trail, a string of green crystals, eddying and curling and melting into the dark water. The breeze was mild, but the boat traveled on very little air, its molded plywood hull shaped like a canoe, flowing back to a gracefully tapered transom. Her touch was expert. She knew every inch of the cove, knew the parts that in afternoon lay in shade, and it was in these that she would often drop a small anchor and spend hours, reading and gazing at the reflections.

In the houses around the cove, distant oblongs of light had begun to appear. She glided on through the darkness, glided with the curve of the shore, following its arc, and the breeze kept coming forward with her. She knew that close to shore the wind, whether it had been fore or aft, tended toward the beam, so that now as she kept sailing around the cove the breeze kept moving forward as she went. She thought of it as the curvature of the wind.

Off to the right was the mouth that led from the cove to the river, and if she so desired she could sail right through the mouth, out into the river, and on into the world. But she knew she would not. She would continue sailing always endlessly around the cove.

Prologue . . .

That afternoon she had described to the doctor what she felt about the cove and its mouth, and he had listened without replying. For a long while they sat in silence, and then she began speaking as if to herself, as if she had no awareness of his presence.

"There was this bird that sang at night and it kept my husband awake," she said. "I think it may have been a whippoorwill. So he'd take his shotgun and go outside and shoot at where he thought the bird was singing from. Only he'd never hit it, and soon it would start singing again. It used to make him furious. He loved to shoot things, loved to hunt. Killing things meant so very much to him. In his spare time what he liked most was to hunt."

"There are many just like him."

"Yes," Daisy said.

Presently she had nothing more to say, and the rest of the hour was spent in silence. Twice a week for the past eight months the doctor had been visiting the house and before that the private mental institution where she had been confined after a marriage befouled by abuse and violence. The marriage had produced a child that had been taken from her because she was deemed emotionally unfit to raise it.

On the elongated dining room table, candles were lit and three places were set. In the candlelight they were moving silhouettes, moving side by side, one towering above the other. Turk held her chair, then gently slid it forward as she sat down. Patting her shoulder, he circled to the far end of the table and seated himself. In the light of the candles, he smiled at her and then sat in silence, a sort of healthy root, a tanned, ruddy, burnished root of a young man.

In the elegant setting, the sedate light, dinner was served with elaborate movements, almost as if in slow motion. Daisy knew that it was nothing more than a stately charade, performed by Noreen for Noreen's own amusement, the small flourishes, the elaborate spooning of vegetables, the circling around Daisy's chair to get to the other end of the table. "What did *you* do today, Nory?" Turk asked, looking up as she approached.

Noreen made no reply, but simply in ebon hauteur held the serving dishes for him one by one until he had taken what he wanted, then took her own place at the table.

Turk had already begun attacking his plate. "Anybody wanna watch *Dallas?*" he asked presently. "Daze?"

"No thanks."

"Nory?"

"I have a book," Noreen said.

"Big deal," Turk said.

For a long while he sat once more in silence, raising his head occasionally to gaze first at one and then at the other. In the candlelight the muscles of his long, tanned jaw lengthened and tightened as he chewed. "I'm gonna watch the Orioles if nobody wants to watch *Dallas,*" he said finally. "Startin' late: Anaheim."

"No point in letting the set go to waste," Noreen said.

Turk grinned at her sarcasm.

"Would you like some tea, Daisy?" Noreen asked.

"No thanks, I don't believe so."

Noreen was on her feet. Turk's eyes were on her rump and thighs as she moved toward the kitchen. Now he looked the length of the table at Daisy. "Did you know your father called today?" He raised his voice. "Did you tell Daisy her father called today?"

Noreen returned and took her place again. "Your father called while you were with the doctor," she said. "He's coming down."

Daisy frowned. "*When?*"

"In September."

"Oh."

"For your birthday. Or maybe the week after. He wants to do a little dove shooting while he's here."

"Yes, of course. September is dove season, isn't it?" Daisy sat lost in thought. Presently she picked up her fork as if to continue eating, then immediately set it down again.

20

"Any dessert?" Turk asked.

"Ice cream, if you want it," Noreen said. "Grapes. Would you like any, Daisy?"

"No thanks, nothing for me," Daisy said.

"I'd like some ice cream," Turk said.

"It's in the freezer," Noreen said.

Turk got up from the table and disappeared into the kitchen.

"Hey, Turkey," Noreen called.

"Yeah?"

"Bring me some grapes."

"Gotcha," Turk called. In a few moments he returned with a huge dish of ice cream for himself and grapes for Noreen.

"Thanks, Turkey," Noreen said.

"It's okay," Turk said. He began eating his ice cream and was nearly finished before he noticed that Daisy was sobbing. He called out, "Hey, Daze!" as she moved swiftly from the room, but he knew better than to follow. He was well trained, like a well-trained dog. He knew not to jump on the beds or the sofa, knew where he could go and what was off-limits.

"Leave her alone," Noreen said.

"I *am* leaving her alone," Turk said. He helped Noreen clear the dishes and then sat smoking until it was time for the Orioles game to begin.

Three

IT HAD BEEN just past 8:30 when Martha Donaldson backed her classic 1965 Lincoln convertible phaeton from the carport of the house across the cove and headed for Carsons Mills to meet the bus. The evening was warm and she had put the top down. The route was filled with by-ways, but it was a trip she had made many, many times, and she knew it well. It led over back roads, narrowed by curtains of dense foliage, and she drove with her bright beams high, alert for deer. In this part of the world, deer could be a menace to cars and drivers as well as to themselves. They crossed roads in great unheeding leaps, and sometimes a leap landed them smack in the middle of a car hood.

Martha was scheduled to leave the next day with a tour group on a chartered flight to Italy. As she drove she was filled with uneasiness and doubt, knowing that her plans hung by a thread. Solid enough until that very afternoon, they now depended upon a young man she did not know and knew nothing about, the young man whose bus she was meeting. She prayed that she would like him; yet she knew that if there was even a shred of doubt in her mind, she would not hesitate to cancel her trip.

In early winter her husband Warren had suffered a massive heart attack. Warren was recovering nicely. He felt he was perfectly capable of being alone, and it was true that in most ways he needed no help. The person most in need was herself, and what she needed was to avoid waking at four o'clock in the morning in some Italian village, gnawed with fear that her husband might be on the floor with another heart seizure, alone in the house, stretching a hand for the telephone, not quite able to reach it.

The headlights picked up an opossum, and Martha shuddered, mostly at the thought of Warren suffering another heart attack but also because of the opossum. Opossums always made her shudder. Dazzled by the headlights, the opossum paused next to a ditch and she sped on, glad she had not hit it. Hating them as she did, she would have hated still more hitting one. On she went, threading her way over the intricate network of bypasses and shortcuts learned over the years, past fields in which her headlights shone over tiny sprouts of new corn and past imposing entranceways that, although her speed was too great to read them, she knew were hung with signs that said *His Majesty's Indul-*

22

gence, Troth's Plight, and other Elizabethan-sounding names bestowed upon stately homes that dated back to the 1600s. It was an unusual area of the United States, but Martha's mind was not upon her surroundings. She was thinking instead of the sequence of events that had led her to this moment.

Years earlier, Martha's unfortunate sister Agnes had made the mistake of marrying one Roy Bender, of Teaneck, New Jersey. It had been a poor choice, a poor marriage. Roy Bender as a young man had slick black hair, a pencil mustache, small black eyes, and skimpy eyebrows that he made skimpier still by shaving and reshaping them. From early in the marriage he had a look of pallor, of ill health; yet he had lived on and on and on. Roy once sold billiard tables for a living and later, washing machines. In the infancy of television, he was an addict of roller derbies and wrestling matches. He had also bet on trotting races and picked up bag girls in supermarkets.

Over the years, Martha had received many a disquieting letter from poor Agnes. In her letters, Agnes always tried to put a brave face on things; yet envy and self-pity ran through them like a river of arsenic. Toward the end of each letter, angling for an invitation, she included the wish that "our paths may soon cross," sometimes varying this with the hope that "we may see each other ere too many moons have passed."

The union of Agnes and Roy Bender had been afflicted by a son, Eliot, now somewhere between thirty and thirty-five. Martha had not seen her nephew for many years. She knew him only through the letters of her sister, who spoke of him as a bright young man, rich in promise, but one who was having trouble finding himself, "like so many of your bright young kids today."

In a phone conversation in May, Martha happened to mention her forthcoming trip to Italy and the problem she was having in finding someone to be with Warren while she was away.

"What a shame," Agnes said. "Well, heavens, I'm sure Eliot would be *glad* to stay with him."

Martha was startled into a few moments of silence. Then: "I never *thought* of Eliot. . . ."

"I'm sure he'd love to spend some time in the country," Agnes said. "New York can be awful in the summer."

"What's . . . Eliot doing *now?*" Martha asked.

"Helping his father. Roy has a little bookshop in New York and Eliot helps out."

"*Book* shop?" The idea of Roy Bender having any connection with books seemed inconceivable.

"Religious books," Agnes said. "Religious books and articles. They're doing very well."

Martha was stunned. "How nice," she managed.

"I think it would be so wonderful if Eliot could get to know . . ." Agnes's voice broke. "It's always seemed so strange, so sad, that two families . . ."

Martha was beginning to feel pinned to the wall. She had never stopped feeling sorry for Agnes, feeling guilty that her own standard of living should always have been so high and her sister's so meager.

Agnes by now was sobbing. "Mother would feel so disappointed if she knew our families had had so little contact over the years. It's as though we . . . weren't even a family."

Martha by now was thoroughly miserable. All the guilt she had felt for so many years now came rolling up and overwhelmed her. "The years slip by so quickly," she said.

"Oh, they do, they do!" Agnes said.

"We'll have to see if we can't do something about it," Martha said. "How about his job at the bookshop?"

"I'm sure Roy could spare him for a couple of months."

"*Well,*" Martha said brightly. "I don't see why it might not work out. I don't see why it might not work out at all. I'll talk with Warren and you talk with Eliot and I'll call you. Or you call me. How is your arthritis, Agnes?"

"Worse," Agnes said. "I don't get out much. Not even to the city. I haven't been over to New York in three years."

Prologue . . .

Warren Donaldson was a man known for his kindliness, a man of goodwill toward the human race, but he had a blind spot on the subject of Roy Bender. He couldn't stand him, and Martha knew that the prospect of spending the summer with Roy's son would strike him as no great bargain.

Listening as Martha explained her predicament, her feelings about her sister, Warren patted her arm tenderly. For months she had devoted most of her waking hours to nursing him back to health, and to have her deprived of her trip would be unthinkable. Warren took a deep breath. "Okay, let's try it. If it doesn't work out, I'll tell him I've decided to close up the house and go up to Maine for the rest of the summer. Hell, I don't need anybody in the first place."

"Unless there's somebody here, I won't go," Martha said.

It was Agnes who called back to say that Eliot would be delighted to come.

Martha said Warren would be delighted to have him.

A couple of weeks later Martha was briefly tempted to change her mind, for out of the blue came a call from a young man who said he had heard they were looking for a caretaker for the summer. Confronted so unexpectedly with this embarrassment of riches, Martha hesitated a moment and then said, "Oh, I'm so sorry. We've already made arrangements with my nephew from Teaneck."

"Teaneck, New Jersey? *Really?* I have relatives in Teaneck. What's his name?" The young man had a pleasant voice, a pleasant laugh.

"Eliot Bender—do you know him?"

"Eliot Bender . . . Nope. Afraid not. Well, thanks very much, ma'am. Sorry to disturb you."

Thus the matter had stood until that very afternoon. With her departure for Italy less than eighteen hours away, Martha was in the yard pruning rosebushes, glancing about the cove, happily looking forward to her trip, knowing that Eliot would just about be boarding his bus and would very soon be barreling down the Jersey Turnpike. Then the call came from Agnes—telling her that Eliot would be spending the summer in California instead of with his Uncle Warren.

"Oh dear!" Martha wailed. "Oh, *Agnes!*"

"Don't worry. He's found a wonderful young man to take his place. We wouldn't leave you high and dry, Martha."

Martha was doing her best to fight back her anger, feeling foolish, feeling victimized, remembering that it was only out of pity for her sister that she had agreed to Eliot in the first place.

"It was such a marvelous opportunity that he simply couldn't turn it down, dear," Agnes was saying. "He'll be producing movies! Can you imagine?"

Martha's voice was cold. "I wasn't aware that he knew anything about movies," she said. "What kind of movies?"

"Religious themes," Agnes said. "I told him I was sure you wouldn't want to stand in his way. Please don't be upset, dear. I'm sure this other boy will be just fine."

"When can he be here?"

"He's on the bus right this very minute. The same bus Eliot was taking."

"How long have you known about this, Agnes?"

"Not until yesterday," Agnes replied. "It was a last-minute thing, honestly, Martha."

"What's the young man's name?"

"Mark. Mark something or other."

"Have you met him?"

"No, but Eliot and Roy both speak very highly of him. They're sure you and Warren will like him."

Martha by now was nearing the end of her drive. Over a bridge she sped. The water was dark, but here and there along the shore lights twinkled. Presently she entered another dark stretch of road, tunneling through dense foliage, and then far in the distance, at the very end of the tunnel, she saw the receding bright red taillights of a bus. She heard the roar of its motor as its gears were shifted and it strained

for speed. As she neared the darkened Gulf station that
served as depot, a car was just pulling away, taking the same
direction the bus had taken, following the taillights of the
bus down the road.

Now in the full glare of her high beams, she saw old-
style gasoline pumps and a sign that said "Continental
Trailways," and then she saw, seated on the steps of a sloping wooden porch, the figure of a man wearing a backpack.
He got to his feet. She gave the horn a light tap. "Hel-lo,"
she called in a singsong. "Are you Eliot's friend? I'm his
aunt, Martha Donaldson."

"Good evening, Mrs. Donaldson. . . . I'm Mark Travis."
In the high beam of her lights he was circling the car, a tall,
rangy young man with dark hair. Reaching across, she
opened the door and it swung wide. "Hop in, Mark. You
can put your knapsack on the backseat if you like."

"Thank you." Slipping the backpack from his shoulders,
he did as she suggested, then got in and closed the door.

"I can't imagine what happened to the bus," she said
with a nervous laugh. "It's *never* early. That's one thing we
can count on around here."

"I was only waiting a few seconds," he said. "It was very
nice of you to come for me." His voice was soft and low. She
liked the way he sounded. "I really love this car." Turning,
he glanced at the tonneau. "They don't make them like this
any more. What is it?"

"It's a 'sixty-five Lincoln. I simply hate to let it go, so
I've kept it year after year."

By now Martha had circled the gasoline pumps and was
headed back the way she had come. The headlights ate up
the center line; the wind rushed by. She glanced at him
sidelong. His elbow was on the doorsill; his eyes on the
road. "I don't know how much you were told about our
problem," Martha said.

"As I understand it, you plan to go to Europe and need
somebody to be with your husband."

"That's about the size of it," Martha said. "And I'm
supposed to be leaving *tomorrow.*" Again she laughed nerv-

ously. "So I suppose it might be a good idea if we spent a little time getting to know each other."

"Of course," he said.

"Tell me a little something about yourself, Mark."

"Sure. What would you like to know?"

"Is New York your home?"

"It has been, for the past six or seven years. Before that I lived in the country, and I must say it's nice to be back." He sniffed the air. "When Eliot told me about this, I jumped at the chance. I realize, of course, that I'm a complete stranger to you and to Mr. Donaldson. It was too late to get together any references, but I can certainly get them if you like. Gosh, I can't get over this car. It's so tight. It rides so smoothly."

"Do you drive?"

"Oh, sure. I don't get much chance in New York though. It's very expensive to keep a car there." He sighed. "I sure do love this one."

On impulse, Martha removed her foot from the accelerator. "Would you like to drive it?" As one step, it might be worthwhile to find out how well he drove.

He seemed surprised. "Well . . . sure! If you don't mind."

She pulled off the road, and with the motor idling she could hear the sounds of the night—the undulant sound of the peepers, the soft, shrill *cheep-cheep*, a rhythmic rise and fall, and above the sound of the peepers and beyond the soft sound of the idling motor and the scrape of their feet as they circled the car, beyond all these the vast sound of the deep country summer stillness.

The two doors slammed, one after another, loud in the silence.

As he drove, Martha was content to sit and watch, interested to notice the way his hands fell loosely over the steering wheel, to observe his profile, to see his hair lifted by the wind. "Left at the stop sign," she said.

Coming to a complete stop, he looked carefully in both directions before turning left into the wider and more smoothly surfaced state road. "What a great car," he said.

28

"Do you mind if I give it a little gas?"

"Go right ahead if you like."

His foot went down on the accelerator. His head lifted. His hands were tight on the steering wheel. His face had a look of intensity. The car poured down the road, and when she looked at the speedometer the needle was flickering under and then over seventy. Although it was a straight and perfectly flat road, she had a sense of a steep incline, an impression of flowing downhill, and she was reminded of the long, sheer, breath-snatching first drop on her very first roller coaster ride, taken when she was a girl in high school.

"Watch out for deer," she said.

Gradually he let the speed fall back to fifty. "Sorry."

"They jump right out in front of you," she said. "With the top down they could land right in our laps."

"Sorry," he said again. "This thing is so smooth it runs away with you. Would you like it back?"

"No, you go right ahead. I'll tell you where the turns are." Martha settled back into the seat. "Where did you live before New York?"

"I was born and raised in Virginia. On a farm."

Only the softness of his voice seemed Southern. If he had once had a country accent it was gone. She liked his voice.

"Why did you decide to go to New York?" she asked.

He smiled. "Sometimes I'm not sure it was such a great idea. I don't know. I suppose mainly because I wanted to go to school there. To take some courses in photography. I like it there, but the city can get you down after a while. The idea of spending the summer down here was something that appealed to me very much. How about Mr. Donaldson? Is he . . . bedridden?"

"Oh, no, not at all," Martha said. "He can do a great many things. He's recuperating beautifully."

"Did I understand Eliot to say he had a heart attack?"

"Yes, about six months ago, and that's why I didn't feel it was a good idea to leave him alone. But he's doing just fine. He had a doctor's appointment late this afternoon in

Baltimore, a big checkup. I wanted him to have it before I left. He'll be home about eleven or so. By the way, I've saved you some supper. I knew you wouldn't be able to get anything on the way down."

"That's awfully kind of you, Mrs. Donaldson. Thanks very much."

"I don't know what Eliot told you about salary. We weren't planning to pay a great deal. Room and board, of course, but not much beyond that."

"I'm not worried about making a lot of money," he said. "Just being down here is worth a lot to me."

"Were you working when this came up?"

"I was doing some free-lance work. Nothing that I wasn't perfectly willing to leave."

"Photography?"

"Yes."

By the time they reached the house, Martha was feeling something very close to optimism. The young man seemed intelligent. He had the manners and speech of a gentleman. She was also impressed by the dominant, sure-handed way he had handled the car.

She led him from the carport into the kitchen and turned. She smiled and he smiled back. He was nice-looking, very nice looking. His dark hair was shaggy. She had feared it might be hanging to his shoulders. A headband would not have surprised her. He seemed altogether conventional and totally presentable.

"A few weeks ago," she said, "I had a call from a young man who was looking for a job for the summer. That wasn't you by any chance, was it?"

He shook his head. "No, I didn't know a thing about all this until I heard about it from Eliot."

Looking into his dark eyes, she had an instinct about him and felt sure she was going to obey it. There was still Warren, of course, but she knew the kind of young people Warren liked and she felt sure he would like this one. Feeling less guilty about Warren with every passing second, she said, "Okay now, Mark, I'll show you to your room and then how about a little supper?"

While she fixed it she missed him, and when she called he didn't answer. Going outdoors, she found him down near the water, standing in the darkness, looking at the lights across the cove.

Part II

The Cove

Four

WARREN DONALDSON, a man nearing sixty, had spent his adult years as a benign, tolerant professor of history at a small college not far from his home. During the winter, as he lay recuperating from his massive heart attack, he knew even before his doctor told him so that the active part of his life was over. He was less depressed than he might have expected. Comfortably fixed (he and his wife came from moderately wealthy families), he faced his remaining years with gratitude and pleasure, envisioning a contemplative life of quiet pursuits and serenity.

When he thought he would be spending the summer with his wife's nephew Eliot Bender, it did little for his sense of serenity. Warren Donaldson was no snob, far from it, but for years he had nursed what he felt was an entirely justifiable aversion to his brother-in-law Roy Bender, and he felt certain that Eliot would prove to be just as irritating to have around as his father. He agreed to have Eliot because he knew how much going to Italy meant to Martha and because he realized she had gotten herself into a bind with her sister.

When Eliot dropped out at the last minute, Warren asked himself what he had done to be so lucky. Mark Travis, Eliot's replacement, was far from irritating. He was a quiet, sensitive, occasionally dreamy young man, pleasing in manner and appearance, and with a romantic fixation that for a time made Warren wonder if he might not be watching some sort of reenactment of *The Great Gatsby*.

Mark's fixation was not apparent all at once. During the first week there seemed nothing particularly significant in the dreamy way he sat on the white bench in the yard and gazed across the water. Warren found it fascinating to think of what Scott Fitzgerald's book had done for two promontories facing across a body of water—yet the appeal would have been there without Fitzgerald. There was something magical about sitting at dusk and watching darkness fall over a river and watching lights appear on the far shore, and for a while it seemed that this was all Mark was doing, sitting and gazing out over the water at nothing in particular.

In that first week Mark asked no questions about the girl and if he had asked, Warren would have been unable to give him much of an answer, for along with many others in Craddock County he was mystified by the setup across the cove. The young man and young woman, hardly more than children, living in one of the showplaces of the county. Who were they, and who was supplying the money? The girl had a Thistle, a seventeen-foot day sailer, one of the most graceful of boats, its hull a gleaming powder blue, and Warren had seen her out in it a couple of times in early morning, sailing around on her side of the cove. Since summer began he had also been aware that someone was ghosting around the cove at night. Whoever it was carried no lights, but occasionally he had caught a glimpse of white moving in the darkness, occasionally heard the rustle of the jib as the boat tacked away. He had no way of knowing whether it was the girl. He rather thought it might be.

Meanwhile he and Mark had begun their life together. Warren's goal at the beginning was to keep out of Mark's way as much as possible and to have Mark keep out of his, an attitude that might have seemed supercilious but from the older man's viewpoint was simply precautionary, for at first he had no idea what to expect. He had even made it a pre-condition that each would take his meals when and as he liked.

Warren long since had grown strong enough to climb stairs again and had resumed sleeping in the bedroom he and his wife had shared for twenty-five years. Mark slept downstairs in the small room Donaldson had used for his convalescence. It contained a daybed, a television set, and shelves filled with books. The television set was important to Mark. The day after his arrival he borrowed Warren's Toyota and drove to the village for the *TV Guide,* something he would do each week thereafter. In the evening, once it was dark, he lay on his bed and watched television, having carefully checked the listings for old movies, muttering about the selections available, and from his muttering it was apparent that back in New York there was, for whatever reason, a veritable parade of old movies featuring the likes of Erich von Stroheim, Joseph Schildkraut, Mae Marsh, Billie Dove, Lila Lee, and others of their vintage. Asked if there was a particular channel that featured such fare, Mark said no, that it was simply a matter of checking the listings and being alert for the sort of pictures he considered worth watching. Most of these, it soon became evident, were made in the twenties and thirties.

He also seemed particularly interested in a set of photographs, black-and-white shots that had been mounted in matching mats and frames and that now hung in groups of four in the Donaldson library.

"These are very nice, Mr. Donaldson," he said one afternoon. "Did you take them?"

Warren said that he had.

"Nice," Mark said. "The one of the gull is terrific. I love the shadow."

It was Warren's own favorite—a gull skimming the water close to sunset, its shadow elongated over the water's surface.

Mark's eyes roved over the rows of books. "Help yourself to anything you like," Warren said.

"Thanks." His eyes were still moving.

"In Eliot's bookshop . . ." Warren began—Mark turned —"what do they sell? Religions of the world, things like that?"

For a moment Mark was silent. "Those," he said. "Also religious philosophy. It's a fairly broad selection."

Donaldson was having great difficulty picturing his old nemesis Roy Bender making a living on, say, the Upanishads.

"This is a beautiful room." Mark's eyes were now on the burgundy leather chair that stood before the fireplace, the chair in which, during his waking hours, Warren had spent most of the winter and spring. "A truly beautiful room. I'm certainly glad to be here, Mr. Donaldson."

His voice as always was soft and deep, and in his dark, deep-set eyes there was a look of sincerity and gratitude. His dark hair was shaggier than it had been when he arrived. In build he was slender, although his body had a wiry strength that Warren, in his admittedly parochial view, found difficult to associate with people from New York.

The young man had brought very few clothes, principally a pair of white denim slacks and several navy blue shirts with short sleeves. He wore this combination almost every day, and it was this outfit that he wore when, toward the end of the week at breakfast, he offered to ride the tractor and keep the expansive lawn mowed and trimmed. By then Warren was no longer avoiding him and they were taking most of their meals together. "Keeping you company is not exactly my idea of a chore, Mr. Donaldson," Mark said. "There's no reason why I can't help with the yard work and whatever else you'd like me to do."

After many years of doing the mowing himself, Warren had no great eagerness to turn down the offer, and very soon Mark got to it, mowing the lawn to the rear of the house that morning and then after lunch attacking the sides and front. He performed conscientiously and well, mowing systematically, always in neat parallel overlaps. He seemed very much at home on the tractor, and this was hardly surprising considering his farm boyhood.

It was toward late afternoon that Warren saw him down close to the water's edge, tractor idling. Warren was reading on the screened porch. The sun glinted on glass, and it was this perhaps that caused him to glance up from his book to see Mark, a pair of binoculars raised to his eyes, looking out across the cove.

Presently, as he continued to sit there without moving, Warren crossed the porch to the screen and looked. It was too far across the cove to see much with the naked eye, and he stepped just inside the door to pick up his own binoculars from the shelf where they were kept. They were gone, and it seemed clear enough that these were the ones Mark had taken with him aboard the tractor. With a pair of weak opera glasses that Martha sometimes took to the Kennedy Center, Warren went back out to the porch and advanced once more to the screen. Focusing the glasses, he saw, at the end of the dock across the cove, a young woman wearing what appeared to be a white middy blouse over a bathing suit. As he watched, she stepped into the Thistle, hoisted the sails, and soon was moving away from the dock. Mark was still watching intently. Although the breeze was light the boat was already moving well. For a few minutes it seemed that she was headed straight for the Donaldson dock, but then she fell off and headed eastward, deeper into the cove.

Only then did Mark resume his mowing. Placing the binoculars behind him on the seat of the tractor, he made a long sweep toward the house. As he approached, he kept looking back over his shoulder. Reversing direction, he picked up the binoculars again as he headed back toward the water. He steered with one hand, holding the binoculars with the other, but by now the young woman was deep into the cove, and her sails were barely visible against the far shore.

Martha had left innumerable food packets in the freezer, and that evening Mark and Warren were on the porch eating twin chicken potpie dinners when it began. For most of the meal Mark had been silent, looking now and then over the lawn.

Finally he spoke. "That girl over there, the girl in the sailboat," he said, "I have a feeling I've known her before, sometime long ago, maybe in another life." He smiled, looking Warren now full in the eye. "Did you ever have that feeling, old sport?"

Frowning, Warren looked at him closely. Who did he

think he was—Jay Gatsby? Mark was smiling a smile he could not interpret. Dreamy. Wistful. Both, but something more. In the argot of his generation, the young man seemed to be "putting him on." Mark's smile faded. His fist pounded his palm. "I've gotta meet that girl, Mr. Donaldson. That's all there is to it. She's just the loveliest thing I've ever seen. By the way, I already know her name."

"How did you find it out?" Warren asked warily.

"In the village," he said. "It's—Daisy." He grinned.

By then Donaldson felt sure he was being conned. Daisy her name well might be and this could be overlooked as coincidence. But certainly not the "old sport." All along, Mark had been respectfully addressing his employer as Mr. Donaldson. Suddenly it was "old sport." But no coincidence here. "Old sport" was Jay Gatsby's favorite phrase, his favorite mode of address. It seemed clear enough. At some point in his life Mark had fallen in love with a book and through the book with an era and finally, inevitably, with a girl whom he was determined to know as Daisy.

Warren was amused. "Daisy Buchanan?" He paused. "Daisy and Tom Buchanan?"

"Buchanan?" Mark sounded perplexed. "No. Daisy King. I don't know what the guy's name is, but her name is Daisy King."

His face had a look of perfect innocence.

Warren asked himself what he was to believe. Clearly Mark was lying. To watch him feign innocence was to suspect that he was up to something dishonest, however harmless it might be.

After supper Warren went into the library and checked the shelves. His venerable copy of *The Great Gatsby*, with its tattered jacket, was in its place, in perfect alignment with the rest of the books on the same shelf.

Before the end of the evening he stood in the doorway of the small downstairs bedroom. Mark was stretched full-length in the dark, looking at a movie. Warren recognized Lizabeth Scott and Dick Powell. For a few seconds he watched and then said, "Tell me something, Mark. Did you ever read *The Great Gatsby?*"

"No, I never did," was the reply. "What's it about? Is it a good book?"

His eyes had not left the screen, and after a moment Warren turned away without replying.

For whatever reason, he decided, Mark was playing a game with him and obviously with himself. It was quite evident that he preferred not to be called on it. He wanted Warren not to notice; wanted him to accept it, or ignore it; wanted his employer to let him have his little charade and not to take exception, not to spoil it.

It seemed not only harmless but also not even terribly important. If this romantic kid wanted to spend his summer fantasizing that he was a man named Jay Gatsby living on an estate on Long Island in the year 1922, and that across the cove lived a Southern belle who was his lost love—again Donaldson asked himself where the harm could be. Obviously it was a matter of an overnourished sense of fantasy, all of a piece with his fixation on old movies. In another month he might be living out a dream of Lizabeth Scott or he might be playing Richard Barthelmess in *Dawn Patrol* or Charles ("Buddy") Rogers in *Wings* and the object of his fantasy would be Billie Dove or Colleen Moore.

But for now it was Daisy Buchanan—or Daisy King, if that in fact was her real name. For however full-blown the rest of the Gatsby fantasy might be, what did remain was that he had most definitely fallen in love. He loved Lost America, he loved the idea of lost beauty, he loved the idea of the girl, and he loved the fact that she lived across the cove. At times it struck Donaldson that this last was most important of all. It gave rise to all the rest.

Five

IF MARK WAS YEARNING for Lost America, Warren reflected, he had come to the right place, for in certain aspects and among certain folk there was in this elegant neck of the woods a great deal of Lost America. In an epoch of denim, pizzas, and scatalogically inscribed T-shirts, the area stood as one of the final resting places of what some might call refinement. Not merely wealth, for the refined were not always wealthy, and the wealthy, God knows, were not always refined. Of the two, refinement was the more important. Scandals were hushed. Affairs were conducted discreetly. Dress was important. The men still came to parties clad in green linen jackets, in maroons and yellows and plaids, and here one still saw beautiful dresses, creations as white and billowy as the dresses worn by Daisy and her friend Jordan Baker on Long Island in 1922. Things were done with elegance. To go with the Japanese lanterns and the Japanese automobiles, there was always a Rolls Royce or two, along with a couple of Bentleys. The parties were invariably catered. There was valet parking, handled by a trio of black men who knew and were known by the guests.

It was to just such a party that Warren now would take Mark. The party was held next door. Although the phrase *next door* had a cozy sound to it, in Warren's case *next door* meant the adjacent estate. It differed from the Donaldson place in a number of important respects. Instead of five acres it had forty acres, enough to have accommodated at one time a small railroad system. It had an heirloom house —and it had a cornfield. In this part of the world, one standard of prestige was whether the house simply appeared amidst its setting of lawn, there to be seen with the naked eye from the highway, or—much more impressive—

whether it was hidden from view by a front line of corn or nestled beyond a vanguard of soybeans, so that only after one traveled down a long lane did the corn or soybeans give way to the well-tended lawn. It all, of course, ended up one way or another at the water. Thus, although Warren's far less imposing property had no outlying stand of corn to give it class, it did have the lawn and it had the waterfront and it had very easy access to the adjoining property, so that to go next door he had merely to sideslip through sentinel cedars planted in a long line many years earlier by his friend Burton ("Bucky") Baker to mark the boundary between the two properties.

Bucky Baker had been one of Warren's favorite eccentrics and as good a neighbor as a man could have. Before his untimely passing, there had been many a happy hour with Bucky, drinking with him, listening to what his wife dubbed his "Buckyisms." On meeting new people: "I don't want to meet any people, I already know some people." On people in general: "If there's anything I can't stand, it's others." On driving: "That's what I hate about driving— there's always some other son of a bitch coming."

Many were the happy evenings Warren spent with Bucky Baker riding over the narrow-gauge tracks through his cornfields, Bucky's hired man in the cab of the small locomotive, Bucky and Warren in the miniature caboose when the weather was poor and in a gondola car with seats when the weather was fine, getting slowly and with dignity quite drunk, retracing the circuit over and over as the cocktail hour moved slowly toward dinner and the shadows fell long down the aisles of corn. The locomotive had a whistle, and the hired man now and again would reach up and give a little toot to punctuate Bucky's political opinions, always the same hired man, always the same toot, and Warren listening over all the many years as Bucky declaimed against John F. Kennedy, Lyndon Johnson, George McGovern, Richard Nixon, Gerald Ford, and Jimmy Carter. It was a shame that Bucky passed on to his reward before the election of Ronald Reagan. Warren always felt

Reagan might have been Bucky's man.

Bucky then was a part of Lost America and so too was his railroad. After he died his wife sold out and moved to a condominium in Manhattan. The new owner, one Rex Calabrese, was a forty-year-old wunderkind who had made a small fortune in small computers and whose main residence was elsewhere. Rex Calabrese saw little to recommend the railroad and soon it was gone, even the tracks.

The Calabreses entertained a great deal, particularly considering the limited time they were in residence. Their parties were theatrical productions, although in this they were not alone. Martha often lamented that in this area one did not have a party, one *produced* a party, with a set, a director, props, stagehands, and audience participation. It was a production that started punctually, usually at six, and that had if not a preannounced then at least an implicit closing time, usually no later than nine. Rarely did one encounter the on-into-the-wee-hours spontaneity that one had known back in the city in one's earlier days. This would have been virtually impossible in any event. The caterers, for example, left; the bartenders left; the parking attendants left; and before you knew it the theater was closing down and you and your wife faced the embarrassment of suddenly finding yourselves the sole surviving guests, confronting a host and hostess who with frozen smiles and feeble stabs at conviviality were offering a nightcap—which under the circumstances might be construed as somewhat more delicate than suggesting one for the road.

Warren's invitation to the Calabrese party had come in the mail not long after Mark's arrival. At the time he would have found it hard to believe that on the evening before the appointed day he would be calling up Jan Calabrese and asking if it would be okay to bring along his paid companion. But in the nearly a month since his arrival Mark had become much more friend than employee. Warren was influenced moreover by the excited and undeniably wistful expression on Mark's face when he heard the party was to take place and when he heard the sort of party it was to be. It was to be a *huge* party. He was intrigued as well to learn that it was one of *two* parties. The Calabreses were entertaining on successive nights—on Thursday and again on Friday. In the area this was not uncommon. If one was in the social swim and one paid back, one ended up with a tremendous number of people on the payback list, and with parties on successive nights there was a cachet that was lacking when one gave merely one.

Mark was impressed by all this, but most of all he was entranced and excited by the expectation that the girl might be among the guests, and Warren was reminded of the way Jay Gatsby kept hoping that Daisy Buchanan might some night appear at one of the huge parties at his estate on Long Island. Dreaming of his own Daisy, Mark mentioned the possibility at least three times, pondered the chances, asked Warren's opinion, and then kept quiet about it, but it was clear that the thought was sustaining him all day Thursday. It was the Thursday party to which they were invited.

In the area people tended to arrive at social occasions with rather astonishing punctuality, so that just past 6:30, as Mark and Warren sideslipped through the sentinel cedars, they found the party already in full swing—or, as Warren wryly reflected, as fully in swing as a party in the area could ever be. In this case *full swing* meant that handsomely clad people were drinking in clusters, standing about in the area staked out for the occasion. The stakeout area was an emerald rectangle approximately the size of a tennis court. At each baseline stood a bar and behind each bar stood a man in a white jacket, serving drinks.

For the occasion Mark wore his white denim jeans and a blue blazer that no longer fitted Warren because of the weight he had lost after his heart attack. Mark's hair was carefully brushed and his face by now was tanned and ruddy from the long hours spent on the tractor. His eyes were filled with excitement, and as they stepped through the cedars it was as if he had stepped into a scene long dreamed of. The afternoon was windless. On the right the blue water of the cove had a smooth, unruffled surface. On the left stood the handsome redbrick house with its facade of slim, delicately wrought white columns. The sun bathed the lawn. Its rays glinted on glasses, on moving rings and bracelets, on tanned faces, glinted on the chrome of arriving automobiles. In the late afternoon light, Mark's eyes were shining. For a moment they held a mysterious look. The dazed, bemused expression passed, and now he was on the alert, his eyes roving quickly through the crowd, all around the curve of the shore. He watched cars arriving. He scanned the faces of each new arrival until there were no more.

Instead of clinging to his benefactor's elbow, Mark mingled freely. Once Warren saw him trapped near the water's edge by Cornelia Lipton, surely the most bombastic of the area's resident moralists. Cornelia had once been a Broadway actress of some note and she never let anyone forget it. She was passionately and often, Warren felt, histrionically perturbed by what she saw as a national drift into amorality, particularly as evidenced in motion pictures and fiction. There she stood in a shapeless pink dress, slouched against a table, with her thick white hair, her bushy white eyebrows, face florid, drink in hand, by now profoundly and irately drunk, glowering and growling. "Where is the pacing?" she demanded. "I ask you, young man, what has become of the decorous pacing? What has become of the long quest? The treasure hunt! The heady joy of suspense and doubt! The target layered o'er with camisoles, the veritable roadblock of undergarments, and the delicious uncertainty of whether the man would ultimately have his way, would lay aside the final, the innermost camisole!"

Draining her glass, Cornelia tossed it into the water, watched it bubble and gurgle and sink. "Instead what do we have? Everybody on the fellatio-cunnilingus express, going like sixty!" Her voice was like thunder. Far from finding her hysterical, Mark seemed impressed, not only by what she was saying but also by the way she was saying it. He was replying earnestly. Cornelia gave ear only haphazardly, partly because she wanted to get on with her tirade and partly, Warren had no doubt, because of a surfeit of scotch. "All the movers and the shakers!" Mark by now was listening raptly once more. "Hard put to know where the next variation is coming from! Adrift in a sea of orifices—*whereaway!*" Cornelia reached along the table for her glass, forgetting that she had thrown it overboard. She then moved uncertainly toward the nearest bar, Mark watching with concern until her outstretched, heavily jeweled fingers made contact with the white tablecloth.

An hour later, as the light began to fade, Warren saw him in a conversational knot nearby, and although he could not hear his question its nature was apparent from Jan Calabrese's reply. "Yes," she said, "they were invited. Just for the hell of it we mailed them an invitation for tonight, if only to try and—you know—flush them out of hiding. I understand it's the girl's parents who have the money. Do you know anything about them?"

Mark's reply was inaudible. Jan Calabrese was nodding and then saying: "At bridge at the yacht club the other day, somebody said that she's—you know—just the tiniest bit cuckoo." Jan's laughter ran up and down the scale. She touched her temple with her fingertip. "Somebody saw her in town the other day in a straw hat with ribbons that tied under the chin."

Jan drifted off and Mark drifted toward the shoreline, his face a mask.

At 7:30, strings of Japanese lanterns were lit. By 8:00 it was dark. Torches flanked the bars, their flames standing erect in the still air. On the far shore of the cove, lights appeared in some of the houses. A few of the guests had arrived by boat, and soon, with tipsy laughter in some cases, they carefully embarked, embarked with the care of the tipsy, skippers proclaiming their sobriety and their fitness for navigation. Running lights were switched on, lines cast off, and slowly, one by one, with laughter and thank-yous floating back, the boats moved out over the dark water toward the mouth of the cove and the twin flashers that led one out to the river beyond.

The next evening Mark took a stand in the line of cedars, himself a sentinel. After an hour or so he headed back toward the house, his Giacometti shadow falling long over the lawn behind him.

Warren was on the porch reading about the Federal Reserve Board's stand on discount rates, a hot topic that summer. "If they were invited to the Thursday party, they're not likely to show up for the one on Friday," he said, looking up from his paper.

Nodding, Mark took a seat in the opposite rocker. "I suppose not."

Warren folded the paper, refolded it, and tapped it against his knee. "If you want to meet them . . . or meet *her* . . . why not just go over there and introduce yourself?"

Mark's eyes were cast down. He seemed evasive. He muttered something to the effect that he wasn't very "smooth" about things of that sort.

With a doleful look he went on into the house, fixed himself something to eat, and disappeared into his room. Warren didn't see him again the rest of the evening.

The days passed. August approached. Mark mowed and watched television and waited. Warren marveled at his patience, then realized that it should not have been too surprising. Perhaps, he thought with amusement, the young man was content to proceed at the pace recommended so indignantly by the flamboyant Cornelia. In a love affair a little bit at a time would do; a little bit at a time was to be preferred. It had a civility, a chivalry perhaps, in any case an old-fashioned quality that Mark probably preferred, so that a first kiss, if it came, would be elysian, but long before even the first kiss there was the breathless joy and suspense of merely glimpsing her sails in the dark, of watching her face through binoculars.

Warren himself was perfectly content with the pace of their life. At his age and in his state of health, the fire was banked, the flame turned low. He rocked on the porch. He read. He listened to music. He drove to town for groceries, sometimes lunching with friends. He lay in the sun by the pool; he swam laps as the doctor had recommended. He had Martha's itinerary and wrote her a couple of times a week, describing the life he was living in her absence and invariably devoting a few paragraphs to Mark, telling her how nice he seemed to be, how well they were getting along together, how fortunate he considered himself to have missed out on Eliot, and telling her of the torch Mark was carrying for the mystery girl across the cove. Mark's quest had provided amusement during what might well have been a boring summer.

For curiosity, Warren read here and there through *The Great Gatsby*. Even from a cursory reading one might guess Mark's next move. If he was indeed playing a Gatsby game and trying to keep it to himself, he would continue to feign innocence—yet it was increasingly obvious that the person who would ultimately make the trip across the river would be not Mark but Warren Donaldson, even though Warren lacked the egregious qualification enjoyed by Fitzgerald's narrator: Daisy was not his cousin from Louisville.

It amused Warren to think about it and amused him to realize that if Mark did in fact ask him he would probably go, since at that time it all seemed so perfectly harmless.

Warren waited and at supper on August 3, two full weeks after the parties next door, Mark set down his fork, carefully wiped his mouth with a paper napkin, and looked up with a troubled frown. "Mr. Donaldson," he said, "I'd like to ask a favor, if it's okay."

"What sort of favor, Mark?" Warren had put down his own fork and wiped his own mouth.

"I've got to meet that girl—that's all there is to it." He sounded desperate and his eyes were clouded. "Will you please help me? Will you get me an introduction, Mr. Donaldson? Please?"

"Mark—from what everybody says, she's *living* with that young man. I mean—how can you expect—?"

"I'll take my chances," he said.

Warren sat looking across the water. "Don't you think it's something you'd be far better off doing for yourself?"

He looked up helplessly, as if he were in the grip of something beyond his control. "I just don't trust myself, Mr. Donaldson," he said. "I've never been very good at these things. I've never had much what you might call social flair."

To hear him say this was of course disarming and so too was the look in his stricken eyes. Donaldson realized that he was making too much of it, too much of a simple call upon newcomers by himself, one who had lived on the cove for so many, many years—particularly when it was so obvious that Mark wanted him to do it so very badly.

Six

AND SO IT WAS that the next afternoon he found himself passing between brick columns, peering up a long graveled lane, the house still out of sight beyond a distant curve. Obeying a sign that said, "5 MPH Please," he moved slowly up the drive between tall, lacy deodaras standing in matched pairs, deodaras now fifty years old, planted, one might guess, by an owner who never suspected that his chateau, his dream house, would be inhabited half a century later by two kids who were—in what doubtless would have been his phrase—living in sin.

On either side of the drive, the ornate deodaras gave way to thick stands of loblolly pine. As he looked left and then right, he was surprised to see a man moving slowly down one of the aisles of pine, a rifle or shotgun under his arm.

The man glanced over his shoulder, veered off, and was quickly out of sight among the pines. Warren concluded that he was headed for a skeet-shooting range. Certainly there was no game in season.

Slowly he continued up the drive, and as he rounded the final curve the house stood facing him, perfect in its architectural balance, with its facade of mellowed brick, the center doorway so massively beautiful, its pediment glistening with fresh white paint, the small glittering panes of the mullioned windows, the luxuriant tendrils of ivy climbing the bricks in long streamers.

Almost as quick to catch his eye was a silver Mercedes convertible, a forty thousand–dollar automobile that year. It was parked squarely and precisely beneath the roof of a porte cochere. Angled off carelessly to one side was a scarlet Honda.

Pulling in alongside the Honda, he got out and stood for a moment, conscious of moving shadows, of leaves stirring, of the faint salt taste of the breeze from the river, and, in the intervals between zephyrs, of the smell of August heat and the faint lingering scent of grass mown perhaps the day before. There was the deep, hot silence of early afternoon, a siesta stillness, with no sound except for the low whistle of a chickadee that he could hear but not see, an excited sound at once mournful and hopeful, a little like the sound of a small boy whistling between his teeth.

Dressed for the occasion in his new, size-smaller blue blazer, his thinning white hair carefully combed, he approached the front doorway and mounted the curved brick steps. Through the double screen doors there was a view of a dim interior—the suggestion of rooms cool and gladed, an interior cool without the benefit of air conditioning.

He tapped.

"Who is it?"

The voice was that of a young woman, and although the question was one he had been raised to consider impolite, and had so trained his own children, the melodious sound seemed to do away with any suggestion of rudeness. The question was a song, three notes—G-sharp, D-sharp, and C —a lilting musical murmur, exciting and beautiful, and he was impressed by it. It was a voice that went with the Daisy loved by Gatsby, and, hearing the voice, sensing the dim interior, he half expected to see the setting in which Fitz-gerald had so beautifully introduced his own Daisy: white curtains lifting in the breeze from Long Island Sound, and the enormous couch on which the two young women, Daisy Buchanan and Jordan Baker, sat so buoyantly, their dresses rippling and fluttering in the breeze, a feeling all so languid, a time when even the very wealthy were forced, for cool-ness, to depend upon breeze and shade and walls and blinds that blocked and deflected the sun, conserving whatever cooled air might have been stored.

"Warren Donaldson." He paused. "Your neighbor from across the cove." It seemed a stupid way to identify himself but he could think of no other.

Now he could hear hurried whispers, murmurs of inde-cision. Presently, instead of the girl, a woman appeared, a handsome black woman wearing a flowered kaftan. Her feet were bare, her toenails painted silver. Having lived so long in the area, having known so many of its black families, and having been friends with so many, he was surprised to find his receptionist unfamiliar. He had never seen her before. She shoved open the screen door and he entered. "This way, please." He followed her down a hallway beneath a twelve-foot ceiling, past walls of aqua, walls paneled in white, bordered and freshened with white embossing and scroll-work, all looking as if it had been painted only yesterday.

The door stood open. The room was light and airy, but the girl was hardly Fitzgerald's Daisy. A book in hand, she sat on a sofa slipcovered in watermelon pink. Instead of a gown of white parachute silk she wore blue denim cutoffs and a yellow blouse. Her feet were bare; her tanned legs were of delicate bone structure, as fragile as the legs of a little girl. Laying aside the book, she was rising, saying, "Mr. Donaldson? . . . I'm Daisy King."

She looked into his eyes. Her own were a deep, dark

blue, and her off-blonde hair was pulled back and tied haphazardly with a yellow ribbon. "I hope you'll forgive me," he began. "I was on my way back from town and I—"

"I'm so glad you came by," she said, although nothing in her manner indicated that she meant it. "Suppose we go out on the porch, shall we? It's a little cooler out there."

The porch was filled to overflowing with white wicker furniture. An electric fan blew warm air against his legs. A ceiling fan revolved slowly. In one corner of the room the entire surface of a card table was covered with a jigsaw puzzle, perhaps a third completed.

She was standing at the jalousied windows, pointing. "I know where you live." She looked over her shoulder and then again out over the cove. He moved to her side. "You live—right *there*. Where the man is mowing the lawn."

The man mowing the lawn was, of course, none other than Mark, visible as a figurine on a child's toy tractor, and at this great distance he seemed to be in slow motion. Warren considered it fortunate that he had not told him he was making the visit so soon. Had he known that at this very moment Warren was standing at the frail shoulder of his lost love, his Daisy, there seemed some danger that he might have become so excited as to run the tractor over the bank, right into the water.

And yet for Warren Donaldson the fantasy was fast dissolving. To him, the glamorous Daisy in the Fitzgerald novel was one of the more fetching females in fiction. The poor child facing him was something less. Once again he had an impression of fragility and of a childlike quality. Her shoulders were narrow and in the frilly yellow blouse she seemed flat-chested, or nearly so.

"I love your house," she was saying. "A week or so ago you had a very big party—two big parties, one one night and one the next. Was it you? Or the people next door? Did you invite me? Somebody invited me and I was so pleased. I'm sorry we couldn't come. It was so beautiful, the torches and all the lights and the sounds across the water. I could hear the people leaving on their boats. It sounded like such fun. Everything seems like fun from a distance, doesn't it?"

This last she had said with no change in inflection, but now, having said it, she turned from the window with a sad smile. "What would you like? Some iced tea? May I get you some?" She started expectantly from the room, and when he said, "No thanks, none for me," she turned back with reluctance. "I just wanted to say hello," he said.

"Oh, I'm so glad you did. It's very kind of you."

With a smile she sat on the arm of a white wicker chair, looking again across the cove.

"The young man on the tractor over there," Warren said, "he works for me. He's been watching you sailing your Thistle. I think he might like very much to meet you sometime."

She nodded gravely. "Thistles are such lovely boats," she said. "Have you ever sailed one?"

"When I was much younger," he said. "We had one of the early ones. Long before fiberglass."

She nodded but seemed not to be listening. Her thoughts were elsewhere, and now it all seemed to be falling apart, and he sat there thinking how silly it had been, silly of Mark, of course, but silly of himself to go along with it, no matter how good his intentions. No glamorous girl in white silk, just a sad, frail, terribly nervous girl who was in pain. The hollowed-out sockets beneath her eyes looked bruised and discolored, not from a blow but as if from something within, from sleepless nights or bad dreams.

Donaldson deliberated. He had stated his business most clumsily to be sure and she had not responded. She had instead said something about her sailboat. He told her a pointless anecdote about his old Thistle, something about the day he and Martha broke the centerboard. She smiled a fixed smile, as if waiting for him to leave. For all her attempts at politeness, he had seldom felt so unwelcome, so mistrusted, as if she automatically mistrusted anyone who was nice to her, automatically found that person an object of suspicion. "When you're out sailing," he pressed, "why don't you tie up at our dock sometime and come in? Mark would be delighted to meet you. Are you interested in old movies? Mark is something of an authority. . . ."

She said no, she was not a fan of old movies. All the while she had remained perched on the arm of the white wicker chair. Wisps of her hair moved in the air being stirred by the ceiling fan. Nervously she fingered them, terribly ill at ease. Why?

"It's time I got along. . . ." As he spoke he was aware of a rapid tread, and then, stepping heavily into the room, there loomed a young man, whom he judged to be the live-in everybody had heard so much about and whom no-body, even in the village, had seen. Here, presumably, he stood, a young behemoth. She was performing introductions. "Mr. Donaldson . . . this is Turk. Mr. Donaldson lives over there, in the gray-shingled house with the swimming pool." She was pointing across the cove.

"Hiya doin'?" Turk had taken Warren's hand in his and applied pressure. Donaldson managed not to wince. For a fleeting second he was amused. Here at last he had found some shred of resemblance, recalling of course the description in *Gatsby* of the almighty Tom Buchanan and the way he had been portrayed as bursting with muscle. The boy who—for so much longer than necessary—stood now gazing into his eyes, gave off a similar impression of raw power. He wore a faded blue work shirt, the sleeves sheared off at the shoulders, the better, one might guess, to show off his powerful bronzed biceps. From these and from the breadth of his knobbed shoulders, the set of his thick neck, it was safe to surmise that he lifted weights.

He was looking Warren up and down, and Warren was doing the same with him. The boy's chunky bare feet were firmly planted. He had the thighs of a middle linebacker, bursting with muscle against the white sailcloth cutoffs, with calves to match. His eyes were dark, his hair long and thick, and the deeply bronzed face was dominated by a thick drooping mustache.

Having, all in a matter of seconds, judged his visitor no threat, he slumped into a wicker settee with such force that he seemed to threaten its underpinning. "Nice house," he said, responding finally to Daisy's identifying remark about the Donaldson house.

"Thank you."

There was a long pause, which finally Turk broke. "We watch you sometimes with binoculars." He chuckled. "Hope you don't mind being watched."

"Turk!" the girl said, obviously in reprimand.

The young man shrugged.

She looked at him with disgust.

"I doubt if we're ever doing anything worth watching," Warren said.

There was no reply. By now two things were apparent. The first was that Turk had hurried to the porch from wherever he might have been, hurried in to be with the girl, stand guard in a very possessive way.

The second was that he had absolutely no intention of leaving until Donaldson left. This became steadily more apparent as the silent moments passed.

Warren got to his feet. "I was about to leave." He turned to the doorway and turned back. "Maybe you'd both like to drop over and have a swim some afternoon. Love to have you, and meanwhile if there's anything I can do for you . . . anything you need to know . . . well, we've been living here now for better than a quarter-century, so try me. I might be able to help."

The boy nodded. "We're doin' okay," he said ungraciously.

"Thank you so much," Daisy said. For no reason that was apparent, her lip trembled as she said it. Tears filled the dark eyes. She made no attempt to dry them or dash them away. "We don't leave the house a great deal," she said.

"No, we don't," the boy said quickly. He was frowning at her. She turned away. "No, we don't."

"Do you expect to be here long?" It was not a question Donaldson had intended asking. It popped out.

"We don't know what our plans are yet," Turk said, and

his eyes said to lay off, that it was nobody's business. None of it.

Unwilling to risk another handshake, Warren held up his hand, palm outward, in farewell. The girl, having wiped away the tears by now, walked with him only as far as the threshold and there stood awkwardly watching as he moved away. Before he reached the end of the hall he was intercepted by the black woman, who held open the door for him. "Good day," she said.

"Good day," he replied, and a few minutes later he was moving at the requested five miles per hour, back down the graveled lane, between the twin rows of deodaras, wondering what he had accomplished. From Mark's viewpoint, he knew it would seem very little.

Seven

Mark was grateful for the attempt but disheartened when he heard how possessive Turk was of Daisy.

"If they're living together," Warren said, "what other attitude can you expect? He's not going to be very happy about having her take up with somebody else."

Mark's nod was disconsolate. He brightened a little at the unflattering portrait Warren painted of Turk.

"Do you really think she could be in love with a guy like that?" he asked.

Warren shrugged. "It's obvious that he has some degree of control over her. Certainly that much is true."

"Yes, but do you think she's really in *love* with him?"

"I really can't say."

"Then that must mean you're doubtful," Mark pressed.

"There's certainly some strong bond between them.

Whether it's love on her part is something I couldn't really judge."

"Damn him," Mark said.

Warren smiled. "He's big. He has the dimensions of a California redwood. When he shook my hand he almost broke it."

Mark looked grim. Presently he sighed. "Well anyway, thanks for trying. I must say I really didn't expect you to go over there so soon. I really do appreciate it."

"So what now?"

"Just wait and see, I guess, and hope."

For a week the weather was poor and there was no sign of the Thistle. The weather cleared. A fine northwest wind scoured the skies and brought brightness to the cove again. Stirred by the stiff breeze, the tossing leaves turned their pale undersides to the sun, all of it presaging autumn.

Mark mowed, or he lay in the August sun, his lean, tanned body stretched flat on the diving board.

Each morning one or the other walked to the end of the lane to pull the mail from the RFD box. Mark had not mentioned his family except to say that he was unmarried and that he had a brother and sister and some cousins still living in Southside Virginia. So far as Warren knew, he had received no mail the entire summer. Every few days there was a letter or postcard from Martha. One morning there was one saying she had eaten too much lasagna in Bologna.

Mark was amused by the message. "What day did you say she was coming back?" he asked.

"September sixteenth," Warren replied, aware that it was the second time Mark had asked the question. "If all goes well."

"You mean? . . . "

"I mean assuming she doesn't get sick and have to come back early."

"She's very healthy though, isn't she?"

Donaldson smiled. "Yes, my wife is very healthy."

Mark's interest in the date of Martha's return had not escaped him. It was simply that at the time he gave it no importance. He thought it might mean that Mark would be sorry to see the summer end, because with Martha's return, of course, there would be no further need for him.

"Maybe she should go easy on the lasagna," Mark said.

Warren smiled. Levity was alien to Mark. He had become increasingly dogged, increasingly preoccupied. Warren asked him once if he would like to go out to a restaurant noted for its soft-shell crabs, and on another occasion to a steak place of local repute. In each case Mark turned him down, and it seemed to confirm what already was apparent —that except for his weekly trip to pick up the *TV Guide* he had no intention of leaving the property. What Warren began to perceive now was a young man who was something more than merely lovesick. Instead he had become a fanatic, as single-minded in his determination as was Jay Gatsby himself, without, of course, Gatsby's resources. No fruiterers arrived with cases of oranges and grapefruit, no vintner with cases of champagne, and there was, of course, no one who was Daisy's cousin, available to arrange a rendezvous.

The days passed. Stoically Mark pursued his dream— even though the avenues of pursuit he had chosen seemed pitiably limited. Yet how simple, Donaldson thought, as he watched him down on the dock one afternoon, how simple to view life in this manner: the pursuit of a dream and all else shut out—to the extent that one gained on the dream, to the extent that the dream became real, and then one day perhaps even gloriously attainable.

Mark's, of course, would be like all dreams. Once attained, once real, it would—self-destruct. What beauty would flow from it? What dreams beyond dreams would unfold? Or would the simple attainment be the end of it? Would tomorrow simply pass into yesterday? Questions for the old and the mordant, Warren thought, not for the young, hardly questions for those still in ardent pursuit.

There came the day that Mark must have been praying for, with perhaps, little hope that it would ever arrive.

Having had a Thistle of his own, Donaldson knew the girl's boat well by now, could recognize it from afar, with its blue hull, large mainsail, and small jib. He didn't even realize that she was out, although with the beauty of the day she might well have been. The day was benign. Fleecy clouds dotted the blue sky, and below on the water the pattern was repeated, with so many sails that the surface of the cove was a gingham of blue and white.

Toward three o'clock he saw a boat on a course that would take it straight for his dock. He saw that it was Daisy's Thistle but remained skeptical. There had been other times when she had approached, only to tack away. All summer long she had been doing it, and indeed was about to tack away this time as well. It seemed clear that she would have done so had it not been for the hullabaloo raised by Mark.

Mark had seen her. From the swimming pool he had spied her and was running across the lawn, headed for the dock, pulling a dark blue terry cloth shirt over his damp head as he ran, and now yelling and beckoning and gesticulating. About to change course, she veered once again toward the dock, and when she was perhaps fifty feet away she slacked both sails, letting them luff to lose speed.

The landing was a good one. By then Mark was there to help. He knelt, grabbed the gunwale amidships, and held the boat off while she tossed him a line. With far more seamanship than might have been expected, he secured the boat fore and aft.

Daisy wore what evidently was her favorite sailing costume, the white middy blouse over a flowered bathing suit. She had already dropped the sails and now Mark handed her lightly up to the dock. His face was filled with rapture. He looked as benign as the sky.

In another moment they were moving up the lawn, the girl smiling shyly, Mark eager. He led her toward the pool, and for the first fifteen minutes or so it appeared that he had no plans to share her, that he wanted to keep her to himself.

But then they were heading for the porch, Mark still in his damp swim trunks, his hair still wet from the pool.

"Well!" Warren got up from his rocker as they approached, determined to do his own part to make her feel welcome, secure, attractive, whatever it was she seemed to need so desperately. "Come in! Sit down. I'm so glad you decided to sail over. Have you ever seen a more beautiful day?"

He offered her something to drink. Iced tea? Wine? Diet soda? "Nothing," she said with her shy smile.

Mark was pointing toward the Calabrese house, explaining that the party had been over there, beyond the line of cedars. Warren's thoughts for a moment were upon Turk, the rugged live-in. Was she here without his permission? How had she summoned the daring to sail across the cove? Had she truly intended to come? Or was it the prodigious welcome, the exuberance and enthusiasm of Mark, that had kept her coming when she had no intention of doing so? Or had she simply presented herself, knowing that Mark would do the rest? Had Mark truly known her before?

To this last question, Warren's answer had always been no. But now for a fleeting second he wondered. For the first time, as he looked into the girl's eyes, it struck him that what was important to her was simple survival. Was that what made him think she might have spent time in an institution? Was it possible that she and Mark had been in one together?

These questions lingered in his mind as he excused himself, leaving the porch to them and going over to the pool, swimming his laps and afterward lying on the diving board and staring into the pure blue of the sky.

They were still there when, half an hour later, he went up to shower. After dressing he made some phone calls from the bedroom, and when he got downstairs Daisy was just leaving, moving slowly over the lawn, already halfway down to the dock, Mark at her elbow. Warren called goodbye. She turned and waved. They moved on and from the porch he watched Mark help her into the boat, saw the sails go up and luff, saw Mark shove the bow away from the dock. As he did so, the sails filled and soon she was moving swiftly away, looking back, waving, and then, fifty yards out into the cove, waving again. Mark was standing at the very end of the dock, as far as he could possibly get without falling overboard, watching her go. Only when she was far across the cove, nearing her own dock, did he turn and move slowly back up the lawn. Drawing near, he smiled at Warren watching from the porch.

"Well!" Warren said as he stepped up to the porch. The screen door closed behind him. "Well!"

He nodded, still smiling.

"Eureka!" Warren exclaimed.

Mark plopped into one of the rockers with an air of exhaustion, as if the tension, the tension wrought of sheer joy, had left him drained—yet Warren ventured to guess that at this moment he was as happy as he had ever been in his life. And all because of this sad little girl, who had seemed if anything more gaunt, more hollow-eyed, and more angular than when Warren had seen her on his trip over to her house.

"I can see that you're not disappointed," he said.

"I found out one thing," Mark said with grim satisfaction. "That guy's no live-in. I found out that much. I mean, he lives there but he's no live-in."

"What a blow to the county gossips," Warren said.

"He's just there to help her," Mark continued. "To look after her in case she needs help. Her father wanted somebody to be with her."

"To keep watch over her in other words . . ."

Mark nodded. "I suppose you could say that."

Warren could not forget Turk's custodial attitude, his hostility on the afternoon of his visit. Why was she deemed unfit to go forth? to have visitors?

"Do you plan to see her again?" he asked.

"I sure do," Mark said.

"Will she be able to?"

The question did not please him. "He has no claim on her. He can't tell her what to do."

"Where is she from? Did she say? Where did she live before they came here?"

"We didn't talk about anything personal. Just mostly about—sailing. She said maybe she would teach me to sail."

"That sounds like progress."

Mark looked pleased. "I hope so."

Before Warren Donaldson fell asleep that night, it struck him all over again that there was something about the summer beyond his comprehension, something he didn't quite understand.

He could, he supposed, have stopped it at any one of several junctures, this being one of them, right there and then on the screened porch on that afternoon of Sunday, August 22.

But he didn't because yet again it all seemed so perfectly harmless, a lonely romantic young man falling in love with a sad, neurotic little girl. Love was not meant solely for Apollo and Venus, not intended exclusively for the beautiful people. The others, the sallow, the sad, the weak and the haunted, the losers, they too could take part.

Eight

NOT SURPRISINGLY, Mark now was interested only in the girl, in their next meeting, the time and place; his duties, such as they were, went largely disregarded. Mowing the lawn was a thing of the past, although this was hardly a problem. The days were dry, as they so often were in late August, and the grass had all but stopped growing. The ground, particularly around the base of the trees, was hard as cement, and the birds had gone off to the deep woods for damp earth and water.

For the most part close-mouthed, Mark talked at length one evening of what he had learned about the household across the water. Warren found that he had been right in one surmise—Daisy indeed had been institutionalized, in a state of deep clinical depression. She still saw a psychiatrist twice a week, not in his office but right there in the house. He drove down twice weekly from Washington. Warren found this impressive.

"He charges the hourly rate plus travel expenses," Mark said. "A four-hour round-trip plus an hour with Daisy. Five hours."

"Who pays?"

"Her father." Mark's eyes had a faraway look. "He pays for everything. Including the baby."

"The baby?"

"Daisy has a baby. It's being raised by a couple in Ohio because she's not well enough to have it with her."

"My God!"

"She was married when she was nineteen. Her husband left her when he found out she was pregnant."

"How old is the child?"

"Not quite two."

"Boy or girl?"

"A girl. Named Cindy. She hopes to get her back as soon as the psychiatrist says it's okay."

They were on the porch after supper. Warren rocked for a while in silence, thinking of Daisy's face on the day he met her. The stricken look. The eyes that seemed filled with the memory of bad dreams.

"Is she better now?" he asked presently. "Is she less depressed now that she's met you? I mean, are you helping her, would you say?"

"Maybe," Mark said. "Maybe." Warren found it strange

that he said it in a way that suggested regret, sadness, rather than the pride and satisfaction one might have expected.

"Does she like you, Mark?"

He nodded. "Yes." He looked down at the porch floor, at a point between his dirty sneakers. "Yes, I think she does."

"You don't seem very happy about it."

"Of course I am," he said. "Of course I am."

"What are the prospects?"

"Who knows? A lot of it depends on her father."

It was her father's feeling, he told Warren, that she was unfit for normal life. She was, as it were, still institutionalized.

"Is it Turk's job to see that she's confined to the property?" Warren asked.

Mark smiled. "Turk is being handled," he said.

"Handled?"

"By Noreen."

"The maid?"

"That's not what we call her," he said. "We call her Daisy's friend. They met at Shepherd Pratt. Noreen had a drinking problem."

Warren thought it over. "Let me get it straight," he said. "Because of Daisy's mental illness, her father saw fit to set her up in one of the most expensive houses in the county, and with her he installed a staff of two—Turk and Noreen."

"Right. Plus a gardener. Also the Huntsman." Mark's smile was now ironic. "That's what Noreen calls him. He's a caretaker. He was the man with the rifle you saw. He lives in a caretaker's cottage. You can't see it from the road."

"Why is *he* there?"

"Protection, I suppose." Mark for a moment seemed lost in thought; then he shrugged. "There's also a woman who comes in twice a week to do the cleaning. Noreen doesn't clean."

"She's a companion to Daisy. . . ."

"Yes. I'm not quite sure what she is to Turk. All I know is that she's making a monkey out of him. He's her love-slave. She calls him 'Turkey-man.' She says, 'Wheah dat Turkey-man?' You know, in a put-on black dialect. 'Wheah dat sweet Turkey-man?' " Mark was smiling faintly. "Noreen studied at the Sorbonne. She looks like Lena Horne in her prime."

"I noticed."

"Daisy says Turk's in heat twenty-four hours a day. It's comical."

"And just why is Noreen willing to go to such lengths to—shall we say—rob Turk of his vitality?"

"For Daisy. She loves Daisy. She started doing it when she knew Daisy wanted to get away from the house to be with me."

Warren let it hang for a moment, slightly addled by the aspect of triangulation that seemed to suggest itself. He had a fleeting impression of fox-goose-grain—knew it was hardly analogous, but there it was. Perhaps a roundelay—Turk to Noreen to Daisy to Mark. A severed roundelay. "I don't mean she loves Daisy in any lesbian way," Mark was saying. "Not in any Old Mammy way either."

Again Warren thought it over. He found it comical to think of Turk, the behemoth, his crankcase drained twice daily, watching glassy-eyed as Daisy came and went as she pleased.

"No," Mark said when he mentioned it. "I don't think Noreen is sleeping with him. She may be, but I think she's just—teasing him. Distracting him. They work on the jigsaw puzzle together."

Warren smiled. "How does the psychiatrist feel about all this?"

"He thinks it's good for Daisy to get away from the house. And good for her to see me."

"Do you agree?"

"Why not?" He was frowning. "Why wouldn't I, Mr. Donaldson?"

He got to his feet and moved to the screen, standing with the tip of his nose all but touching it. "Well . . ." He turned away. "I've got to get going."

The Cove

"You're seeing Daisy?"

"She's picking me up. We're going to the movies."

Warren smiled again. "How do you like the movies being made today?"

"Mostly I don't." He stood for a moment next to the rocker and then: "See you later, Mr. Donaldson."

By now Mark was away much more than he was home. Although he was never gone overnight, it was clear that watching over his invalid employer, being his companion, was something that no longer seemed so important. There were other things on his mind. He was undeniably taking liberties with his employer's hospitality, taking advantage of his good nature, and Warren wondered how Martha might have felt about it. For himself he cared not at all. He was happy for Mark, happy for the girl. His own pleasures, the soft, mild pleasures of convalescence, remained the same. He read. He sat watching the boats move through the cove. He paid bills, answered letters, bought two new speakers for his stereo, had a small drink each night and sat listening to music.

Of all the pleasures at this time of his life, he found listening to music by far the most gratifying. Out in real life the times were alarming. Dumfounded by the world and its persona, its mores and incomprehensible economics, dumfounded by his illness and by what had happened to him, he was, in his convalescence, finding solace and deep pleasure in being dumfounded by music. Legitimately and gloriously dumfounded, for example, by the massive mountain of music left to the world by Antonio Vivaldi, the vast trove of treasure; but his dumfoundment and bewilderment were things of pure joy.

This language, ethereal other-language, at once beyond him and profoundly within him, throbbed in his vitals and delighted his senses, while at the same time remaining incomprehensible. And simply because he could not understand, the music remained a glorious mystery, touching him in some unfathomable way.

67

As the days passed, for all his absorption with Daisy, Mark began once again to be concerned for Warren's welfare, to be interested in how he was spending his days and in whether he was taking his pills on schedule. Once again he expressed interest in Martha's return. Had there been any changes in her schedule? Warren told him none so far. Mark saw and read all her postcards. Her letters were often quite intimate and these, of course, were not shared with him. They spoke of how glad she was that Warren had not died in intensive care and of how much she looked forward to their remaining years together, which now seemed abundant rather than few. Warren felt very close to her and in the evening, listening to his music, he felt a pleasant serenity about his marriage and his life. He and Martha had been fortunate. They often told themselves and each other that they had lived in a good time. From here it was but a short step to be reminded of Mark and other young people in today's world, with the state of its economy, everything so badly tilted against the young. Daily one read in the press of how difficult it was for a young couple to become established. Buying a house was beyond the reach of most.

Unless, as Warren reminded himself, one member of that young couple should happen to be a Daisy King, who, it was safe to guess, had or would have access to substantial wealth. However, he didn't think that her financial prospects had any effect on Mark's feeling for her. It was some other quality about her, perhaps her very frailty, that appealed to him, and as the days moved along in that first week of September he was with her more and more. At first they had sailed a great deal. Warren had watched them morning and afternoon, moving around the cove, but lately the boat had remained at her dock and wherever they went it was not by water. On rare occasions Mark asked to borrow the Toyota, but more often Daisy drove over to pick him up in the silver Mercedes convertible, the top always down, the days always fair. She was better. Her eyes were no longer so sad. Even the circles beneath them had softened. There was color in her cheeks and a trace of hesitant joy in her eyes and around her mouth. It obviously was all because of Mark.

Off they went in those bright early September days, driving once to Annapolis, once to Washington to the Kennedy Center, and all around the bucolic and often picturesque Eastern Shore: Down to Princess Anne and thence westward, following fingers of land to the edge of the bay; over to Assateague where one swam in the ocean under the eye of wild ponies; to the dark waters of the deep narrow Pocomoke River; to all the places neither of them had been and that they now saw at Warren's recommendation. And when not driving to these places they sat, so far as he could judge, mainly on the jalousied porch of the chateau, where they watched television or worked on the giant jigsaw puzzle and from where, Mark said with an ironic smile, he had once looked across the cove and seen Warren riding the tractor. "I'm sorry, Mr. Donaldson," he said. "I've been goofing off."

Warren assured him that having done the mowing for so many years he could do it again any old time, and that in fact he rather enjoyed it.

Mark was sitting on the porch in one of the rockers. He hadn't heard.

"Does Daisy ever talk to you about her marriage?" Warren asked.

Mark's eyes looked pained. "She's begun to. A little. It shattered her. God!"

Warren waited.

"She says she had no will to live," Mark said. "I find that hard to understand, don't you? Or do you?"

"I suppose so," Warren replied. "I've never really experienced it. When I had my heart attack I was very, very close to death, but it didn't occur to me that I was close at all. I was—interested. Curious. Dying didn't seem to be at issue. Because I didn't feel at all close to death—even though I *was. Very* close. Does any of this make sense? I don't see how it possibly could."

Mark laughed softly, and his look for a moment was

affectionate, a brief moment out of context, away from the thoughts foremost in his mind.

Then his brow furrowed. He ran his fingers through his hair, looked at the ceiling, out over the lawn, and then shook his head. "Poor kid," he said softly. "The poor little kid."

"Daisy?"

He nodded. His eyes were clouded. "Yes. Daisy."

There was something odd in the way he said it, something odd in the way his eyes looked. For a moment Warren felt he had detected, in spite of the words, a note of indifference, even of coldness. The moment passed, but he was left with a feeling of puzzlement. Poor Daisy, Mark had said. It seemed hard to believe that he entirely meant it. How could he, when under his touch she had flowered so? His love had transformed her. He had made her into a princess by treating her as one. Warren Donaldson considered himself eminently old-fashioned, old-fashioned enough to believe that people should still dream dreams, that young women unblessed by nature should dream of beauty, the poor of wealth, the weak of power, the lonely of love, and all be the better for it. Perhaps it was only when one stopped dreaming, moved beyond such yearnings, that one reached maturity, but when this happened the loss could be very great.

For Daisy a dream had come true. The very next day, in early afternoon, when she drove over to pick up Mark, she looked more joyous than Warren had ever seen her, as she sat at the wheel of the convertible, the top down, her hair freshly washed, soft and shining in the sunlight, a young woman gravely ill but who was now daring to hope.

Nine

LABOR DAY was late that year. It fell on September 6, which also happened to be Daisy's birthday. She would be twenty-two.

For the birthday dinner, Mark had chosen a restaurant that had been open less than a year and that had given the area the touch of class that its wealthier denizens felt they eminently deserved.

To avoid what promised to be a huge Labor Day evening crowd, he chose to celebrate the following night. Warren was surprised that morning when Mark asked him to go with them. When Warren thanked him, Mark said it was Daisy's idea. "I mean I was all for it too," he said, "but she's the one who thought of it."

Since the Mercedes was a two-seater, Warren volunteered to take Martha's phaeton. To save him the trouble of picking her up, Daisy offered to drive over to the Donaldson house in the Mercedes. When Warren said it was no trouble, she insisted, and he decided it was the better part of tact not to make an issue of it.

The day was beautiful. He put the phaeton's top down and toward six o'clock, with the day still bright, they were tooling along the highway, all three in the front seat, the wind blowing through their hair, the sun still high, Daisy in her white dress and the two men flanking her in blue blazers. The car was beautifully preserved, with its white real-leather upholstery, the rear seat as commodious as the front, and although it was a 1965 model, seventeen years old by then, it gave the impression of having been a part of a much earlier America. Daisy seemed delighted by it, as for that matter was Mark, who had fallen in love with it on the far-off night when Martha met him at the bus stop.

They moved slowly up the cindered drive, beneath an

arched canopy of huge trees, to an opening where cars were lined up side by side. Warren slipped between two VW Bugs, a fact noted by Daisy with a giggle. He had never heard her giggle. He might have thought she was incapable of it. To hear her gave him pleasure.

Although the restaurant made a policy of accepting no reservations, the table to which they were led was splendidly placed. Daisy seemed thrilled—by the occasion, by their table, and most of all, to be sure, by Mark. Her eyes rarely left him. His face was swarthy from his weeks in the sun, accenting the smile lines near his eyes. It all seemed somehow to make him look older and wiser than he had on the day he arrived.

And as for *Gatsby*, Warren mused, it no longer seemed relevant. If Mark had been acting out a charade he had long since dropped it. If he had had a purpose, the purpose was long since served. Perhaps much of it had been in Warren's imagination, nurtured by the phenomenon of the cove, by the two houses facing across the water, the fact that a young girl lived over there and that a young man had found it romantic to know she was there and had found it thrilling to look over the dark water at the lights of her house, or to sit by day, waiting for the sight of her sailboat. Never at any time did Warren doubt that Mark was in love. This much had always seemed authentic.

Daisy was holding her glass of white wine, smiling. She too was tanned, not so deeply as Mark but with a smooth color that contrasted attractively with her flaxen hair and white dress. "I think we should drink to Mr. Donaldson," she was saying shyly. She hardly seemed accustomed to proposing toasts, but here she was. "Because without Mr. Donaldson . . ."—she was smiling at Mark—"we would never have met."

Warren touched his Scotch to her wine, and Mark after a moment did the same with his ginger ale. During the entire summer Warren had not seen him drink anything stronger.

"I'm sure you would have met," he said. "It was only a

question of time. Mark was very determined."

Mark's smile seemed halfhearted. Daisy's slim hand lay on the white tablecloth. He covered it briefly with his own. On her wrist there was a silver bracelet; around her slim, tanned throat a string of pearls. They looked real.

Another round of drinks was served. Of the three, it was Daisy and Warren who were having a good time. Mark was somber. When he joined in, he seemed to do so only with an act of extreme concentration. Warren felt good. Not since his heart attack had he drunk more than a single Scotch, and always very weak ones at that. Perhaps, he told himself, his view of the proceedings was exaggerated. Perhaps Mark was not self-engrossed but merely sober. Warren tried for a sense of order, tried to see things more clearly. What he saw was that if any animation existed it was flowing between Daisy and himself. She was charmed by the place, charmed by the Williamsburg decor and by the added charm of the broad expanse of blue water visible through the window behind Donaldson's head. He had insisted that she have the seat with the view of the water.

Mark now, as their entrées arrived, seemed to make a conscious effort to discard whatever mood was upon him. "Gosh, Mr. Donaldson," he said, "this sure is an attractive place. I'm glad you suggested it. You couldn't have picked anything nicer."

For a long moment Warren sat frozen. Mark had sounded so—he wasn't quite sure. Insincere was not strong enough. Downright phony was more like it, and for the first time that summer he found himself feeling a twinge of dislike. It was as if Mark were changing before his eyes into an entirely new person, one he did not think he was going to like.

"I thought it might appeal to you, Mark," he said. "Knowing how you feel about—"

"The past," Daisy supplied. From the way her eyes played over him, it was plain that she too was vigilant for every nuance. "Mark was born about a hundred years too late," she said.

Mark demurred. "If I'd been born that long ago I'd never have met *you*," he said with a smile.

"Who knows?" She patted his hand. Warren looked from one to the other. Something was going on. Within his state of mild intoxication, he was overcome by a sense of sadness that had to do with the spectacle of a sad young woman of vast wealth, newly emerged from a prison, a tomb, even, seduced and led out by a Mark who now had lost his ardor and seemed merely to be putting on an act. She seemed taken in, but only because she wanted to be. Warren for his part was not, and he noticed that Mark had begun to realize it.

They had arrived early. The room was now beginning to fill up. Out on the river, visible through the window, boats were dropping anchor one by one. When Warren looked over his shoulder, he could see them being met at the channel's edge by the restaurant's tender, a spick-and-span white launch that ferried the visiting yachtsmen back through shoal waters to the restaurant's own dock. By now, there were quite a few of them at the tables nearby, talking of the joys and miseries of cruising and all quite happy, it seemed, to be eating ashore instead of in their respective galleys.

Daisy seemed pleased by all this. For someone brought up in wealth she seemed so appreciative that in his haze, his Scotch mist, Warren was once again overcome by melancholy. Then suddenly he felt a stab of suspicion, prompted this time by the sight of her pearl necklace. Was it her money after all that had attracted Mark? Could he be such a bastard? Warren had long since decided not, yet how much, after all, did he really know about him?

For the rest, Warren had managed, with no little persuasion and a few dollars, to exact from the management something they at first professed an unwillingness to provide— the implication being that it was beneath their level of sophistication, that it was folksy, and that folksiness was hardly their thing.

Nonetheless, as a result of Warren's wheedling, in it

now came, borne aloft by an unsmiling, jaundiced young man in a gold linen jacket, his face solemn above a cake with white icing and five white candles, the flames of which bent double, so swiftly was he moving, the sooner to have done with it.

In Warren's relaxed state he began singing "Happy Birthday" even as the young man approached. Mark smiled and managed to join in. There were amused glances from neighboring diners.

"Happy birthday, dear Daisy . . . happy birthday to you."

Mark and Warren clapped, and there was scattered applause and even a couple of "hoorays" from the room at large.

But Daisy was not noticing. Her small face was buried in her huge gold damask napkin. Mark frowned. He reached for her hand. She let him take it. Still her face remained hidden behind the napkin. Warren asked himself what he had done. "Daisy," he said feebly.

"She'll be okay," Mark murmured. He gripped her hand, patted it, then held it in both of his.

Gradually the sobbing subsided. The napkin fell to her lap, and although tears still glistened she was doing her best to smile. "I'm sorry. . . ." She touched her eyes. "I'm—sentimental. It was so very nice of you."

"It was Mr. Donaldson," Mark said. "He did the whole thing."

"Thank you, Mr. Donaldson, thank you so much. . . ." With quick motions, she picked up a knife. "I'll cut it, okay?"

One by one she removed the five candles. "I think that's what did it," she said. "The five candles." Suddenly her eyes were filled with tears again, but she was managing to smile now, even as she wept. "I felt like I was five years old again."

"How did it feel?" Mark asked gently.

"Very good. It was a good birthday. I think this is my nicest birthday since I was five years old. Funny you should have picked five. Because my fifth was the first I have any memory of, and I know it was a happy one."

Shoving back her chair, she got up and circled the table, bent and kissed Warren's cheek. "Thank you, thank you, Mr. Donaldson."

Warren was touched. His voice was about to break. "Many happy returns, Daisy," he said.

She was bending now to kiss Mark, then returning to her seat and picking up the knife again. "And now let's eat it," she said. Looking up from the cake, she managed another smile. "Happy birthday," she said. "To one and all."

She was looking long and hard at Mark, a searching look. Once again tears blurred her eyes. She did not like what she was seeing. Mark's eyes dropped. He looked away.

Ten

THE SUMMER WAS DRAWING to an end. The waters of the cove and river were blue and sharp, and the days cool with bright, filtered sunlight. Soon one would be hearing the first cries of the Canada geese that for so many years had arrived with October, but that seemed now to arrive earlier and earlier, as if perhaps to live through as many bright, beautiful days as possible before the hunting season began.

Warren Donaldson had always felt autumn was a time of renewal, but it was also a time of sadness with the changing slant of the light and the shortening days. Across the cove Daisy, he felt sure, was feeling all this and something much worse. Since the birthday dinner, Mark had seen her twice, but neither time for long. When Warren questioned him he was evasive. He obviously had no desire to talk about it. Nothing lasted forever, he said, and the summer was ending. Her father was due on the fifteenth, which happened to be the day before Warren would be driving up to Dulles to meet Martha's plane. "Will you be meeting her father?" Warren asked. Mark shrugged and made no reply. By now this was characteristic and apparent not only in his indifference toward the girl but even toward Donaldson. Civil enough, he was not making the effort to ingratiate himself that he had made all summer.

He planned to stay long enough to tell Martha goodbye. Warren told him he was welcome to stay on for a few days more if he liked, but Mark thought not. Would he be returning to New York? He shrugged. He supposed so.

On the evening of the fourteenth his attitude seemed to soften briefly, and for a few minutes he was the young man Warren had grown to know and like during the summer. He had spent the evening quietly in his room, reading probably. Warren had spent it on the porch, listening to the music that poured out from the speakers in the living room.

Toward eleven o'clock he looked up to see Mark standing in the doorway. "Mr. Donaldson . . ." The words seemed difficult for him. They seemed to die in his throat. But then he recovered. "It's been a nice summer." He paused. "And whatever happens, I'd just like you to know that I think you're a helluva nice guy."

He turned and went inside.

Martha was flying in from Rome. She was due at Dulles at five, and Warren knew from experience that it would be at least an additional hour before she cleared customs. From the house it was about a three-hour drive up to Dulles, and he had planned to leave shortly after two.

It was still morning when, seated on the porch, he looked up from the newspaper in time to witness the arrival of a vehicular phenomenon that he knew to be increasingly popular on U.S. highways and for which he had an intense distaste.

What he beheld easing to a stop in the parking lot was a huge vehicle of the type used for chasing wild game over the African veldt. It was pitched high off the ground and was supported by four of the fattest tires he had ever seen.

It was black with random, wavery orange stripes, a color combination perhaps intended to suggest something tiger-ish.

From it now emerged a young man with what Warren had come to recognize as a laid-back California look, his legs sheathed in gray denim, a matching gray denim jacket swinging wide to reveal a chest sprinkled with a stubble of hair. A silver chain encircled his neck and from the chain hung a silver medallion. His face was tanned and his bleached hair was of medium length, cut in what in Warren's youth had been known as a Dutch bob.

He was approaching now with a grin, closer perhaps to a leer, wary, defensive. "Uncle Warren? . . . Are you Uncle Warren? Hi. I'm Eliot."

"Well, *Eliot,*" Warren said. "Well, I'll be a son of a gun."

"I guess maybe you're surprised to see me," Eliot said.

"Maybe a little. How did things go in California?"

Warren was looking at the impossibly fat tires of the vehicle and then up at the steering wheel, thinking how superior at that elevation it must make the driver feel to an eland or zebra or other pedestrian.

"Pretty good," he said. "I was on my way home and I just thought I'd drop by to say hello and see how things went."

"Everything went very well." Except for the color of his hair, Eliot looked very close to the way one might have expected a son of Roy's to look at this age. His small piglike eyes were very much reminiscent of Roy's.

"I know it was a dirty trick to play on you at the last minute like that," Eliot was saying. "But I hoped you and Aunt Martha would understand. It was just too good a chance to turn down."

"It was perfectly understandable," Warren said.

Eliot now was looking about with an unsettled expression, as if it had dawned upon him for the first time that they were still standing in the parking lot. "So what do we do?" he asked. "Go up and sit on the porch, or what?"

Warren moved toward the screened porch. "Come and have a seat," he said.

"Where's what's-his-name?" Eliot asked. "Mark?"

"He's around somewhere," Warren said. He sagged into a rocker and Eliot into its counterpart. The jacket fell open, and now Warren could see the tattoo on his sternum, a tattoo depicting the full-blown body of a nude woman, the head hidden by the silver medallion but the remainder easily discernible through the stubble. For a moment Warren regarded it with fascination, realizing that his age made him feel she bore a resemblance to the late Jayne Mansfield. Someone less stricken with years might have said Dolly Parton.

"How did he work out?" Eliot was asking. "Was he okay?"

"He was just fine," Warren said. "Just fine."

"Well bleep, that's a bleeping relief anyway. I was afraid for a minute back out there on the parking lot that you were bleeped with me."

The words he was using were, in actuality, *bleep, bleeping,* and *bleeped,* as if he felt the real thing might be unfit for anyone of Warren's age, or had been so admonished by the home folks.

"Okay if I use the phone a second, Uncle Warren?" He was on his feet. "I oughtta call the old man and let him know I'm back."

Warren led him inside to the kitchen phone. A moment later Eliot was telling the operator he wanted to make a collect call to New York City. He gave her the number and then immediately hung up and began dialing, having been told by the operator, of course, that even though it was a collect call he could dial it himself. Now, from the throaty chuckle coming from the kitchen, Warren could tell that the connection had been established. "Roy, you old son of a bitch, how the hell are ya, anyway?" Spoken albeit with affection. And then, eschewing *bleep:* "Hell yes, more ass than you could shake a stick at. . . . Yeah . . . Yeah . . . How about Aggie? Does she know anything? . . . Good . . . Yeah,

that's where I am. That's where I am right *now*. . . . Yeah
. . ." Another chuckle, followed by a burst of laughter.

Warren moved stolidly out of earshot, passing Mark's
room. He was not there. He moved onto the porch and
slumped into his rocker, finding it necessary now to face a
very practical problem.

"The old man says to say hello," Eliot said as he returned.

"Tell him I said hello," Warren replied.

"Yeah, I'll do that."

"Eliot," Warren said, facing the problem, "your Aunt
Martha is flying in from Rome this afternoon, and I have
to leave in a couple of hours to drive up and meet her."
He paused. Eliot was rocking with considerable speed.
"I'd ask you to ride up with me, except that she's got a lot of
luggage—"

"No problem, Uncle Warren, no problem . . ."

"And I'm afraid there's hardly going to be room enough
even for us. I mean the *two* of us. By that I mean for Martha
and myself."

Eliot was waving his hand in dismissal. "No problem,"
he said again. "I gotta get going soon. I promised Aggie I'd
drop by on the way back and offer my apologies in person
—and, like I say, to see how everything went."

"Your apologies are accepted," Warren said. "And everything went just fine. No need to apologize, none at all.
Martha and I both felt that what you were doing was a very
worthwhile way to be spending the summer."

"I'm gonna let you in on a little secret, Uncle Warren,
if you promise not to tell Aunt Martha."

"What secret is that, Eliot?" From the phone conversation he had overheard, Warren felt reasonably certain that
it had nothing to do with religion.

He then sat listening as Eliot recounted how he had
spent the summer in a billowing sea of willing flesh, making
pornographic movies aboard a yacht somewhere off the
coast of southern California.

"I was planning to spend the summer with you, Uncle

80

Warren, I really was," Eliot said. "And then this guy Mark keeps coming into the arcade and getting real friendly. . . ."

"Arcade?"

"Yeah. So one day he brings this other guy with him, Tex Poffenberger, the director, and Tex offers me the chance to spend the summer in California acting in pornies. So—I mean, what am I—flesh and blood, or what?"

Warren paused. "Flesh and blood, I should think," he replied. "So then Mark—"

"Mark says he'll be glad to take my place because he likes the country a lot and he's got nothing better to do." Eliot grinned. "Wait just a minute, Uncle Warren, I got something for you."

From somewhere inside the house there was a sound that Warren took to be a footstep. Eliot by then was out in the parking lot, climbing until he reached the driver's seat level, reaching into the car, and now returning with a broad grin.

In one hand he carried an enlargement of a color photograph. The other held something that he stuffed into the pocket of his denim jacket. The photograph was of a yacht. In the cockpit, leaning over the after-rail, stood a bevy of topless beauties. On the cabin roof stood three more, these not only topless but bottomless, gaily waving against a bright blue California sky.

Across the transom, in large black block letters, was the vessel's name:

S E A - R A G L I O

"I mean," Eliot was saying, "what would *you* have done if a guy comes up to you and says how would you rather spend your summer—mowing your uncle's grass or mowing yourself some ass?"

"I think you did the right thing," Warren replied.

Eliot grinned. "That's kinda the way I was hoping you'd feel about it." Now he reached into the pocket of his jacket. "Here, Uncle Warren, I brought you a little present. Here."

Warren looked at the object Eliot had transferred to his

palm. It was, if he was not mistaken, a flesh-colored plastic phallus.

"The batteries may be a little weak," Eliot said. "It just takes those little transistor batteries. There. Press it. Right there. It's a blast."

Warren did as directed. The end lit up and from somewhere within a weak voice said, "Hello!"

Warren looked at it for a second and placed it on the table. "Very nice," he said. "Thanks very much, Eliot. That was very thoughtful of you."

"You can pick up new batteries at the drugstore, or almost any place," Eliot said.

"Yes, I should think so."

"I thought you might want to spring it on somebody at a party or something like that," Eliot said. "We have all kinds of stuff like this at the arcade."

Warren looked at him thoughtfully. "This arcade you speak of. . . ."

"You know—like adult books, adult items . . ."

"Is this the bookstore that your mother mentioned to your Aunt Martha? Does your mother think you and your father are running a bookstore?"

"I'm not really sure what she thinks," Eliot said. "Sometimes I think she's onto it and doesn't want to admit it."

"Does she know how you spent the summer?"

"*Hell* no! And I don't want her to. If she thought Aunt Martha knew I ran out on you to spend the summer making pornies, she'd have my ass. You gotta promise not to tell, okay? Man to man. Besides, I'd never have done it if it hadn't been for Tex Poffenberger and Mark."

By now Warren was no longer listening. He had heard the kitchen door close, softly but unmistakably. "Excuse me a second, Eliot. I'll be right back."

Warren was reasonably confident that what he had heard was his friend Mark, his friend of the summer, taking his leave, taking flight.

By the time he reached the kitchen door Mark was halfway across the parking lot, leaving on foot, dressed in his white jeans, the backpack strapped over his shoulders, just as it had been the night Martha met him at the darkened bus stop in the deep country.

"Mark . . . ," Warren called.

The look he gave Warren held no fear. Instead it contained a great deal of affection, and a sad apology. In it there was gratitude, and in the faint, sad smile he seemed to be saying that they had been through something together, and he was asking Warren to understand.

When Warren called to him he turned and started jogging down the driveway.

Whatever he had done, and for whatever reason, it was over.

Warren watched him disappear. Going back into the house, he glanced into the small downstairs room. The bed was smoothly made. The television screen was dark. No blue shirt hanging on the back of the chair. It seemed strange to find it empty.

Then he noticed something he had overlooked. On the dresser in a neat pile were the weekly paychecks Warren had given him during the course of the summer. They were all there. Not a single one had been cashed.

Eleven

WARREN LEFT FOR DULLES just after two. By then Eliot had taken his departure, after asking him once more not to reveal the nature of his mission to California.

Warren had allowed himself plenty of time. All the way to Washington and through the city to the Beltway and thence to Dulles, he drove at a modest pace, thinking his thoughts, feeling less and less interested in Eliot as the miles passed. What interested him was the young man who had spent the summer beneath his roof, eating his food, mowing his lawn. Mark had set it up. Why had he done it? What had he been up to? He hardly seemed a hippie parasite and obviously had no interest in robbing the house. Nor had there been anything sleazy about him. Certainly he had not given the impression of someone connected with pornographic movies. Yet he had obviously arranged the entire thing, perhaps even Eliot's (Warren could not resist it) abduction to the *Sea-raglio*.

The plane was on time. Warren stood with a throng awaiting the arrival of international passengers, watching the faces as they came around the corner from the customs area. When he saw Martha he dashed forward and embraced her. Then he picked up her bags. Both were light. From years of excursions with her travel group she had learned how to travel light.

There she was smiling in her black suit and white blouse. He was enormously glad to see her, as he always was when she returned from one of these trips. They had had a long and checkered marriage. Whatever flaws it may have contained, they had ended up liking each other a great deal, and they held hands for almost the entire distance from Dulles to the Beltway. Her hands were long and slim and quite beautiful, by far the nicest hands he had ever known.

All this while she was telling him about her trip, about the people on the tour, about the generosity of the Italians, their cathedrals and galleries and fountains, their mad traffic patterns, the caloric content of their food. When she seemed for the time being to be finished, he said, "Okay. Now I have something to tell *you.*"

They ate at a place on the Annapolis side of the Chesapeake Bay Bridge, lingering with an after-dinner drink and then another. He told her everything there was to be told. She kept shaking her head in wonderment, frowning, pressing for more details. "What a strange-sounding boy," she said. "Riding home from the bus that night, I thought he was so nice."

"He *was* nice. What gets me is why he manipulated Eliot the way he did. Obviously he engineered the whole thing. Why was he so hell-bent to spend the summer in *our* house?"

"There's something that makes me uneasy about it," she said. "Do you suppose he was setting us up for something?"

"I can't believe that," Warren said. "He seemed—decent. I didn't much like the way he treated Daisy toward the end, but he was always more than decent to me."

"He struck me the same way. . . ." Martha shook her head. "As for Eliot, he sounds perfectly disgusting."

"He was," Warren agreed. "A real chip off the old block. Hell, I guess things could have been a whole lot worse. I could have had *Eliot* with me this summer. But I wouldn't have. I'd have sent him packing after one day."

Martha's eyes moistened. "The way they treat poor Agnes. As if she were some kind of moronic invalid. You're right about Roy. You've always been right about him. He's despicable."

It was past eleven when they got home. Setting down Martha's bags, Warren took his pills and then for the first time that summer locked all the doors.

Martha was in the living room, examining the plastic phallus. "Where on earth did you get *this?*"

"A little present from your nephew," Warren said. "Just think—I might have had it weeks ago if Eliot hadn't decided to go off to California."

She seemed unsure whether to show disgust or laugh. She did a little of both.

"Here," he said. "Press it."

She did as directed.

"Hello," it said.

"Just like a momma doll," Warren said.

"I suppose it works on the same principle," Martha said.

"I really wouldn't know. Or care."

Complaining of jet lag, she was soon in bed. Warren crawled in beside her, tried to engage her in conversation about the young man who had spent the summer in their house, but she was too sleepy to talk about it.

When he awoke the next morning, the room was filled with sunlight. Martha was up, and from downstairs came the smell of coffee. Contentedly, he lay there thinking what a pleasure it would be not to have to provide his own meals. He bounded from bed. Martha brought him breakfast on the porch. When he had finished he sat looking around the cove, searching as he had so often searched for the sight of the Thistle. But there were no boats out; the cove was empty; and he sat wondering about Mark, wondering if he had stopped long enough to tell Daisy goodbye.

Toward two that afternoon, he heard the sound of sirens across the water, still a long way off, still very faint, but getting steadily louder.

He got up from his rocker and looked across the cove, frowning curiously. The sound, if he was not mistaken, was coming from the direction of Daisy's house.

He slipped inside and grabbed the binoculars, already raising them to his eyes as he hurried down the lawn. He saw an ambulance near the porte cochere, then the flashing red dome of a police car, and then two more pulling in behind the first.

Two men were hurrying with a stretcher. He was at the very end of the dock by now, and the view through the binoculars was sharper. The ambulance was backing around so that its rear doors now faced him. The doors swung open. Two state troopers headed for the house. Then, for a few minutes, nothing except for the flashing red domes of the police cars. Now the stretcher reappeared. Two men in white slid it carefully into the ambulance and the doors closed behind it. Lights blinking, the ambulance moved away, and as it passed from view among the trees its siren began to sound.

One of the police cars followed. The other two remained behind.

Hurrying back up the lawn, Warren called to Martha. She appeared as he stepped into the kitchen. "What's going on across the cove?"

"Daisy's house," he said. "An ambulance. Cop cars. God knows what-all." He handed her the binoculars and she stood in the doorway, training them on the house across the cove.

Long ago, Mark had written Daisy's number on a slate that was kept in the kitchen. It was still there. He dialed the number and it was of course busy.

"See anything?" He snapped on the radio and turned in the local station, noted for its singing strings.

"Just two patrol cars," Martha said.

"Keep watching." He dialed the number again and once more got the busy signal.

The singing strings abruptly went silent in midbar. "We interrupt this program to bring you the following news bulletin," the familiar voice of the staff announcer said. "A man has been shot and fatally wounded in a home near Mills Landing. The dead man has been identified as Hamilton Carver, age about sixty. His alleged assailant has been tentatively identified by police as Mark Travis, age about thirty-five, of New York City. The gunman, according to police, made his escape on foot after being shot at least once by an armed guard who was stationed on the premises."

"Police have broadcast a lookout," the news bulletin continued, "for a white male, who when last seen was wearing white jeans and carrying a backpack. We will bring you further details as they become available."

In the days that followed, the details became plentifully available. They filled the local newspaper, and the story was played prominently in Washington and Baltimore as well as New York. Hamilton Carver, Daisy's father, was a prominent financier and developer. He was shot in early afternoon of the day following his arrival for the visit Mark had mentioned more than once, and of which Mark had obviously been aware for weeks.

When the plainclothesmen came to question him, Warren told of Mark's fascination with Daisy, of his ardent desire to meet her, and of his own role in making it possible. He also told of the elaborate way Mark had maneuvered Eliot off to California for the summer so he could take his job.

Warren's remaining thoughts he kept to himself. The problem Mark had faced was of course formidable. He had had not only to meet Daisy but to become a part of her life, to become someone she would trust completely, indeed fall in love with. He must hve been well aware that the precautions taken by and for her father would be elaborate, almost impossible to crack, unless he had the entrée to the household given him by his close relationship with Daisy.

So that the whole thing was clearly a scheme to commit cold-blooded murder.

Although Warren told her he had discounted *Gatsby* in the end, Martha found the idea intriguing enough to reread the novel. One evening in the living room she came upon a passage that she read aloud. They were indoors by then. The summer was long gone. The days were short and the nights chilly.

"Listen," she said. "Listen to this: 'He had . . . paid a high price for living too long with a single dream.' "

Jay Gatsby, of course. Yet it seemed to have relevance to the young man who had lived in their house that summer. What had the dream been? And was it dream or nightmare?

Part III

Flight

Twelve

THE GLITTERING HIGHWAY stretched to infinity beneath the blue flame of the Mexican sky.

From the window of the speeding car he could see mountains rising beyond the open range, their molded peaks blending with dense white clouds; the mountains giving substance to the clouds; the clouds in turn making of the peaks more than mountains.

In late afternoon the road curved through the foothills and, looking upward, he caught glimpses of upland valleys, majestic with their many shades of green and all known patterns of line and curve, darkening greens against lighter greens, curving boundaries of color, spokes and haphazard oblongs and random crescents, some a blazing rich green high up toward the sun, and the rest curving away into shadow.

On he moved in headlong flight, a man driving through a landscape of magical luminosity, a man whose flight path carried him through the most gorgeous landscape he had ever known.

He was aware of a strange mixture of beauty and horror, Blake's marriage of heaven and hell. He could not have been so deeply stirred by the beauty and grandeur had his senses not been so raw, had he not come to it as a man filled with horror, a man more in flight from his life than fleeing to save it, for there had been nothing to save ever since the day, months earlier, when his wife had thrown herself in front of a subway train.

For so long, all through the summer, living with the gullible, kindly, courtly person named Warren Donaldson, he had survived on hatred, burning with the need for revenge. He had shot to kill; yet aside from what he had done to poor Daisy he felt no remorse. He had willfully, cynically duped a mentally disturbed girl into thinking that he was in love with her. He had made love to her mechanically, untouched by his own deceit, desensitized, untouched by the hurt it would ultimately bring her, convinced that what he was doing was the only way.

He was not sorry that Carver was dead. The man deserved to die. At times he felt it might have been preferable that he had lived, for only by living could Carver have known the enormity, the fierceness of another man's hatred; only by living could he know that another human being hated him so violently and heedlessly that he was willing and eager to commit murder, and then willing and eager to accept the consequences, whatever they might be.

Flight.

Exile.

Extinction.

He could see Carver's face, the shock, the fear, abject fear as he looked at the pistol. Daisy was on the porch and Turk was away. Only Noreen saw, and he remembered not caring that she would be there to witness what was about to take place. She had met him at the front door, looked at him with doubt. In spite of the frequency of his visits, there was a new quality in her expression, and it was all quite clear. The master was in residence. Things were not the same. "I'm not sure Daisy is home. Wait here just a minute and I'll see. . . ." And then she was looking beyond his shoulder, through the screen door, out toward the parking lot, the driveway, seeing no car in which he might have arrived, wondering for those fleeting seconds how he had gotten there; and looking too, it was clear, for some sign of the Huntsman, concerned and puzzled; but then turning away even so and starting down the long hall with its fresh aqua and white paint; and then the sound of footsteps, a heavy tread, a man, *the* man, moving slowly down the stairway—and abruptly falling the rest of the way, clutching his chest where the shot had entered and where his white silk shirt was already stained red. He was on his back for a second, mouth open, the insides of his yellowed teeth visible, and then trying, crabwise, to move, clutching at his assailant's feet before collapsing into death.

And then, or surely before, surely at the sound of the shot and the muffled sound of the body falling down the thickly carpeted stairway . . . but when? It was blurred, the shot, the fall, the screams from Noreen and then Daisy, the single glance at Daisy, the look in her eyes, and then he was bolting, he was outside, running, entering the woods, dodging, veering, although he heard no one in pursuit, saw no sign of the Huntsman, who had failed at his job but who, of course, could be forgiven, so skillfully had it all been done during the course of the summer, so intimately had he linked himself with the household. Failed—but now: first the whine and only then the sound of the shot and with it the searing pain as the slug grazed his scalp, just as if it had carefully parted his hair. Another whine, crack, the thud of slug in loblolly, and then no more, only the sound of his own gasping as his lungs fought for air and as, with rasping sobs, he tried to supply it, never slowing his pace and finally, when he was beyond the estate grounds, finding the strength to sprint along the shoulder of the road to where he had left the rented car, then driving at eighty miles an hour down the tree-canopied county road, eyes on the mirror, headed southward, ever southward.

Without sleep, he had driven deep into Texas, crossed the border at Brownsville and was now almost a thousand miles into Mexico. He drove as if mesmerized, with no aim save motion. Flight was a way of life, a condition of the human spirit.

Often he felt an infinite loneliness, a longing for the company of the Mexican peasants he had never known and would never know—figures in the passing landscape, men slung in hammocks visible in the oblong of space that served as a doorway for their clay huts.

As he hurtled past the huts and hovels, the people, the faces, were sometimes a blur, but at other times for a fleeting instant he saw them in sharp detail, feeling a pang of compassion and longing—a desire to know them, to eat with them, to join their herdsmen and drive home the lean Brahman cattle that strayed over the open range and grazed so perilously close to the highway.

A desire to live in their huts and play in their caked yards with their children, taking love wherever he might find it.

His loneliness became most acute as twilight approached. At tiny crossroad settlements the highway came to life. All the young men at evening, when the day's work was done. The road was their link with the world. As in earlier civilizations boys had stood on the banks of rivers and watched sailing ships bound for far places, these stood at the side of the road and watched the cars speed past—to Tampico, to Vera Cruz, to Ciudad Victoria.

At twilight in their white shirts and black pants they gathered along the road, sat along its edge, stood bent, elbows on knees in the dimming light, etched against the dark blue glory of their mountains, talking and laughing at day's end, convinced for now of their immortality.

Thirteen

WHEN NIGHT FELL the beauty was gone, and he was alone in the darkness, following the high beam of the headlights. His sleepless brain had begun to play tricks. Along the edge of the path of light, the outlines of trees and outcropping of rock became figures in his imagination. Ahead loomed the house in which he had been born, a single light burning in its window. He had almost reached it when he slammed on the brakes, heart pounding, shaken to find that he had been speeding toward the rear of a lumbering, top-heavy truck that traveled with no lights save a kerosene lamp hung from its rear bumper. He sounded his

94

horn, swung past it, and drove on.

Half an hour passed. Shadows fled by. Anne's silhouette, arms outstretched, and beyond her the shadow of Carver. Anne's waxen face, pale white in death. He was standing in the morgue and the drawer slid slowly open to reveal her mutilated body, her face seamed with blood. There was a flash of white, and he swerved to avoid a man galloping a white horse toward him along the narrow shoulder of the road.

By now it was past midnight, and as he drove he prayed for the village that he knew from the map could not be far away. When he reached it, the highway became a muddy, rut-filled main street lined with the dispirited silhouettes of dark houses. He could drive no more. Wearily he pulled to a stop before a cantina in which a dim light burned, but when he climbed the broken steps and knocked there was no answer. Descending the stairway, he stood for a moment looking up at the blazing stars and their unfamiliar constellations.

Getting into the car, he let his head fall back against the seat. When he closed his eyes he could see the horseman reign up sharply and the face of the horse, white in the headlights, wild-eyed, and then gone as the car sped onward.

Soon he slept and his last waking thought was of falling deeper and deeper, down an endless flight of steps into the city morgue, into the subway tunnel, and finally deep into the cavern with its sloping walls and low ceiling, rough and pitted, contoured by deep shadows.

Down the long stone stairway she walked into a circle of blue light and for a moment stood motionless, the blue light touching her face and dark masses of hair, a slim young woman in a white pleated dress drawn in at the waist by a strip of lavender. The headwaiter beckoned and she followed, moving with graceful strides that drove her thighs against the soft material of the white dress. Seated at the next table, she glanced at him and then away as a waiter approached. She was asking the waiter about the well, and when the waiter looked at her without comprehension she shrugged, gave her order, and began to inspect her surroundings, her eyes luminous, fringed with heavy, dark lashes. She was searching the ceiling and then, with a frown, glancing all about the grotto, as if perhaps looking for an airshaft, and now at the stream, as if gauging its depth. He followed her gaze. The stream traced a narrow course, widening into a pool at the bend where they and a handful of other patrons sat, then disappearing left and right behind a wall of rock. The stream's limestone bottom was visible as if through a sheet of clean glass. So clear was the water that it doubtless was deeper than it looked; yet the ceiling arching above it was unbroken. Flying in that September afternoon from Mexico City, leafing through a pamphlet on the attractions of Mérida, he had read of a nightclub where nightly at ten o'clock a young girl was thrown into a well, an act patterned after a ritual of human sacrifice once highly popular among the ancient Mayans. The girl's body was painted blue and the act was replete with high priest and eerie screams, but already it had struck him as obvious that whatever act they might witness could not possibly include someone being tossed down a well.

The young woman's smile and shrug seemed to indicate that she had reached the same conclusion. Her drink arrived. Raising the glass, she touched the rim with her lips and set it down. He found it hard not to stare. As their eyes met, she smiled. "I think we've been had," she said. She was still looking into his eyes, gently moving a forefinger down the stem of her glass, up and down, up and down, again and again.

She was American and so was he, but they were in Mexico. He summoned the waiter and listened as, a moment later, the man, bending deferentially from the waist, said: "*Por favor, señorita* . . . the gentleman wonders if he might join you."

She smiled, looked into her glass for a moment and then looked up. "Tell the gentleman, why not?"

Flight

The waiter held a chair and he sat down. "Hi," she said.
"I'm Anne Myatt."

"Charlie Ellis . . ."

She extended her hand. He held out his own and it was
grasped firmly with long, slim fingers. "Hi, Charlie . . . ,"
she said. "Did you come here expecting to see a girl thrown
into a well by any chance? Do you see any way?"

He shook his head. "Not unless they get a well-digger
in here in a hell of a hurry."

"We could sue them for false advertising. . . ."

He had photographed fashion models by the score, beautiful girls with high cheekbones, perfect skin, perfect
mouths. She was their equal, but already what he felt for
her had to do with something beyond her beauty.

"How long have you been in Mérida?" she was asking.

"I flew in this afternoon. I asked the waiter at supper
what there was to do here at night. It was either this or sit
in my room and watch Mexican television."

She smiled. "Are you on your vacation?"

"Assignment. I'm leaving tomorrow for a place called
Chichén Itzá to do a picture layout."

She laughed.

"Why so funny?"

"A place called Chichén Itzá . . ." Her eyes danced. "A
place called Chichén Itzá . . ."

"A bunch of Mayan ruins," he said.

"I know, Charlie," she said softly. "I *know.*"

"I'd never heard of it before," he said.

"I have." She was looking into her drink and her voice
seemed faraway. "I've been waiting to go there for years."

"Is it where you're headed?"

"I'm doing the circuit." She looked up. "Tulum. Uxmal.
Palenque. Chichén. I'm waiting to hear tomorrow morning
where I start. . . . So you're a photographer? . . ."

"Yes."

"Well . . . I'm in publishing."

"Magazines?"

"No. Castle Press."

"Oh, sure . . ." He sipped his drink. "Do you live in Manhattan?"

"Yes. You?"

He nodded. "Just off Washington Square. The corner of Waverly and University Place."

"I know where you mean. I love it down there. You must be right across the street from Washington Mews."

"Almost."

Again she was moving her fingers lightly up and down the delicate stem of her glass. "Where are you staying in Mérida?"

"Excelsior."

She laughed.

"You too?"

"Sure. It's where the travel agents send all us gringos. Aha! What have we here?"

The lights had dimmed to a deep blue. Her hair swung as she turned and peered into the darkness. There was the distant sound of a drum, a ceremonial *thump-thump*, then an interval and another *thump-thump*, two understated notes of portent.

She was looking toward the stairway. "I believe that something solemn and grim is about to take place." She paused. "Or perhaps merely ludicrous."

"Maybe the well-diggers are here," he said.

Down the stairway advanced the sound, and then from the deep shadows at the foot of the steps a figure emerged, a man holding a vertical tube of a drum. Still *thump-thump-ing*, he backed against the grotto wall as two barefooted girls appeared in red dresses with miniskirts, each carrying a bowl of fire. Setting the bowls on the floor, they took up posts flanking a large stone slab that jutted out over the now-darkened stream, turning toward the stairway as another girl appeared, this one clearly the intended victim, for she stared straight ahead as if at doom. She wore a long, loose white dress and in her hands were white flowers. Someone at one of the other tables made the kissing, chirping sound frequently addressed in Latin America to comely, and uncomely, females. The girl took no notice. She was trying hard to achieve the look of one about to be sacrificed, shrinking theatrically away as the two miniskirted handmaidens advanced and conducted her to the slab.

Anne watched with a rapt smile. Her hands were clasped on the table. Her nails were clean and unpainted. In the dim blue light her lashes shadowed her face. She was watching the young victim, who was now draped supine over the sacrificial slab, striking an attitude of fear and passivity, raising the flowers to her face and registering wide-eyed dismay at the appearance of two prancing males in breechclouts.

"The crew," Charlie said.

"Shhh, Charlie," she murmured. Eyes still intent on the spectacle, she reached across and touched his hand.

The two men, bells jingling at their ankles, had kicked over the bowls of fire and now danced about the bowls, occasionally thrusting their feet into the flames and withdrawing them with soles ablaze. They took turns grimacing at the victim, then pranced to the foot of the stairway, drawing apart to leave a path for the climactic entrance of the grand executioner, the high priest. As the tempo of the drums increased, he appeared from the shadows and paused dramatically on the bottom step, neck rigid, as though hard put to sustain the weight of the priestly headdress, a convex sheet of gold fanning high and wide and apparently so heavy as to make the head wobble.

His approach touched off a show of panic in the victim, who had been sprawled over the sacrificial slab in moody resignation, but who now, at the sight of her malefactor, leapt to her feet as if bent upon flight, only to be restrained by the handmaidens. Each grabbed a wrist, and after a brief tugging match she was subdued and draped once more over the slab.

Again, as a dagger appeared in the hand of the high

priest, Charlie noticed Anne's reaction. Her smile had faded. She sat tensely forward, lips parted, fists knotted on the table.

The lights went out. In the darkness there was a scream and then another as the beat of the drums accelerated. When the lights came on again, the victim was sprawled over the slab as if dead and the high priest was wiping the dagger.

There was a loud echoing laugh, and all eyes now turned to the stream where, bathed in brilliant white light, a man stripped to the waist stood in water up to his shoulders. He wore a huge square mask with heavy painted eyebrows and huge painted teeth. Once more he laughed and his laughter echoed around the cavern.

Again the lights went out, and when they came on again he had disappeared, apparently around the bend of the stream beyond the wall of rock into a neighboring chamber.

The drum thumped. The victim rose from the slab and filed with the others toward the stairway, making an exit. As she passed the table her eyes met Charlie's. She was smiling a little, looking sheepish. He smiled back and clapped lightly.

Anne took no notice. She was following the girl closely with her eyes, eyes filled with fascination and something more.

Not until the girl had disappeared up the stairway did she relax. "That would be Chac, I suppose." She smiled.

"Shock and chaos," he said.

"The guy with the mask. Chac. The rain god. C-h-a-c. Pronounced 'shock.' Short for Chac-mul. A god familiarly known as—Chac."

"So what was with Chac? What was he yelling about?"

"He lived at the bottom of the sacred well at Chichén Itzá. When the girls were thrown in, he was waiting for them. It was a very high honor. The girls wore their best clothes, their gold bracelets and rings. Stuff like that."

She took a deep breath. "Wow. Crazy, huh?"

"Yeah. I wonder what was on TV?"

She laughed. The other patrons were filing away, and they were left alone in the bright blue light. "Well . . . I guess that's it, Charlie. Shall we go?"

He followed her up the long stairway, his eyes on her slim ankles and the curved strength of her calves. Upstairs at the entrance she confronted the headwaiter, saying a few words in Spanish, lightly chiding him for false advertising. The headwaiter spread his hands, smiling apologetically. "*Otra noche, otra noche* . . . ," he said.

She smiled. "I'll bet you say that *every noche*," she said.

Uncertainly, the headwaiter smiled back.

Outside a few taxis waited. On the hood of the one at the head of the line, the driver was curled up fast asleep. Someone yelled and he slid down as they approached.

In the cab she was silent, and once again he felt that she was under the spell of what they had witnessed. The cab drifted past the darkened facades of old buildings. He was aware of her perfume, acutely aware of her leg next to his own. In spite of her silence, he felt emanations, sensory hints. He reached for her hand, touched it lightly, and then held it in his own. As they neared the hotel she removed her hand and ran her fingers lightly over his wrist.

"I'm glad we ran into each other, Charlie," she said as they drew to a stop.

"Me too." Opening the door, he handed her to the curb, paid the driver, and followed her into the lobby. "Would you like a drink?" he asked.

"It's late. I guess not. Thanks anyway."

At the elevator she turned to face him.

"Sure you won't change your mind?" he asked.

Smiling, she shook her head. They stepped into the elevator. "Fourth please," she said. "*El cuarto.*"

His room was on the third. He touched her button and then his own. The elevator climbed and then shuddered to a stop.

"Good night," he said.

"Good night, Charlie. . . ." She touched his arm as he stepped off. The door closed behind him.

With a feeling of frustration and bafflement, he unlocked the door of his room. In the bathroom he stood before the mirror. He was wearing a mustache then. His face was deeply burned, his dark hair shaggy, his eyes glowing with the intensity of what he had felt for her in the cab. It was a handsome face, a face filled with confidence that year.

In the bedroom he turned on the lamp and sat on the edge of the bed. Five minutes passed. With a shrug he picked up the phone and when the operator came on he asked the number of her room. "*Señorita Myatt . . . cuatro cientos ocho . . .* four-o-eight," was the reply.

"*Gracias. Muchas gracias,*" he said and headed for the elevator.

When he knocked at her door there was at first no answer. He knocked again. "Just a minute . . ."

He waited and was about to tap again when the door swung open. She stood facing him, wearing a white raincoat, buttoned primly to the chin. There was dim light from the bathroom.

He walked in and closed the door behind him. She faced him with a smile. "Hi, Charlie . . .," she said. "Listen, it's very late. . . ."

"I know." He unbuttoned the top button of the raincoat and then slowly, one by one, the rest. The raincoat fell to the floor. Naked, she moved into his arms.

Now, in a Mexican village he was sleeping in a car. When he awoke and looked from the window the constellations had moved down the sky. It was 3:30 in the morning. Refreshed, he started the car and drove on through the village out to the open highway, a man following a flight path that at first had seemed aimless. Mexico was a land for fugitives; yet he had known from the first that he had a destination. He was being drawn as if by a magnet to the city of Mérida, where four years earlier they had met, and beyond Merida to the Mayan ruins at Chichén Itzá, where he had fallen in love with her, fallen in love with the woman who had been the love and riddle of his life and ultimately its ruination.

Fourteen

FOUR YEARS EARLIER he had come to Mexico in style, flying first class, eating and drinking on an expense account, a young man, twenty-nine then, who found life glamorous, relishing his assignment, self-assured, attractive to women, idealistic enough, yet amused by the world, filled with the confidence and pleasure of being twenty-nine.

Now, with only the car and a backpack, he was a fugitive from justice, speeding at eighty and ninety along the near-deserted arrow-straight highways of Mexico, freezing on the rare occasions when a Mexican patrol car appeared in his rearview mirror, slowing to sixty and staring straight ahead as the patrol car sped on by and soon disappeared into the nimbus of shimmering heat waves far down the road.

He reached Vera Cruz after dark on a Saturday evening, caught up in a fiesta celebrating Mexican Independence Day. The city was jammed. At hotel after hotel he was turned away and toward midnight found himself in a huge floodlit square, seated alone at a sidewalk cafe, sipping coffee and perusing the Mexico City newspaper, looking as always for mention of his own name, finding none.

Well past midnight the fiesta was still going strong. The streets were filled, impassable to auto traffic, the sidewalks still thronged with Mexican families, with young children and infants in arms. Strolling guitarists roamed the plaza, stopping to serenade the patrons at each sidewalk cafe. Men in rags sold Chiclets. On the far side of the plaza the air was filled with the swelling sound of marimbas and trumpets and heavy, deep percussion. Occasionally an operatic voice rose above the trumpets and the noise of the crowd, an amplified voice of nationalist pride, filling the square, bouncing off the gleaming faces of the floodlit buildings that bounded the square.

Watching, listening, drowning in sound and light, he found himself surprised and deeply touched by the simplicity, the unquestioning fervor of patriotism, the thundering sound of joy, belief, and triumph. It left him thrilled and soon sad. Never had he felt greater loneliness.

His coffee was long since gone. The fiesta surged on. From time to time during the course of the evening it had given him pleasure to gaze at the young girl who stood just inside at the cash register. In her white peasant blouse, with her wide dark eyes, her black hair in shining braids, she looked no more than fourteen, but her English was excellent. As he paid his check she told him of a hotel where he might rent space in a parking lot and sleep in the car. When he found the place, the clerk said that some patrons would be checking out early and promised him the first available room. In the parking lot he pulled in between two huge recreational vehicles and slept fitfully on the backseat. The sun was just up when he was awakened by a tap at the window. A room was available.

Within ten minutes he was sleeping profoundly in a bed just vacated, on sheets still damp from another man's perspiration, and, four hours later, showering and drying himself with a towel still wet from the same man's body.

By noon he was on his way again. Ahead lay another thousand miles or more of driving. Just beyond town, at a Pemex station where he stopped for gasoline, he was told the route now would include five ferry crossings over rivers often so swollen in the September rainy season that ferry schedules were erratic. At any one of the five crossings, several days might pass before the ferry even made the attempt.

At each of the rivers there were long waiting lines, but

Flight

the crossings were made and on he moved, curving north-
ward finally into the Yucatán through terrain that became
ever more tropical. He arrived in Mérida exactly a week
after his arrival in Vera Cruz. Again it was a Saturday
night. After a telephone call to make sure of a room, he took
a taxi to the Excelsior Hotel, leaving the car parked at the
Mérida airport, where it would remain.

The room he was given was not the same one he had
occupied four years earlier, nor was it the one where he had
first made love to Anne. As before, he stood in front of the
bathroom mirror, looking at his face, a face now haggard,
a face dazed with exhaustion and despair, a much older face.
Lightly he touched the hair at the crown of his head, gently
separating it to reveal the nearly healed slash made by the
bullet. An inch lower and there would have been no problem, no flight, no decisions to make.

He awoke to the sound of church bells ringing far and
near, rolling and tumbling and reverberating all through
the city.

It was eleven o'clock. For a while he lay staring at the
ceiling. When the last of the chimes had died away, he
dressed and went down to breakfast, looking at the corner
table where they had sat on a Saturday morning four years
earlier. It was occupied now by an American couple who
spoke in low voices, smiled a lot, sipped coffee, and touched
hands across the table. He forced his eyes away and let them
rove over the elaborate iron grillwork, the profusion of
greenery, the slim oblongs of morning sunlight that lay
over the tiled floor, all of it so engraved in his memory.

For a long while he lingered over coffee and the Mexico
City newspaper, raising his eyes once to watch as the young
couple left the room hand in hand.

When, soon afterward, he wandered out to the lobby, he
found them talking to the desk clerk about Chichén Itzá.

The clerk was a young woman who seemed uncomfortable with their questions. "Chee-chén Eetzá," she said, giving it the Spanish pronunciation. "From 'Chi,' meaning

mouth, and 'Chén,' meaning well. 'Itzá' was the name of the Mayan tribe that lived there. So what do we have? We have 'near the mouth of the well of the Itza.' " She looked at them with a shy smile. "Or you could say here is where the Itzas lived because there was a nice well there and they could get plenty of water for their needs."

Still smiling, she shoved a booklet across the desk. "This will give you some information about the various ruins. If you would like to go, there is taxi service. Not today because today is Sunday. But tomorrow."

"*Mañana,*" the young man said affably. Leafing through the booklet, he mentioned something about the Toltecs.

"*Sí,*" the clerk said with a frozen smile. "In a number of centuries the Mayans were conquered by the Toltecs, and after this things were not so nice again."

When the young couple turned away, he approached the desk, made arrangements for taxi service the following morning, and was given one of the booklets.

With the afternoon before him, he sat for a while in a small park across from the hotel and then went up to his room, sprawling on the bed and glancing through the booklet. It contained a sanitized version of history, but a feeling of the ancient, sunbaked civilization was there between the lines, so much of it savage and bloodthirsty, filled with cruelty and evil, much of it imposed upon the Mayans by the mindlessly murderous Toltecs who had subjugated them. Human life was brief. It was held cheap.

At times he found his mind drifting away in midsentence; drifting to Anne and the strange fascination the place had held for her; drifting to Carver, to Daisy, and to the summer.

But in the booklet that he held in his hands it was the first millennium A.D., and Chichén Itzá was a place that curdled his blood.

It was a civilization that sanctified evil.

It gave murder the status of a blessed act.

Evil gods had constantly to be appeased. They were not

content with the rituals of worship or righteous behavior. They accepted nothing less than human blood and human hearts torn from the victim's breast and offered fresh, warm, still palpitating.

They were a people of great accomplishments, with skill at mathematics and building and even an understanding of astronomy. But they were also people of bestiality, with their unbridled willingness to toss young virgins, children, into their "sacred" well as a tribute to Chac, their insatiable rain god. It was a place of grisly human sacrifice. Down in the well, in the minds of the parents and cheering spectators, the children would be eaten by Chac. Chac-mul. Eaten? Wedded? Ravished? Torn asunder? In fact, to drown, and end their beautiful young lives, lives barely begun.

Chac, of course, was merely a word and a notion. He was the creation of the high priests. It was the high priests who had the power to persuade the parents of the children that they were singularly honored, for only the most beautiful of the children were chosen. It was the high priests who ordained that the beautiful young girls should be dressed in their finery, painted and bespangled, and spend the night inhaling incense as an aphrodisiac—the night before they were given the supreme honor of being thrown into the well for their marriage with Chac.

The supernatural was a human creation.

Carver was Anne's.

Tossing the booklet across the room, he lay motionless.

Presently he went out into the city, walking aimlessly for block upon block, filled with his thoughts, looking at the faces of the people. It was a city full of dust, and on this Sunday evening it was a city of lavender light. He walked through parks filled with people who sat on benches in their Sunday clothes, black for the men, white for the women. As the light waned he reached a vast church, Gothic rather than Spanish, a cathedral fashioned from limestone and topped with a spire that pierced the deepening lavender light of the sky. He stepped into the vestibule. The church was lit only by candles. The pews had no kneeling benches, and the people knelt directly upon the stone floor.

Mass was just ending, and he withdrew to a vast plaza across from the church. A breeze was stirring the dust. People emerged in ones and twos and then in a throng. Most were women. Oval faces in frames of black lace. Somber faces touched with lavender.

At dark he walked past the nightclub where he had met Anne. Its doorway was boarded. It no longer existed.

The cab he hired the next morning was an ancient American used-car discard that, in Mérida, had reached the end of the line. A 1956 Plymouth, he thought. From parts of the seats some of the upholstery had been skinned away like hide skinned from an animal. In the floor there was a hole the shape and nearly the size of a football. Slumped in the backseat, he could look straight through the hole to the surface of the road. On the floor next to his right foot was the backpack that for so long had been his companion, the container of all the remaining tangibles of his life.

The driver had brought his wife, and for the most part they drove in silence. All the way from Mérida the cab had been proceeding at a modest forty miles an hour. Lining both sides of the road was dense, junglelike foliage that at times gave way to cultivated fields of yucca-like plants. Now and then amongst them appeared a huge straw sombrero, the only sign of the man beneath, except occasionally the flash of a blade in the sun.

Looking left and right, he could sense everywhere an aura of antiquity, of lush jungle, of life lived in steaming heat, of a world of lush greens covered by a lush sky of steaming blue and white.

From the driver he now learned that the yucca-like plants were hemp, and that the crop was being harvested with less profit each year because of the increasing and—to the people of the Yucatán—deadly dominance of synthetic fibers.

The driver and his wife were speaking in Spanish now, something about Chichén Itzá. Understanding none of it, he looked down through the hole in the floor and watched the paved road fleeing beneath the car. It became hypnotic and finally he looked away.

The other two were silent again. It was an eighty-mile trip, and they had already been gone an hour and a half. The old car thudded over a pothole. From the rear there came a loud rattle that sounded like a loose tailpipe, done in by the pothole. The driver muttered angrily. Smoke drifted back from his cigarette. And then, tossing the cigarette from the window, he was pointing. *"Chi-chén,"* he said matter-of-factly. *"Chi-chén."*

As the cab rolled by there was a glimpse of crumbled masonry, of ancient gray stone buildings scattered about a broad plain, the highest and most readily visible a pyramid with a temple resting on its flattened top, so well remembered. And then it all disappeared behind a screen of foliage as the cab moved on and pulled to a stop at the hotel.

Fifteen

CHICHÉN ITZÁ . . .
Crumbled and weathered, the ruins of a civilization frozen in time.

Nothing had changed for centuries. Even the relatively modern hotel was just as he remembered it. With its quiet splendor and luxury, its cool, gladed lobby, it was an elegant anachronism, an island surrounded by intense heat, deep jungle, and the echoes and relics of barbarity.

He was assigned a spacious corner room, and as with the lobby it was impossible not to feel amazed by its pristine beauty. It was light, airy, surprisingly cool, a large room that, with its high ceilings, its stark white walls and spare furnishings, seemed even larger.

The bedstead was dark and massively Spanish; the heavily scrolled headboard and footboard limned a vast expanse of embossed white counterpane. As he opened his backpack and began to remove its contents, he paused, overcome by a feeling of emptiness. Standing above the vast white expanse of the bed, he could see her lying there, dark auburn hair strewn over the pillow, staring pensively up at the slowly revolving blades of the ceiling fan.

From the backpack he took her picture and stared at it, torn, as he had been for so long, between hatred and love, between bitterness and nostalgia. Here, as he had known he would, he felt her presence more acutely than he had at any time since the day she told him she was leaving him for Carver. He looked into her eyes and slipped the picture deep into the backpack.

Through the open window he could see the pyramidal structure called The Castle—*El Castillo.* Through the other there was a view of the old observatory. Rising above and beyond The Castle were fluffy patches of dense white. The moist blue sky was beginning to fill with the enormous cumulus clouds that in the Yucatán often began to form in late morning, so quickly and intensely did the ground become heated—the sky one minute a pure spotless blue, filled five minutes later with the vast clouds spreading forth above their heat-baked thermal columns. During the storms that took place virtually every afternoon, they had gone up to the room and made love to the rumbling sound of the thunder, the heavy rains splatting against the leaves of the trees, running through gutters and downspouts, and gradually trickling into silence.

Four years ago he had stood just this way, looking from the window, noticing the sky, thinking of the beauty of the room and of the night in Mérida with Anne. Up from the courtyard drifted the sound of people conversing in Spanish. The rooms along the corridor fronted on the courtyard, each with its own balcony.

He stepped outside. In his memory, four balconies away, four years away, she stood, hands on the iron railing, looking down into the luxuriously planted, heavily shaded courtyard. As he moved to the railing, she had turned with a smile.

"*Buenos días, señor,*" she called, and then: "Hi, Charlie."

He grinned. "You changed your itinerary. . . ."

"It worked." She was wearing a man's white shirt, open at the throat. Her face was nearly covered by huge dark glasses. "Give me a few minutes and I'll meet you down at the bar for a drink."

For a long while he stood at the rail, looking down into the mini-jungle of the courtyard, almost able to imagine that downstairs at the bar she would soon be meeting him for a drink.

It was by now nearing noon. The guests were coming back to the hotel, coming back from the ruins, and whatever eeriness they might have perceived in Chichén Itzá, whatever fascinated horror they might have felt, was overshadowed by heat and sheer discomfort. Wearily they drooped in, shirts plastered to their backs, faces damp with sweat, cameras slung over their drenched shoulders, feet dragging over the huge square butterscotch tiles. Not yet accustomed to the dim light of the lobby after the noon glare outside, they were groping and in a few cases even gasping their way toward the small bar. He looked in. All the small round tables were filled, and at the bar people were standing three-deep.

Turning away, he went outside and walked through the courtyard. Looking up through the heavy foliage, he identified his own room, his balcony—and the one that had been hers. Passing on through the courtyard, he circled to the swimming pool. It was an old-fashioned pool, long and narrow, bright blue, spotless, and for the moment empty. When she was not wandering among the ruins, Anne had spent long hours sunning by the pool. She had returned to New York with a deep tan.

Next to the pool, offering protection from the sun, stood a thatched dome resembling half a coconut shell. There was a chair beneath it, and here for a few moments he sat in the shade. Above the pool an armada of yellow butterflies sailed in the bright sunlight. Four years ago he had photographed the butterflies, and they had been used in the magazine layout. From here, through the swarm of butterflies, he could look into the dining room. In its darkened recesses sat the waitresses, tiny Mayan maidens, flounces of flowered embroidery edging the hems of their fresh white skirts. They laughed and chatted as they ate lunch in this time before the doors were thrown open and the guests were admitted, in this respite while the guests were either drinking or up in their rooms repairing the sweat-ridden ravages visited upon their bodies by *las ruinas.*

When he saw them start pouring into the dining room he went back inside. There were empty stools at the bar now and he took one.

The bartender was dressed in white trousers and a white tunic. Like so many of the staff, he had a round, moonlike face and an attitude of friendly deference. "*¿Señor?*"

It was unmistakably the same bartender. "*Buenos días,*" he said. "Do you have—a coke?"

"Coke—*sí.*"

Four years ago, as the bartender turned away, she had slipped onto the adjoining stool. His hand lay on the bar and she touched it lightly with her fingers, "Hi, Charlie."

"I'm glad you made it," he said.

"So am I...." Removing the huge sunglasses, she looked into his eyes. "So am I."

The bartender set the coke on a circlet of white paper and smiled at her questioningly.

"Margarita, *por favor,*" she said with a smile.

"*Señorita . . .*" He inclined his head.

"What is your name?" she asked. "*¿Como se llama usted?*"

"Pepe," he said with a grin.

"*Me llamo* Anne."

"Hi." Pepe was hardly the cool, laid-back bartender. His round face was filled with creases and crevices as he grinned. He was still grinning as he turned away to mix her drink.

"So here we are, Charlie. . . ." Again her hand brushed his. "Have you gotten any work done?"

"Not much so far. I went out to the sacred well, the so-called sacred well, but the light wasn't much good."

"How did you like it?"

"The most grisly place I've ever seen in my life. It gave me the creeps. This whole damned place gives me the creeps."

"Don't leave," she said.

"I can't until I'm finished."

"Just don't leave." She was looking into his eyes and then away as the bartender placed her drink before her. "*¡Gracias,* Pepe!" She smiled and again the bartender's face cracked with pleasure.

He sipped his coke, looking sidelong at her profile as she raised the frosted glass to her lips, lowered the marvelous dark lashes. She was beautiful. Beautiful and confident. He felt himself falling in love with her and was not sure he wanted to. Even then there was something that seemed to warn him against it, although that afternoon, sitting at the bar, the reasons had to do with power, not traits of eeriness. Never before had he met a woman who could place him under her power. That afternoon he was still cocky enough to believe that he never would. During the long hours of lovemaking on Saturday night in the hotel at Mérida, he had felt in control. He had met a beautiful unattached woman in a foreign country. The exotic setting was acting upon her as an aphrodisiac. He had merely been making the most of it, and although it had been powerful and marvelous it was only sex and she was only a beautiful woman from New York with a big thing for Mayan culture.

She was asking the bartender his age. "Pepe, how old are you? *¿Cuántos años tiene usted?*"

Grinning, the bartender held up the five fingers of one hand and the index finger of the other.

"Hmmmm," she murmured. "Fifty-one. Poor Pepe. Only a year to go."

In a low voice she explained what she meant as they finished their drinks; she continued the explanation in the dining room.

"For the Mayans, fifty-two was very significant. They divided everything into segments of thirteen. Four times thirteen equals fifty-two. They felt that at fifty-two a man was ready to die. He had lived long enough. Four times thirteen was his life span. In fact it was the end of their calendar. After fifty-two years they started their calendar over again. Kind of like starting *life* over again."

She set the dark glasses on her nose, then folded them carefully and placed them on the spotless white tablecloth. They had been given a table looking directly out upon the blue strip of the swimming pool. Yellow butterflies danced and drifted above the glittering water.

"The high priests had it all figured out. They felt that at fifty-two a man had reached the age of maturity and wisdom and therefore was old enough to see through them, see what they were up to. Anybody fifty-two had wised up enough to be a threat to the high priest hierarchy, so they had him killed. . . ."

"The bloodthirsty, heart-eating bastards," he said.

She nodded. "They were. They really were. Not the Mayans nearly so much as the Toltecs. It was the Toltecs who turned this place into a slaughterhouse."

"How do you know so much about all this stuff?"

"We did a book a couple of years ago. I was editor on it but I'd been interested a long time before that."

"Why?"

She shrugged. "Who knows?" Now with a smile, she said, "It just occurred to me that I still haven't asked you if you're married. Are you married, Charlie?"

"No."

"Never?"

"Never. Are you?"

"No," she said.

He looked into her eyes. "Would you like to save money and move into my room? Or—I could move into yours and knock down on my expense account."

She laughed. "We'll visit," she said.

"So when's the first visit?"

"Who knows? This afternoon I'd like to get out and look around."

The memory faded and, leaving the bar, he wandered through the lobby. He remembered being impressed four years ago, as he was impressed now, by the ability of the Spanish to combat heat with natural means, without the aid of air conditioning, taking what breeze there might be, creating shade to cool it, and then using the principles of draft to pull the cooled air along shaded passages and into shaded chambers. A masonry wall laden with vines blocked out the sun. The vines, or so it seemed, gave moisture and oxygen to the passing air as it traveled along the wall, drawn to the next arched opening, drawn, in this particular section of the lobby, down three tiled steps, past the huge black cage of an angry blue macaw. Now, freed from its cage, the macaw stood on the topmost of the three tiled steps. The breeze here was traveling fast enough to ruffle the big bird's bright plumage as it lowered its curved black beak to the tile floor and, with a furious pigeon-toed waddle, long tail sweeping the tiles, took out after an imaginary adversary.

The dining room, like the rest of the hotel, gave the same impression of soft muted tones and cool moving air. Above the entrance hung a small balcony, just large enough for three musicians. He looked up at them over his shoulder. He had been able to hear them from the bar, and now, up on the tiny balcony, in their black trousers and white blouses with puffed sleeves, they were playing "La Paloma" for the third time in the past half hour.

He was given a table overlooking the swimming pool. One of the Mayan waitresses stood by, smiling. His eyes strayed to the flowered hem of her skirt, her sandals, the slim tan ankles, the fragile bones of her wrists. As he looked up, she asked, "Will someone be joining you, *señor?*"

He shook his head.

Sixteen

ALL THAT AFTERNOON and the next he tramped about the ruins, revisiting the temples, the portals, the arches, the broken columns where four years earlier he had so patiently composed his shots, waiting for hours for the right clouds, for the shadow of a feathered serpent's head to move until it was more sharply delineated against a block of ancient limestone.

Now, save for a young Mexican and a group of Americans he was conducting on a tour, he had the place to himself. With the silence of the vast bare plain, the blank blue sky, the ocean of surrounding jungle, and particularly when the tour group disappeared behind one of the crumbling temples, he had an acute sense of being utterly alone, alone in the world of A.D. 700, under the same furnace sky, feeling the same silence.

Four years earlier he had been intent upon his assignment, intent above all upon Anne. Now, a murderer and fugitive, a man with no life ahead, he felt the sad beauty of human hope, the poignant beauty that was present in the thought of these ancient tiny people—the thought that by carrying block upon heavy limestone block, setting them in place, filing again and again, filing like a column of ants up the face of the gradually rising pyramid, each carrying his block, they would somehow convince themselves they were more than dust. If they were building a temple, there must be a god, and if there was a god, they were more than dust. Standing between themselves and that god were the intermediaries, the high priests, for the high priests had told them it was so. Tiny, lonely figurines in the eighth century jungle, sweating and toiling in the cause of immortality. If the blocks were cut straight enough, chipped fine enough, if the honey was mixed properly with limestone dust to make mortar, if the temple kept rising . . .

It was not out of arrogance that they built but out of the deepest of all needs. To build was a plea for the enduring cosmic roles that the high priests assured them would be theirs. They were toiling to be spared the knowledge of their vast unimportance, the devastating knowledge of their mortality.

To propitiate and thereby endure, how willing they were to send certain chosen members of their number to torture and death! Not merely the child-victims thrown into the sacred well, but even as the aftermath of a game played on a vast ball field, far larger than an American football field, paralleled on both sides by long limestone walls with flattened-out tops where the spectators stood and watched, danced and sang. It was the captain not of the losing but of the winning team who was slain on the spot and offered to the gods. As a man of glory and prowess, he would be more pleasing to the gods. In their way of life, it was the best, the most beautiful, who died first.

He looked out over the sunbaked, stubbled plain. Everywhere he looked, at every site, there was such incredible evidence of an obsession with cruelty—as if the people, in constant danger of losing out to savagery, had embraced as idols the very things they most feared and that represented the very most savage threats to their lives. The jaguar *(El Tigre)*; the rattlesnake, which the Toltecs had fantasized into the Feathered Serpent; the eagle, which plucked hearts from living flesh.

Across the plaza the guide was lecturing in his earnest, precise but thick-tongued, adenoidal English. Standing perhaps twenty feet from the base of The Castle, the guide clapped his hands sharply. It was a trick Charlie remembered from four years ago. A single sharp clap, and the echo sounded (as the guide was now explaining to the group) just like the sound of a bird, the cry of a gull, the cry of a nightbird. And all of it of course redounding to the greater glory of the high priests. Another weapon in their magic arsenal, another compelling entry in their roster of runes. We the mighty priestly hierarchy, standing at a certain magic spot, we with the mere clap of our sanctified hands, can summon up the cry of a bird. We are to be held in awe.

The supernatural was indeed a human creation.

God did not create man. Man created God.

Or gods.

He was standing now at the portal of the Temple of the Jaguars. Here in this place, this relic of a lost civilization with its brooding silence, he could have killed Carver and felt nothing. Perhaps because of the aura of death, the fittingness of death, the feeling that death was everywhere, a harvest of death, omnivorous and inevitable, the numbing sense of death everywhere imposed upon life, wherever life dared show its head, and for a brief moment its eager face, its hopeful eyes.

If he had killed Carver here it would have been fitting. It would have been as if some high priest had wanted Carver's death—ordained it and assigned him as executioner.

For the gods.

For the common good.

For rain.

Murder sanctified.

Murder as blessed act.

And yet was not Carver himself one of the high priests —with their power and their alliance with the savage gods they had created?

High priest, or savage, insatiable god?

Something of each, with the dead, pupilless eyes of a figure carved in stone.

He gazed across the field. A couple of men and a woman in white stood at the very topmost level of The Castle. Atop The Castle stood a temple. Through its portals one could enter and, once inside, descend a stairway into the dark recesses of an inner temple, which lay beneath the first. The two men entered and after a moment the woman followed.

The temperature by now must have been easily 110. The air was surprisingly dry, but the thermals were shooting heat into the sky like rockets, and the clouds were forming, gathering, soon thickening. The storm broke quickly. A few claps of thunder; then a deluge. The rain came in huge cool drops. Welcoming it, he walked at an unhurried pace back to the hotel.

It was on just such an afternoon, during just such a storm that he had gone back to the room to find her waiting, her body half-covered by the twisted strip of sheet. Naked, he had stood for a moment, looking beyond the balcony, seeing the flashes of lightning, the rolling, tumbling writhing mix of whites and grays and blacks, as the clouds charged before the wind and fell topsy-turvy.

He turned. She had tossed aside the sheet. He moved into her arms and she rolled on top of him. Her breasts swung toward him, swept his bare chest. She moved closer and the tips brushed his eyelids, carefully traced and re-traced his lashes. Just as in Mérida, the lightness, the glancing touch, there and gone, elusive, fingers sliding off fingers, lips glancing off lips, the tip of her tongue touching his, dampening his face, his fingers moving lightly along the delicacy of her ribs, moving, barely touching; hard, harsh pressure, and then as weightless as the wing of a butterfly, hovering, gliding, membrane to membrane, moving toward and always away, averting the moment, the long moments of eluding, made more ecstatic still by the certain knowledge that it would be there for the taking, yet continuing to move away, glance by, harsh and then delicate, with the tiny, pirouetting movements of hand and touch, palm brushing palm, a dance involving all the tips of their bodies as the thunder rolled and circled and chimes in the court-yard tolled the quarter and then the half hour. She was sitting erect and he was driving deep into her body and with the power of her own she drove him deeper. He was looking up at her face, at her closed eyes, the lustrous lashes, parted lips, body constricting, face drawn with fierce agonized concentration, breath coming faster, and then a moan and she fell forward, burying her face against his chest. Finally falling away, lying at his side, she moved her body close to his, clasped him in her arms, held him close.

He stroked her head, her temple, her cheek, waiting for the moment that would become so familiar. She lay on her back now, the sheet half drawn over her body, eyes smeared with makeup, looking up at the ceiling fan, lost to him, far away. Thunder rumbled in the distance. The storm was over, ended as abruptly as it had begun. The sun shone. The clouds hanging above The Castle were fleecy white; the sky filled with blue. Her face was a mask of infinite sadness.

"What's wrong?" It was the question he would ask so often in all their years together. She shook her head. She was far away, and no matter how close they might seem she was always somewhere beyond.

Seventeen

HE WAS UP AT DAWN and the light was still dim as he moved across the vast plaza, past the softly lit facades of the ancient buildings. A slit in the jungle marked the pathway to the sacred well. All during the previous afternoon he had avoided revisiting it, drawn and yet repelled by a deep aversion, a feeling that coursed through his body and stirred his groin. Even four years ago it had affected him deeply and he knew now that it would be far worse.

Reaching the pathway, he walked with head lowered, his eyes on the flattened grass, a swath of flattened grass, all that marked the path. On both sides he was hemmed in by dense jungle foliage. He stood listening. The silence was complete—an abrupt warble, a brief halting trill, and then silence again.

He moved on. Now only a trail, this once had been a well-kept pathway for ceremonial processions. On the day of ritual sacrifice it was strewn with fresh flowers. Perfumed smoke filled the air. Leading the procession in feathered headdress were the high priests. Next came the victim, dressed in a white gown, borne upon a litter, under the influence of the sacred narcotic, smiling a dreamy smile. Behind her, pirouetting and dancing and singing, came the populace.

Ahead now was their destination, and his own. Trees and foliage described a circular clearing and he could see its outline. In another few steps the huge circular opening of the well itself was in view. Soon he could see its striated sides. He paused. There was a sense of eeriness, of obscene quiet. A well in a jungle, a vast crater, a perfectly cylindrical crater with sides of chalk white, the color of putrefaction, the shade of bodies bloated from drowning.

He moved closer and gradually closer until he stood at the very rim. From here he could look straight down at the surface of the water, an unruffled dark green, looking thick, as though it could be ladled; and from the ladle it would drip, thick and slow, with the viscosity that was fed from the muck below, the muck from which excavators had hauled up gold and silver amulets and bracelets and necklaces, rings and eyes of jade, and the bones of countless children.

He stood motionless at the rim. Horror was everywhere. Horror permeated the deadly silence, the total stillness of the early morning air, the stillness of the water's thick surface, of the leaves that hung limp in the trees that rimmed the well.

Trees so grotesque in formation, their limbs gesticulating, performing crazy dances in the dim light, as if because of their germination in this obscene place, they were destined to perform idiot dances against the sky.

Here they had germinated, here near the edge of a sacrificial well, seeds sprouting amid the semicircular stone slabs that rimmed the well in irregular tiers, fashioned by Mayan hands centuries ago to serve as seats from which the spectators might witness:

The headlong plunge of the blue-painted bodies, the virgin children falling in early morning sunlight, or the silver of moonlight;

Flashes of blue and gold and silver and white as they fell toward the green murk to satisfy the lust of the grotesque god, the lust of the high priests, the lust of the spectators, lusting after rain and immortality.

At the south rim, only a few steps from where he stood, were the remains of a stone pagoda, and this seemed more horrible somehow than the well itself. Drugged though the children were, the anticipation seemed more horrible than the event that would follow. Here in the pagoda they spent the hours before their death, being prepared and anointed in elaborate rites of purification and beautification, with steam baths, copal incense, and narcotics.

The pagoda's outer structure had the squared-off dimensions of a miniature temple. Its inner chamber was rounded and the inner walls charred from the smoke of ancient fires. There was a hole in the ceiling, a chimney of sorts. Inside were stone slabs. On these had sat the children, and he could envision the victim, a child dressed in white, bespangled with precious metals, knees drawn up to her chin, inhaling incense, the smoke pouring up through the hole in the ceiling.

He could imagine her seated there, awaiting the ceremony, being reassured by the high priests and their subalterns, being told that the event soon to take place would be the greatest moment of her life—not the moment of death but the moment when, deep in the well, she would be conjoined with Chac, to be his eternal bride.

From the rear and two sides it was evident from the rubble that stone steps once had led up to the pagoda, but on the fourth side, the side at the rim of the well, there was a small clearing and then a sheer drop, so that it was from this ledge that they were hurled. This was the launch pad. In the first rays of the sun if by day, or by the first rays of the risen moon if by night, the highest of the high priests had taken the fragile body in his arms and held it aloft, offering it to Chac, raised it high, to the level of his feathered headdress, stretched it toward the sun or the moon, and then the horrifying splash, the horrifying cheers.

Part of Anne had wanted to be there, wanted to be painted blue, to be picked up in the arms of the high priest and to be tossed, a blue body falling through the moonlight.

He looked into the well and then across to the far side. Exactly opposite the pagoda, symmetrically germinated and now symmetrically posted, stood two of the crazy dancing trees, the largest in the clearing. Four years ago he had shot them over and over again, at all hours of the day, seeking the light that would portray the horror that he felt at the sight of them.

Still he stood by the well, hypnotized with horror, noticing its perfectly rounded, totally sheer sides, sheer yet striated with marks showing older and higher water levels. He looked for handholds and saw none. Only here and there a vine, a trace of greenery seeking to struggle up the sheer sides, as long ago a doomed sacrificial victim, a terrified child, must have tried.

Finally he turned away and moved as if under a spell back along the pathway. The sun was just rising. The plaza was still in shadow, but far off to the right, toward the hotel, the first rays were just touching the peak of The Castle.

Pausing for a moment, he turned east toward the edifice known as the Temple of the Warriors, wanting to break the

appalling sense of horror that had been cast by the well. As
he approached, he paused to study it. Unlike The Castle and
the smoothly triangulated pyramids of Egypt, its pyramidal
effect had been achieved with setbacks, a series of tiers
receding one by one as they rose finally to a broad flat top.

The base of the pyramid was surrounded by stone pillars that had successfully weathered the centuries. Those in
front had once supported the roof of a colonnaded portico.
The roof of the portico had long since gone and the supporting columns stood naked. To the right marched other stone
columns by the hundred, perfectly aligned in long rows,
each representing a fallen warrior, his commemorative
stone.

Beyond all stretched the immensity of the jungle, its
endless horizon etched against the brightening morning
sky. As he moved closer a half-sun was in view, and the
warrior columns were just beginning to cast their shadows
in long, precisely aligned diagonals. Four years earlier he
had risen at dawn to photograph them as they appeared
now. Anne had been with him.

As with The Castle, the flattened top had been used as
the base of a temple. To reach the top, a stairway had been
built up the face of the pyramid, steps with short risers and
very shallow treads, built to accommodate little red-brown
people with tiny feet. The stairway here was so steep and
the footholds offered by its treads so small that halfway up,
as he glanced down at the rows of warrior columns, he felt
a wave of vertigo. Facing upward, he continued to climb.

Dimly in view at the head of the stairway, and growing
steadily larger as he climbed, was a stone statue of the
diabolical Chac, set before the entrance portal of the ruined
temple. Reaching the top, he stood for a moment before the
clumsily hewn stone likeness. Chac was reclining on his
elbows, one vast stone knee drawn up. On his belly rested
a rounded tablet, an offering plate. He was looking out over
the plaza, master of all he surveyed. For all the coarseness
of the statue and the squared-off lines, its creator somehow
had managed to give the face a cocky look of insouciance,

an expression of arrogant self-confidence.

Circling the statue, he paused. From this height, as far as he could see, stretched an ocean of dense jungle. He turned to face the faraway castle. The sun was higher now, high enough to bathe the entire enormous plaza in light, broken only by the long rectangular shadows of the ruined buildings.

Birds called, greeting the sun. Calls unfamiliar to his ear; one resembled the call of a bobwhite; another, the piercing notes of a cardinal.

High above the world he stood now, at the open portal of the temple. This wall and the two side walls were intact. The roof here too was gone, but as with the colonnaded portico the supporting columns still stood. Weeds grew at the foot of the columns. The weeds stirred in a faint breeze. He watched the moving shadows of the weeds drift over the base of the column.

He turned away. The fourth wall, the eastern wall, had either collapsed or perhaps more likely had never stood. On this side, the side facing the sun, the temple was open to air and sky. Just beyond where the wall might have been, out at the very edge of this plateau in the sky, stood a huge stone slab, an altar, a silhouette still dark against the barely risen sun.

Four years ago her body had been part of the silhouette. She had been stretched out on the slab of altar, hands laced behind her back, looking up at the sky, then looking over her shoulder and smiling.

As he approached she let her head fall back again. "This thing is so big," she said. "It's like a quadruple bed, a king-size bed. It's surprisingly soft. Is limestone softer than other stone, Charlie?"

The vast altar was composed of stone slabs, fitted tightly together. Moss grew in the cracks.

She was smiling again. "If I lie like this and look straight up at the sky, I feel as if I'm absolutely drowning in it, drunk with the sheer unbroken blue of it, the purity of it."

He had moved closer, watching her face.

"Looking up like this, it's like a drug," she murmured. "Looking up deep into the sky gives the effect of a drug. I might not have minded. It might not have been so bad."

"Whatever turns you on," he said.

She was looking at him over her shoulder. "This is exactly where it was done." She lay back again. "See, I'm lying here and here comes the high priest and he rips open my chest." With a sudden movement, she ripped open her blouse, tearing the buttonholes. "He rips open my chest and here is my heart exposed, still beating, and here comes the eagle, here he comes with talons outstretched and he grabs my heart with his talons and flies off with it. . . . Oh God!"

He stood dazzled by the sun, numb with revulsion and desire. By now she had snatched away the rest of her clothing and lay naked on the slab, hips already beginning to rise, back arched, her eyes slits. "Come on, Charlie, hurry! For Christ's sweet sake, hurry. . . ."

Toward noon, shaded by the frondlike leaves of a huge tree, they had sat sipping drinks at a small table in a corner of the courtyard. The ripped blouse she had left on the altar, wearing his faded tan safari shirt back to the hotel. She still wore it.

Behind her head stood a wing of the hotel, a cream yellow with faint streaks of rust. Etched against the soft cream masonry, a black wrought iron stairway spiraled gracefully upward to the level of the balconies. Vines with shiny green leaves were twined among the iron palings, trailing from bottom to top.

The leaves of the trees were motionless, but aloft thick puffs of cloud were moving before the wind. Looking upward through a clearing in the branches, he could see a hawk, perhaps an eagle, soaring, momentarily motionless, a dark spot in the blue sky. Abruptly it was gone from view as a cloud drifted beneath it. The cloud sailed on and the bird reappeared, still soaring high in the wind.

Chichén Itzá was a place of mighty clouds and sharp shadows.

Flight

Birds sang in the courtyard. The Mayan waiters with their greased, slick jet hair moved swiftly about among the tables, through the dappled light, always smiling—short-legged, affable little men dressed all in white, dressed like hospital orderlies. As they walked, their leather sandals squeaked on the tiles.

At a nearby table, people were conversing in Spanish. In the airless courtyard the humidity was intense. Here nature's cooling system was not working. His brow was damp. Bent straws drooped listlessly over the rims of their glasses.

The epaulet on her left shoulder was unbuttoned, and the shirt was unbuttoned at the throat. She had a lovely throat, a lovely, slim neck. In the humidity her hair was tousled, the smooth auburn sheen replaced by a mass of uncontrolled curls. Her eye makeup was smudged. A blue ballpoint pen lay on the table. He asked what she had been writing.

A writing pad lay on her lap. She handed it to him, and he read what she had written in her scrawled backhand penmanship:

> It is life that is unusual. Not death.
> Life is a stone skipped across the water.
> Some feel that death is an obscene transgressor into the sun-filled norm of life, that death is the interloper, the vagrant vandal at the backdoor of the sun.
> But life is the interloper.
> For each of us there is an eternity of darkness before and after; and in between, a small patch of brightness.
> A tiny streak, a rivulet, a blurred arc of light through the darkness.
> The stage is dark. It lights up briefly for a tiny playlet, and then goes dark again.
> Through the void, a ribbon of light.
> I agree with Pascal: Men are so necessarily mad that not to be mad would amount to another form of madness.

He read it twice and then slid the pad across the table. She placed it in her lap.

"Would you like another drink?"

She smiled. "What a reaction! Laid-back Charlie!"

"I'm not as laid-back as you think, not laid-back at all."

"I know you're not, Charlie. You're a good red-blooded American boy who just happens to be very good in the sack."

"Would you like another drink?"

She shrugged. "*¡Sí, cómo no?* That's Mexican laid-back for 'sure, why not?'"

He looked over his shoulder and in a flash one of the waiters stood at his side. "Do you really feel that way?" he asked when the waiter was gone.

"About the sack? You're the best."

I don't mean that. I mean the stuff you wrote."

"Sure, why not?"

"On the other hand, why?"

"If man and woman know they came from nothing and go to nothing—it's not easy to keep your sanity. It's hard to take anything very seriously."

"I don't feel that way," he said.

"Tell me what you feel."

"I don't know. I guess I just like being here." He shrugged. "I just like hanging around."

She reached across the table and touched his hand lightly. "I think I like you, Charlie. . . ."

"I just sort of like being privy to—what's happening. Privy to what's next."

"Umm-*hmmmmm!*" Her eyes sparkled. She was tracing the rim of her glass with the tip of her tongue. "Sometimes Charlie uses big words."

"Where I come from, *privy* is not exactly a big word."

She smiled. The smile faded, and she sipped her drink. "Tell me a few things. I know every contour of your body and I feel I know a little about you soul, enough to like it. But I don't know anything *about* you. I know you left home, came to the big city, and took a film course at NYU. Why did you do that?"

He shrugged. "Because I love film. From the time I was a kid I loved pictures. I was also a movie nut and still am. I couldn't paint, didn't have the talent. I couldn't be van Gogh or Renoir or Andrew Wyeth, so the next best thing was to make pictures, record the way the world looks. I see things in pictures. I see you sitting there. You're a perfectly composed picture I like what I see."

"I'm glad."

"To me, life is a whole bunch of pictures. I love the way things look even if they're ugly. I love the way the world looks—because it's the way the world *looks*. It's what's there. It's what's happening. Okay?"

She was smiling. "Okay."

She took his hand as they circled out to the pool and stood at the edge, her hand still in his. Feeling its warm pressure, its slimness, feeling her palm slide lightly against his own, he looked steadfastly at the surface, at the glimmering, shimmering, twinkling blue water, the bright octagons, self-perpetuating, changing, endlessly flowing, casting octagonal shadows on the bottom, one octagon becoming another and all becoming the same dancing myriad of glittering octagons dancing the length of the pool.

They sat beneath the thatched dome. The view into the dining room was partially screened by a rough-hewn trellis, supported by slim stone pillars. Looking between the pillars, he could see the waitresses at lunch. Bougainvillea vines and blossoms spilled over the top of the trellis. A breeze stirred. A bougainvillea blossom drifted into the pool, then another, and they floated side by side, moved by the breeze, like two tiny crimson boats racing the length of the pool, first one in the lead, then the other.

Presently she arose and walked slowly about the pool, pausing to stand before the trellis, a beautifully contoured woman, moving a step and then another, moving and pausing, as if striking poses.

The profusion of yellow butterflies hurried along, yellow wisps, lighter than air, drifting and gracefully veering and darting above the glittering pool with its endless flow of dancing octagonal lights, an endless flow of yellow butterflies.

The bougainvillea blossoms had completed their race. They had reached the end of the pool, where, barely an inch apart, they clung to one of the soft blue tiles.

Eighteen

HE HAD LEFT Chichén Itzá, his magazine assignment completed, while she continued with her tour of the ruins at Tulum, Uxmal, and Palenque. By the time he reached New York he had begun to wonder whether she was the woman for him. Chichén Itzá had been an idyll, a marvelous memory, a spectacular interlude, and he would let it go at that. She was far too complex, too hung up, too sophisticated for her own good and certainly for his. He was a country boy, born and raised on a farm in tidewater Virginia, with old-fashioned values and a relatively straight view of life. His career was taking shape. Until he met her he had been doing just fine.

In the early years, after completing the film course at New York University, he had taken what he could get, gofering, hanging around with other aspiring filmmakers, shooting remote corners of the city, and even for a very short while working with his friend and fellow graduate Tex Poffenberger, who was finding quick money in making pornographic films, improvising a script and shooting completed works in two days. "Chaucer would have approved," Tex said, "and besides, Charlie boy, think of the money."

But it went against the grain, and after a week, to Tex's good-natured chiding, he quit and soon afterward took his camera and ventured forth into the city. His idol was Jacob Riis, and, pleased to think of himself as a latter-day Riis, he went into the city's bleak areas and photographed its destitute and miserable, piling up stills for which he was told there would be no market but doing it anyway, simply because he wanted to. *How the Other Half Lives.* This was the title of Riis's wonderful book, and the people Riis photographed were the waifs, the beggars and cripples, the blind, the emaciated immigrants of the late nineteenth century. He was trying to do the same for the hapless thousands who inhabited the city a century later.

Through the byways of Manhattan and The Bronx he roamed with his camera, taking shots of the city people, the city children, the child prostitutes, an exhausted mother seated on her front stoop, with thumb and forefinger squeezing a marijuana cigarette between her lips, a baby on her fat knee; men who slept in boxes and doorways, men gaunt and sallow, dead before their time, faces covered with gray stubble that seemed barely to contrast with the gray of their skins. Print by print his collection grew. When he had enough he would approach a publisher.

Until the modeling and magazine work started coming in, life had been meager. His assignment at Chichén Itzá was by far his best to date, and he felt that his life was just where he wanted it. He would not let it be spoiled by an involvement with somebody as overwhelming as Anne Myatt.

He returned from Mexico in late September. Anne returned two weeks later and called him as soon as she got off the plane. That night they had a drink and slept together. Within a week she had moved in with him.

There began the happiest time of his life. He was able to convince himself that at Chichén Itzá she had merely been under a spell and that now he was seeing the real Anne, a wonderful blend of seriousness, passion, intelligence.

At night she brought home manuscripts from the office and read them, seated in the bright, eye-saving light of a floor lamp that stood at her shoulder. She read rapidly, letting the tortoiseshell glasses slide down her nose, absently sliding them back up again, her long, deep auburn hair highlighted beneath the lamp, wearing one of his shirts, this and nothing more, at home never anything else. The photographic darkroom he used was in a loft only two blocks away, and after an hour or so there he would think of her sitting at home and would return and find her just as he knew she would be, legs drawn up, the shirt fastened by a single button, glasses sliding, inserting each finished page into the pasteboard box on the table at her side. "Hi, Charlie". She would finish the page she was reading, slip it into the box, stack the still unread manuscript on the table, take off her glasses, and say, "Anything to show me?"

"They're still drying."

"Any good?"

He shrugged.

"Jeanne? Jeanne again?"

"Jeanne again."

"How much does that slut make an hour?"

"Who knows? Close to a thousand dollars, I guess."

"I make about ten. What was she wearing?"

"More than you're wearing now."

"Bra ad?"

"Yes."

"Frilly, lacy black?"

"Frilly, lacy white."

"The bitch. Did it turn you on?"

He laughed. "It's a job. You don't have any rivals."

"I'd better not." She was headed for the kitchen. "Want anything?"

"No thanks."

In a moment she returned with a glass of tonic and sat once again in the big chair, glass in hand, legs again drawn up, strong legs, solid, fleshed-out thighs, the shirt still fastened by a single button, falling away, and she not bothering, never bothering to hide any part of her body. It was not immodesty. Neither was it exhibitionism. It seemed perfectly natural, and he sat there reading a book, looking up from the page at her body, craving it night after night, and night after night satisfying his own craving and hers.

And then the next morning, beautifully dressed, hair brushed to an auburn sheen, bending for a copy of *The New York Times,* giving a radiant smile to the aging news vendor who was in love with her and who waited each morning for the moment when she arose with the paper and smiled into his eyes. There at the newsstand they would part, she for the office, he for the darkroom, for a modeling date, for a morning with a layout editor, or sometimes merely to roam the streets with his camera, absorbed in his work but always waiting for the day to pass, waiting for the night.

She introduced him to her family and of them all he particularly liked her father, a gentleman who looked and acted the part, successful, well-to-do, retired now in his midsixties, silver-haired, patrician in appearance, full of insight, and deeply concerned for the welfare of his daughter. She had gone to the best schools, an expensive finishing school, graduated cum laude from Sarah Lawrence. A more conscientious father could not be imagined. All through her childhood, her teens, and beyond, he had been bedeviled by her moods, her long brooding silences, her melancholy. He seemed glad she had found Charlie and showed no disapproval of their living arrangement.

In the spring, Charlie's own father died in his sleep at seventy-five. He considered asking her to go to the funeral with him, decided against it, and went alone. His father had continued to live where he had always lived, in the house where Charlie was raised and where he had stayed until he went off to the city. Charlie was the youngest of three children. His sister Janet lived with her husband nearby. His brother Ike and his wife Helen lived in the house with his father. In a country churchyard, beneath the shade of old trees, Charlie's father was buried next to his mother. After the burial there was a reception back at the house, and when the others were gone and he was left with his brother and sister he was kidded as always for having deserted the country for the city and its wicked, cruel ways.

"Nobody could pay me enough to live in *that* son of a bitch," Ike said.

Charlie just smiled.

"Charlie hasn't changed," Janet said. "It's still the same nice Charlie. Did you get a chance to talk to Emily, Charlie?"

"A little," he said.

"I think she's still carrying the torch for you," Janet said. "I think she's hoping you'll come back."

Later he sat on the bank of the stream that ran through the farm, as he had done as a boy. He listened to a redwing blackbird, smiling as he had smiled long ago to realize that from the song of the redwing blackbird had come the opening notes of the old song "Who's Sorry Now?" He kept listening and the bird, off in the marsh in which the stream lost itself, sounded the notes over and over, sometimes slurred, sometimes with a note or two omitted, but the composer's debt was unmistakable. The bird grew silent. A turtle crawled to the bank and slid down into the water. Charlie sat watching the stream, its eddies and currents, the reflections of the trees and the clouds. Near the bank, a twig was caught in a backwater, and he watched as it slowly worked its way free and moved out again into the gentle current. With his first movie camera, from this very spot, he had filmed the stream with its eddies and currents, the bright ripples, the twigs bobbing along the surface.

He had loved his boyhood and loved the farm, but it was no longer where he wanted to be. He missed Anne more than he had thought possible. From his father he had inherited seven thousand dollars, and when he returned to New York he asked her to marry him. She fell into his arms and said yes. The wedding took place in City Hall and the reception at her parents' house in Mamaroneck, where Ike and Helen mingled with her patrician relatives, standing and drinking on a sun-washed lawn. There was something in her father's eyes. Concern. Anxiety. Sympathy. With his eyes he seemed to be asking a question: Will she be all right now, Charlie? And will *you* be all right?

For a while they were, but then it returned, whatever it was, and he began to realize that she was in the power of something she hated but which was no less powerful for her hatred of it. Dismally he realized that he knew his wife not at all, that somewhere in the depths of her being she lived a life that had nothing whatever to do with him or with their marriage.

She still had the power to beguile him. No matter what her mood she was always ready for him. Yet afterward she drifted away, lying there with his semen still in her body, and she would be far off, lying quietly, looking at the ceiling, sometimes turning away to bury her face in the pillow.

He tried, sometimes gently, sometimes angrily, to find out what was wrong, and her answer was always that it was within herself, that it had nothing to do with him. Abruptly she would snap out of it. Smiling, she would slap him on the rump and say, "Come on, get up, I'm hungry," and pad into the bathroom, emerge wrapped in a huge towel, and there in the kitchen he would find her making him a sandwich, and they would sit at the round table with its diagonal view of Washington Square, and she would smile at him tenderly and say, "Don't worry about me. I'll work it out."

"What is it you're working out, Anne? Tell me. Maybe I can help."

"Don't talk with your mouth full."

The towel had fallen away. "Cover yourself up," he said. "I can't concentrate."

"You mean you can't look at me and chew at the same time?" Her eyes danced.

"Sometimes it's easy."

She smiled. "Don't worry about me, Charlie. And don't leave me. For God's sake, don't *leave* me."

"Sometimes I get the impression that you wish you were a thousand miles away."

"Wrong. I love you, Charlie. I love you. I love you,

Charlie. You're straight. You're really the straightest person I've ever known."

"Straight can be boring."

"You and my father. Really straight. Really good. I really love you both." Tears hung in her eyes. "I love what you're doing. The work you're doing."

"Probably at a big fat loss."

"So what? Keep doing what you're doing. I love the fact that you love Jacob Riis. The world would be a better place if more people loved Jacob Riis. I love you for loving the things you love. I envy the way you feel about your eddies and twigs and redwing blackbirds."

He shrugged.

"How do we know if something is beautiful, Charlie?"

"You either know it or you don't." He frowned. "What the hell kind of a question is that? You either feel it or you don't. It's not something you can put a computer on."

She was smiling at him. The towel had fallen to her hips. "Wanna fool around, Charlie?"

"We just did."

Playfully she threw the towel at him and stalked off into the bathroom.

Sometimes it struck him that she was using sex as a veneer. Whatever unanswered and unresolved lay between them was covered over by sex, by the oblivion that making love could bring. It was as if she used it as a means of driving out thought, heading off questions—the mind, the spirit, forced to surrender to the lust and the craving. It was as if it were all she had to give him.

The truth, of course, was that it was all she was willing to give him. Always he was aware of questions beyond questions, and of answers that she pondered but would not talk of. Within the recesses of her mind she was pursuing a secret quest, and in time, as he would learn, the pursuit took more active forms. There was the night he awakened to find her gone. He had not heard her leave, had not heard the door close, but at some point he became aware that the

space next to him was empty. He lay awake and toward five
she returned. He switched on the lamp. She stood before
him, dressed as if she were ready for the office, hair brushed,
eyes freshly made-up. "Hi," she said.

"Where in the hell have you been?"

"Walking. I was out walking. Isn't that okay?" She
removed her jacket and slacks, hung them carefully in the
closet. "Isn't it okay that I was out walking?"

"Great," he said.

By now she had on his shirt and was beneath the covers,
moving against him. "Come on, Charlie, hold me."

"Where were you really?"

"Out walking. Really."

He lay there quietly, hands clasped beneath his head,
tormented by his imagination. Presently she began to sob,
face pressed against his shoulder.

"Anne, what the hell is it?"

"I don't know. I don't know. Hold me, Charlie, for
God's sake, *hold* me, oh please hold me."

"I *am* holding you," he said. "I'm *holding* you."

He stroked her temples softly, cupped the back of her
head with his hand, kissed her brow. Presently she grew
quiet.

"Do you want a divorce, Anne?"

"God no! Please no."

"I'll give you one if it's what you want."

"It's not what I want. It's the last thing I want."

Again he lay there in silence, stroking her head.
"Anne?"

"Yes, my darling?"

"Let's have a baby? Would that help?"

She pressed his hand. "Later. Not now. Do you want a
baby badly, Charlie?"

"I think a baby might be a good idea."

"Give me some time. When I have a baby I want to be
a good mother and I couldn't be a good mother now. I know
I couldn't. Maybe some day I can."

She said she loved him. Did she? Perhaps. She said she needed him and probably did. Mystified by her, he could also pity her. If once he had been her love-slave, he was by now a slave to something else—a slave to pity and to the deep need he felt to protect her against herself, against the deep inexplicable moods that now could send her to bed for hours at a time, where she lay staring at the ceiling, or scribbling in a notebook, and, finally, taking refuge in sleep.

One afternoon as she slept he picked up her notebook and read what she had been writing. "Nietzsche says evil is not all bad! He says we must use the evil, harness the evil, in ourselves, that only by combining the evil with the good can we become a whole person! Nietzsche must have known something!"

The passage was underlined and in the margin there were stars.

Later they were eating lunch in the kitchen. It was a Sunday. Looking down into the square, he could see kids on the swings and seesaws, mothers pushing baby carriages, derelicts asleep on the benches.

When he had finished eating he said, "I was reading what you wrote in your notebook about Nietzsche and evil."

"You were reading my notebook?"

"Just that much, just that one page. It was opened to that page."

She nodded. "So what did you think?"

"I think it's okay for Nietzsche, but in the wrong hands it could play hell."

"I agree—but there's a thought there."

"Are you trying to tell me you find evil—*appealing?*"

"I'm only trying to understand what he meant. Is there anything wrong with trying to understand what the big-time thinkers had in their minds? A person shouldn't fear knowledge."

"A little knowledge of Nietzsche is a dangerous thing. Look what Hitler did with it."

"Are you against knowledge, Charlie?"

"Of course not. I'm just against the way you torture yourself. Whatever you're reading or thinking sure as hell is not making you happy. Why are you so unhappy?"

"I guess because I don't like myself."

"Why not?"

"I don't know."

"My God! You're beautiful, intelligent; you have wonderful parents; you have a good job. No bombs are falling."

"I've also got you. Don't leave that out."

"Yeah," he said sourly.

On a rainy Saturday afternoon they had been to a matinee and were sitting in the Algonquin bar, with no one there but themselves and the bartender.

She told him that what they had just seen had made her start thinking again of Chichén Itzá.

What they had seen was a musical that was as remote from Chichén Itzá as anything could be. "Why?" he asked.

"I don't think I've ever felt so alive as I felt there."

"Why?"

"It had a strange effect on me."

"Yeah, I noticed. Especially early one morning when the sun was rising."

She looked into her drink. "I loved it there."

"Maybe you could go back and get a job as a tour guide."

"Don't be surly."

He was wolfing pretzels. "Tell me what you felt about the place."

"I'm not sure whether it was the place or me."

He was angry. "Tell me what you're thinking. Talk. For God's sake, *talk*. I'm no idiot. Say it. Maybe I'll understand it."

As he watched her face, tears appeared. Taking a pretzel from his hand, she placed it slowly into her mouth. "I can't," she said.

"Why can't you?"

She pressed his hand. "I'll try to get my head on straight.

When I do, I'll try to explain. But please let's not talk about
it any more now, okay?"

A few days later he suggested a psychiatrist, something
he had been suggesting for months. He asked if she would
like to go off somewhere by herself, or with him. Whichever
she liked. She touched his fingers to her lips, touched her
tongue to each fingertip in turn. They were having dinner
in a small, inexpensive restaurant near the apartment. In
the candlelight her eyes were filled with torment. "It's in
me," she said. "It's in *me.*"

"*What's* in you?"

She shook her head. "Something I hate." She stared into
space. "Something I really hate." She tossed her napkin to
the table. "Let's go home, Charlie. I want to get into bed.
I want you to do all the things you've ever done to me, and
any others you can think of. All night long." But when they
got home and he tried, she pushed him away and sat on the
edge of the bed, looking at the floor. When he touched her,
her body went stiff.

It was less than a week later that she flew to Washington
and soon afterward that she started sleeping with Carver.
She told Charlie about it, told him much more than he
wanted to hear. Dry-eyed, she told him they should part,
that she had fallen in love with Carver the moment she saw
him, that what she had thought was sinister she found attractive. She knew it was wrong, but it was too powerful to
resist, almost as if Carver were the Devil himself. He was
dumfounded. He sat listening with pain, jealousy, anger.
He asked how she could possibly throw away their marriage for such a notorious bastard. She said she was sorry,
but she didn't seem to be sorry. She seemed caught up in
the thrill of it all. In her manner there was a strange exalta-
tion, as if she were under a spell. "Sorry, Charlie," she said.
"But you won't be losing anything. You're a wonderful
guy. I'm a bitch." He talked to her long into the night, but
the next morning she moved out and he never saw her alive
again. She had also walked out on her job, and he could only
assume that she had moved in with Carver. He called her

office and talked to Bob Kendall, who gave him the private number of Carver's secretary. He called and was shut off with icy curtness. Mr. Carver, he was told, was accessible to no one. Two weeks later she threw herself in front of the subway train.

She was gone.

He tried covering his grief with a hard crust, tested himself in the role of an embittered man, so mortally pained that he was beyond pain. It was a role he could not fill, and he moved through a blur of days with muted, stricken bewilderment, knowing that he must somehow come to terms with his pain, his grief, his bewilderment, his rage, must somehow take action that would make the rest of his life something more than an idiot-song.

He went back to his boyhood home. Ike and Helen were away and he had the house to himself. There were long intervals when he felt catatonic. He stood on the deep green lawn, embellished with great loops of shade. He stood there and stared, thinking to see the vast shadows move. They seemed frozen, yet he knew they were moving for the sun was moving. He looked at the shadows and they seemed solid, opaque, even though they were composed of leaves and branches. But here and there the shadow showed clearly the line of a limb, a graceful network of twigs. He looked toward the porch. Its shadow was a sturdy rhomboid, frozen in the lawn.

He was obsessed with the moment of her death, the exact moment, and at night in bed he saw himself with a camera pointed at the subway tracks; the shutter clicked and the truth was recorded, accurately and precisely. Yet there was greater accuracy, he knew, in filling in the truth with the infinite, painstaking care that went beyond the truth of the camera. There was need for something more, something that saw and encompassed the truth seen by the camera, yet added an interpretation of its own, so that truth became a particularized truth and thus an act of creation.

By day he sat hour upon hour in the living room and stared through the multipaned window, and the effect was of a group of framed paintings. He focused upon the pane in the exact center. In the painting framed within this pane, the river and sky were separated by a thin horizontal band of green, a strip of shoreline dotted with fat, shaggy willows of lime green and a few cedars, jagged and dark. Beyond the shoreline stretched a farm, and still farther a green haze of woodland—yet because of the distance the entirety was hardly thicker than a pencil line of horizontal greenery, separating the river below from the sky above. Sometimes a seagull would wheel into the picture, beating up into the wind, climbing the wind's steep slope, and then sliding swiftly back downhill, tilting and scudding low over the water, away.

In the basement of the house there was a very small room, a room that once as a boy he had used as a darkroom. It was now stripped bare.

At times he went down into this small room and closed the door behind him. He would lie on the bare floor, or sit with knees drawn up, head lowered. In his mind's eye, in the darkness, he saw a painting, a painting without frame, with neither beginning nor end, neither top nor bottom, so that it seemed to stretch endlessly, as space rolls back upon itself. It was a painting suffused with light. He saw a face, and although he no longer had any explicit religion he felt as one of the great Renaissance painters might have felt as the sunlight fell upon the daub of thick color that the painter was hoping to mold and fashion into a face of beauty, of good-through-God, overlooking the venality of the commissioning pope, overlooking everything except the spots of liquid color, the radiance of sunlight and the radiance of his own inner feelings, for these were all a painter had, his only components.

There in the darkness he listened closely, trying to feel all of it, persuading himself that he could feel the agony begin to soften around the edges and that in horror he could perceive the first faint traces of radiance.

But he failed. As with the endless painting and as with space, the pain stretched in an endless, breathtaking curve.

Nineteen

HIS GRIEF TURNED TO RAGE and the rage to hatred. His quest began.

Carver, he soon learned, was less accessible than the president of the United States. He was a man who safeguarded his privacy and his person as carefully as any Latin American dictator, as carefully as Howard Hughes himself.

Long hours in the New York Public Library at first turned up very little. Carver sat on the boards of six corporations. He had innumerable houses, including a castle in Ireland. He loved Ireland, had been known to do some pub-hopping in Dublin. To himself and his only wife, now dead, two children had been born, a son killed in France in a bus accident, and a daughter named Daisy. Daisy had married a man named Leonard King. The marriage had ended quickly in divorce. Daisy thereafter had spent time in a mental institution but was now out, under the care of a psychiatrist. She was Carver's only living relative. Where was Daisy King?

Day after day he spent in the library, doggedly combing periodicals, business magazines, Sunday supplements, newspapers foreign and domestic—finally finding an answer in a Dublin newspaper. Noting that Carver was a frequent Dublin visitor, a columnist wrote that Daisy King, "his mentally disturbed only child, has been placed away under the protection of caretakers on a waterfront estate in a fancy-folks area on the Eastern Shore of Maryland, U.S.A."

He selected what seemed the most likely area, drove to the county seat, and made inquiries. Daisy King was a recluse. She lived in a mansion. No one mentioned her connection with Carver. No one seemed to know of it.

He located the house and roamed the vicinity, getting

143

names from RFD mailboxes. With a list of names and phone numbers before him, he made five calls without success. On the sixth call a man told him that although he personally had all the help he needed, he had heard that some people named Donaldson were looking for a summer caretaker.

His unwitting benefactress, Martha Donaldson, had a pleasant telephone voice. She sounded terribly genteel, just as self-contained and as trusting as her husband would prove to be. "Mrs. Donaldson," he said, "it's my understanding that you may be needing some help this summer. If so, I'd love to drop over and see you."

Her laugh was melodious. "Oh, I'm so sorry. We've already made arrangements with my nephew from Teaneck."

"Teaneck, New Jersey?" He paused. *"Really?* I have relatives in Teaneck. What's his name?"

"Eliot Bender—do you know him?"

"Eliot Bender . . . Nope. Afraid not. Well, thanks very much, ma'am. Sorry to disturb you."

Although she had no way of knowing it, he was thanking her of course for a great deal more than her courtesy.

From a phone call to the Bender residence in Teaneck, he learned from Agnes Bender that son Eliot worked in his father's religious bookshop in New York City.

After three more days and a visit to the business license division at City Hall, he knew that somewhere in the world, somewhere in fact at an address on West Forty-second Street, there was a man who would be spending the summer in a house directly across the river from the mansion in which Hamilton Carver's daughter was kept a virtual prisoner.

At the address given him there was no religious bookshop. There was instead a porn emporium set between two grubby movie houses on the south side of Forty-second Street. A pink neon sign proclaimed, LIVE GIRLS INSIDE! He walked in and found a huge room filled with glitter and bright blue lights. Not only the walls but the supporting pillars and even the ceiling were covered with mirrors. One end of the room was filled with rack upon rack of pornographic reading matter, encompassing all known sexual combinations and aberrations. The remaining floor space was crammed with rows of cubicles, some offering filmed peep shows, others containing the LIVE GIRLS promised by the pink neon sign.

At a central vantage point, behind a counter with a mirrored facade, Eliot presided on a high thronelike perch, accepting money from those who bought the magazines and books and articles of erotica, making change for those bent upon the peep shows.

Mounted high upon the most prominent wall hung a huge framed likeness of the late Supreme Court justice William O. Douglas in all his black-robed self-assurance, flanked on either side by smaller but no less arresting portraits showing the pink flesh of a pair of reigning porn queens, one known as Désirée Cousteau and the other simply as Seka. The portrait of Justice Douglas, it turned out, had come with the shop, hung by the previous owner, who, because of some of Douglas's decisions on freedom of expression and the like, obviously regarded him as a sort of patron saint, one who—doubtless unwittingly—had helped open up a billion-dollar industry.

Eliot Bender looked to be somewhere between thirty and thirty-five, with light brown hair, long sideburns, and a slack mouth, rarely closed. He wore gray and black jackets with sequined lapels. A double row of sequins ran down his placket shirtfront.

In and out of the place for more than a week, sizing up his quarry, Charlie found that Eliot was spelled occasionally by an older man with a white toothbrush mustache, very small eyes, and gray hair that hung limply to his shoulder. This man, he learned, was Eliot's father, Roy. But it was Eliot who claimed his attention, and day by day he learned a little more.

In such a person the unexpected note might have been the expected. For a person who spent his days thus, the striking touch might have been one that came as an incongruity—a leitmotif perhaps of gum-chewing nonchalance, with almost total indifference to his surroundings. One might have expected a man perhaps studying a racing form, too bored with his work to do more than hand out change, hardly deigning even to glance up from his racing form, or perhaps from his Proust or Plato. So often one in his position might have been expected to tire of the merchandise, simply because of its very day-to-day availability, as perhaps a man working in a candy store might tire of sweets, or a man running a delicatessen might tire of salami.

Not so with Eliot. He was as dedicated as the most febrile of his patrons. There was about him a sort of lazy, lackadaisical lewdness. Every movement, every facial expression, almost every word, seemed suggestive. Up on his throne, his reading matter was invariably pornographic. Now and then he descended from his perch and, sequined jacket swinging out behind him, ducked into one of the cubicles, coming out some minutes later with a silly, vacant smile. When one of the seductively clad LIVE GIRLS emerged for a respite, or at the end of her shift, he always had a lewd bon mot to offer.

If he was genial with the girls, he was equally genial with his customers, a man eager and ready to talk of the things nearest and dearest to his heart. By the end of the week, conversation was free and easy. By the end of the week, it was clear that the ambition of Eliot's life, the thing nearest and dearest to his heart, was to watch a porn film in the making—to go, as it were, on location.

"How about *acting* in one?"

Eliot gurgled with covetous laughter.

For the rest, Charlie enlisted the help of his friend Tex Poffenberger, who would be shooting quickies that summer in a yacht off the coast of southern California.

"How important is it to you?" Tex asked.

"Very important," Charlie said.

Tex nodded. "That's good enough for me. Okay, I'll tell him he's going to be one of the studs; then I'll make him the script boy."

"*Script* boy?"

"A little continuity never hurts," Tex said.

Charlie smiled. "I don't care what you call him just so long as you get him out there and keep him as long as you can."

Eliot being Eliot, the rest, although it took some doing, was relatively easy.

For all his deep-seated yearning to go west with Tex Poffenberger's troupe, Eliot had a problem. He was committed for the summer to watch over a sick uncle.

"Screw the son of a bitch," Roy said.

Eliot frowned. "I sure wouldn't want Aggie to know what I'm doing. What would I tell *her?*"

"Who's Aggie?" Tex asked.

"My mother."

Tex shrugged. "Tell her you're spending the summer with *Up with People.*"

"Tell her you're going to California to make a religious movie," Charlie said.

"Hey!" Eliot said with admiration.

"I'll take care of Aggie," Roy said. "I'll cover for you. She won't know where you are."

"Yeah, but—" Eliot began.

Roy's eyes flashed. "My God, do you mean you'd let that son of a bitch Warren Donaldson keep you from a chance like this? High and mighty bastard. We don't owe him anything. We haven't been invited to the son of a bitch's house since the Battle of Dunkerque!"

"I'm still worried about Aggie," Eliot said. "It's awfully short notice. . . . Maybe I could get somebody to take my place."

Charlie shrugged. "I'll take your place," he said. "I wouldn't mind a summer in the country."

"There you go," Roy said.

It was done.

Taking the place of Eliot Bender was the first step in the furtive way he would be spending the rest of his life. It was the beginning of flight. In flight that summer he had paused to take revenge. With revenge taken, with the bullet searing his scalp, himself zigzagging among the loblolly pines, flight became real. Chichén Itzá was merely a pause in a flight path that would go on for as long as he lived.

Twenty

ON HIS FINAL NIGHT he sat at the bar, slowly sipping a drink, and then went up to his room and lay in the dark. His balcony door stood open. There were lamps down in the courtyard, and their dim light filtered up through the foliage into his room.

When they were turned off for the night, the jungle seemed closer.

Stepping outside, he glanced down the line of balconies. Save for one, all the rooms were dark. On the stone floor of one fell an oblong of dull orange light. He counted. It was Anne's room; had been Anne's room.

He looked away and stared ahead into the darkness, thinking of the past three days. He had come to Chichén Itzá because it was where he had once felt closest to her. It was the place where their love had germinated and exploded into the greatest passion of his life.

He had come because he hoped to see the place with her eyes and perhaps to understand its importance in her life, the part it had played in her torment, her degradation and death.

But what had he accomplished? To revisit the scene of their happiness, to look at the oblong of light on the floor of her balcony, brought only a bitter nostalgia that quickly became pain.

And what insight had it given him into Anne that he did not already have? The allure of the place still escaped him. He felt only its horror, far more this time than before.

The vast sunbaked plaza, the pocked faces of the temples, the rolling, boiling clouds; The Castle, imperious against the sky, and everywhere the evidence of homage paid to rattlesnakes, jaguars, eagles, all elevated into deities.

To him it was a place of infinite horror and infinite sadness. It pained him to think of people who were considered less important than rattlesnakes, jaguars and eagles— the common people, the tiny peasants whose lives were governed by the high priests, by men more powerful than they, and whose power they so freely acknowledged, men who manipulated them, bent them to their will, killed them and killed their children.

High priests. High crimes.

That afternoon he had gone once more to the sacred well. Reaching the clearing, he stood next to the pagoda and looked down at the filthy surface of the water. In the bright afternoon light, some of the eeriness was gone but the silence was still complete, and as he continued to stand there, the horror once more stared at him from the putrescent muck, the cylinder that could never be climbed.

For a long while he stood looking down, and when finally he raised his eyes to the obscene dancing trees his vision was blurred with tears. In an irrational way, he felt that he was saying goodbye to her forever. It was as if she were down there. If he looked he would find her at the bottom, wearing the bloody jeans and blouse that he had been given on the day he identified her at the morgue.

The oblong of orange light had disappeared. He stood at the rail. There was no moon, but there was enough light from the stars to see the domed silhouette of the observatory. He looked up deep into the stars and knew that among them, far beyond them, an unmanned satellite was traveling through an infinity of time and space. To think of its speed and the depth of its probe and the sophisticated data it was sending back—and then to think of a lone Mayan, starting from scratch, with nothing except what his eyes and senses told him.

A tiny man alone at the dawn of history, naked in the Yucatán, and what did he behold? He beheld the sun. The sun disappeared at what he called dark and reappeared at what he knew as dawn. At night, alone under the stars, he stood fearful that the sun would not come up next day. Fearing the sun might not return, he created a special god whose job it was to ensure that night would end and that the sun once more, after a night spent under the flat table of the earth, a night spent down in the unknown nether-world, would slip out from beneath the earth's rim and once more make its journey across the sky.

Standing there in the darkness, he felt a primitive kin-ship with this man and as helplessly bound as he. As with him, there were forces at work beyond his understanding. As with him, he had been manipulated.

And he had killed.

Looking up at the stars, he asked as if in prayer what had happened to him and why.

Tomorrow he would leave. Flight would resume. In what direction, and with what end?

Men in flight changed their names, grew beards, shaved beards; as new men they took women and begat children, lived out their lives in identities they had not been born with, identities forced upon them, or wished for by them. Some failed and were flushed out of hiding. But some suc-ceeded, escaped, obliterating all traces of their former selves, trading one identity for another, becoming someone who had never been.

Joseph Conrad, for whatever reason, had deep interest in such men, in the notion of lost men taking themselves into hiding, deep into the jungle, to the uttermost dark places of the earth. With Lord Jim and Kurtz, Conrad saw flight as having an end—an end that could only be exile, deep in the heart of darkness.

He could go on for as long as he liked, continue to flee

southward, on through Guatemala, Honduras, Nicaragua, onward and onward, by car, by plane, by boat when necessary, all the way to Tierra del Fuego if he liked, a man with nowhere to go and no one to be, with his entire life to roam, to run and hide.

Yet ultimately, as with Conrad's men, he would grow exhausted; out of desperation and exhaustion he would find a place to exist, find someone to be.

Twenty-one

THE SHIP HAD CLEARED the Panama Canal and was moving down the coast of Colombia before he made his first appearance in the main dining salon. He introduced himself as Jim Burke and took the vacant seat at the circular table for six, wearing the maroon blazer he had bought that afternoon in the sports lounge.

There were two married couples from Houston, himself, and a ship's officer. "You got aboard at the Canal Zone?" he was asked politely. He said yes and that he had been under the weather ever since. "I know the feeling." One of the women smiled. "You don't want to do a thing. You just want to stay in your cabin and cover up your head."

The ship's officer said that as voyages went, this one so far had been relatively smooth.

"I'm sure that doesn't help Mr. Burke," the woman said sympathetically.

One of the men ran the food concession at the Houston Astrodome. He and the other man and the two women were all in their sixties. By the end of the meal he still didn't know which wife went with which husband.

For the most part he kept to himself, sitting alone in

remote sections of the ship, often having his meals in his cabin. On the occasions when he took his place at the table, the Astrodome man said unfailingly, "Well, well, well, here's the missing man. . . ."

Once the ship had rounded the shoulder of Ecuador, the coast became a wall of mountain. In the mornings, backlit by the sun, the mountain was a dense purple silhouette, but in the afternoons, when the sun had moved to the west and poured its rays back upon the coast, he could see tiny fishing villages glittering along the shoreline, houses trailing single file up the slope of the mountain.

On the top deck, near the bow of the ship, he spent much of Sunday afternoon bent over a powerful telescope, sweeping the shoreline and the pocked wall of themountain, absorbed in the array of sun-drenched miniatures that he picked up with the glass. A woman, arms folded, stood before a hovel. A lean gray dog looked over its shoulder. A black vulture, wings flapping, rose slowly from an adobe wall.

The Astrodome man's name was Jack. At dinner his wife passed around snapshots of their grandchildren. "Being a grandmother is so much better than being a mother," she said. "You get all the fun with none of the headaches."

"Indeed it's so."

"Life is so short, Mr. Burke. At your age you can't possibly believe how short it really is."

"Each year goes faster than the one before it."

"A year gets to be like a month."

"You wonder where it all went to. . . ."

He swiveled the telescope, seeking a break in the solid wall of mountain to the mountains beyond. The telescope was of such power that he felt he could see anything, anywhere in the world. If he was patient, if he moved the glass with minute, infinite care, focused to infinity, he would be able to see Anne crouched in a tunnel, waiting for the train to strike.

Flight

For long hours each day he stood at the telescope. What showed up in the glass became his world.

At other times he stood at the rail on the top deck, watching the churning, foaming bow wave as the ship cut through the water, raising his eyes to the heavily textured clouds that stretched over the open sea to the horizon, feeling the vastness of the sea and sky, a rangy man alone beneath the clouds. He studied the sea, watched the porpoises that sometimes looped alongside, keeping up with the ship. Occasionally whales were spotted, rolling and spouting off to starboard, and then the passengers would come rushing up from the lower decks to line the rail, and he would stand elbow to elbow with them as they smiled at the sportive whales.

The ship's officer cultivated a cowlick. He seemed bored with his dinner companions. He was always the last to arrive, the first to excuse himself, and betweentimes he stroked his cowlick and smiled a steady smile.

He did not particularly like the ship's officer, nor did the latter seem to like him.

On deck one afternoon Jack, the man from the Astrodome, told him that the ship's officer had a wife and family back in Duluth and that he followed the sea only as a means of sleeping with as many women as might fall his way on the cruises.

"I don't think he's making out much on this one," Jack said, "but I guess it beats Duluth."

That evening at dinner one of the women asked if he was married, for they had of course been talking not only about the ship's officer but about him.

"No," he replied.

She made sounds of disapproval with her tongue. "A nice-looking young man like you should be married."

The ship's officer's eyes were hooded. He tapped his plate lightly with the blade of his knife. As a much younger man, he said, he had worked for six years on an ore ship on Lake Superior.

"And how about you, Mr. Burke," asked Jack's wife.

"Where has your life been spent?" She had a gentle face, a gentle manner, and loved her grandchildren.

There was a lone woman, somewhere in her midtwenties, moderately attractive with long dark hair. In the reading room one afternoon their eyes met. He felt a signal, felt a current, continued to read.

Later that afternoon, staring intently through the telescope, he was startled to find her standing at his shoulder. She had moved without sound.

"Hi," he said. "Would you like to use it?"

"No thanks," she said softly, and with a faint smile crossed the deck and stood at the opposite rail, her hair flattened against her cheek by the breeze, a strand of hair cupped beneath her chin. She tossed her head to shake it free.

He turned away and went below to read in his cabin, but as always the book slipped from his hand and he lay looking at the ceiling.

At night from the top deck, he watched the stars and they seemed misplaced. Here in the southern hemisphere they were not the constellations he had known as a boy. They were different even from the constellations he had seen in Chichén Itzá, the ones the Mayans had studied.

He watched Jack eat. He studied the heavily veined hands as they manipulated knife and fork. His head was framed in a port window, his glistening white hair smoothed over his baldness, his scalp and face ruddy from the Houston sun. Catching his eye, Jack grinned. "Eat up, Jim. Eat up, boy."

The ship by now was moving down the coast of Peru, and the snowcapped peaks of the Andes glistened all day long in the sun. At Callao, the ship would put into port. It was an elaborate cruise. Side trips were permitted. One could leave and fly into the interior of South America and then, at the next port, embark once more. At Callao, the ship would debark passengers who had signed up for the trip to Lima and others who would visit Machu Picchu, the

154

Flight

ancient Incan city high in the Andes.

One evening after dinner he sat in the main salon. The light was deep blue and the floor filled with dancers. He saw the ship's officer sitting with the dark-haired girl at a small table in a remote corner. The ship's officer was more animated than he had ever seen him at meals. He and the girl clinked glasses and the girl smiled into his eyes. Jack, in his white dinner jacket, was dancing with his wife. The band played songs of the thirties. The male vocalist doubled as emcee. Now he caressed the microphone, eyes soft, hair soft, singing:

> I saw you last night and got
> that old feeling;
> Once again last night I got
> that old feeling.*

Jack danced bent just slightly from the waist, his rear just slightly protruding, his cheek against his wife's, her wrist drooping gently against the back of his creased, sunburned neck.

On Sunday afternoon he stood at the telescope. A tiny burro moved up a trail. A child patted its flank. Tilting the telescope, he saw a yellow church that stood at one end of a plaza. Before the church steps, a man in a black suit appeared, carrying a tripod and camera. As he spread the legs of the tripod, two little girls in white dresses came out. The man ducked beneath a black cloth and raised his hand high. The little girls linked arms on the steps. Soon all three disappeared into the church.

At Callao he got off and boarded a bus with ten others. At Lima he took a flight bound for Baltimore-Washington International Airport.

Part IV

Bondage

Twenty-two

IN THE TOWN of Shaftesbury the courthouse was a redbrick citadel rising from masses of boxwood. The building and its grounds dominated a village square, surrounded on three sides by stores, restaurants, and law offices that comprised a sort of lawyers' row. The faces of some of these had been restored and painted to give an aspect of colonial antiquity consonant with the age of the town, which dated back to revolutionary times.

The courthouse was built in the eighteenth century and rebuilt just before the Civil War. Since then wings had been added. One wing contained the state's attorney's office. At the opposite end, another wing shielded from view an ungainly structure that housed the sheriff's office and the town jail.

Above the courthouse towered a steeple containing a huge lighted clock whose chimes tolled the quarter hour day and night in treble tones loud enough to be heard for blocks around.

On the afternoon of March 27, the clock in the steeple had just struck 2:30 when a young man carrying a backpack walked between the rows of boxwood, entered the main building, and was directed to the state's attorney's office. Here, encountering a secretary, he identified himself as Charles Ellis and said he had come to confess to the shooting six months earlier of the multimillionaire financier and developer Hamilton Carver.

Now in her third year as assistant state's attorney, Janice Wood had just hung up the phone. Her door stood partly open, and she heard quite distinctly what was said. Her secretary, clearly rattled, buzzed her phone. "Could you step out here a minute?" her secretary said. "There's someone to—see you."

"Is Mel in his office?" Janice asked, speaking of the state's attorney.

"He's in court," her secretary replied.

"Where's Bob?" Janice asked, speaking of the senior assistant.

"Out getting a haircut," her secretary said.

"Okay . . ." Janice lowered her voice. "Listen, Alma, as soon as I come out, you go pull a guard out of district court. Or anybody with a gun. Grab the first cop you see and get back fast."

Janice hung up.

Through the partly open doorway, she could see the man standing at the corner of her secretary's desk and her secretary eyeing him warily.

Janice Wood was tall and slim and barely thirty-two. She had close-cropped black hair and dark brown eyes. Taking a deep breath, she stepped from her office. "Good afternoon," she said. "I'm Janice Wood, the assistant state's attorney. What can I do for you?"

What she beheld was a slim, rangy man with dark shaggy hair and a deeply tanned face. He wore dirty white sailcloth jeans and the backpack was strapped over a navy blue shirt. Glancing briefly at the secretary as she slipped away, he turned to Janice and said, "I'm Ellis. I shot Hamilton Carver. I'm turning myself in."

Janice rested a hand on a corner of her secretary's desk. "Please sit down," she said.

Ellis said he would stand.

"Okay, sure," Janice said. "Whatever you like. Okay, are you saying you're here to confess to the shooting of Hamilton Carver?"

"Yes."

"Very well." Bit by bit Janice was becoming calmer. She was helped by the young man's appearance, by the look in his eye, a look almost serene in its sadness. Hired as an assistant principally to prosecute rape cases, she had in a very short time encountered some hostile prisoners, some who would have as soon dismembered her as look at her.

Bondage

Because of threats on her life by men she had convicted, and threats by members of their families, she had a permit to carry a handgun that she seldom carried. His appearance told her that this man, in spite of his crime, was not dangerous. His eyes had a tortured look, a look of deep suffering that bespoke resignation, possibly even contrition, certainly not hostility. But she knew she could be wrong.

She had sent her secretary to the district courtroom because the sheriff's office was at the far end of the square. Even though her own office did not communicate directly with the main building—meaning that Alma had to go outdoors and then in again—the district courtroom could be reached much more quickly.

Janice guessed that by now her secretary had been gone three minutes, although it could have been no more than thirty seconds. She wasn't sure. Her eyes kept moving to the doorway, hoping to see someone, Mel or Bob or almost anyone. What she now saw was an armed guard, with her secretary at his heels.

Janice Wood was known for briskness and certitude. She now became brisk. "Billy," she said, "please take this man into custody."

The guard was quick and efficient. "Remove your knapsack, please," he said.

Ellis obeyed. After examining its contents, the guard said, "Extend your hands, please."

Handcuffs were applied. Once this was accomplished, the guard ran his hands over the prisoner's body. Satisfied that he carried no concealed weapons, he stood back. "Okay, Mrs. Wood. Sheriff's office?"

"Yes," Janice said, and then to her secretary: "Alma, call Clark Adams at the state police barrack, please, and tell him to get up to the sheriff's office as soon as possible. Then bring me a copy of the grand jury indictment."

A few moments later the three of them, prisoner, guard, and Janice Wood, were outdoors, moving along a brick walkway, past masses of boxwood. A pale sun shone. The air was damp. The clock in the steeple struck 2:45. As they

161

passed the central building, a few people were looking down at them from open windows. There were sounds of excitement; and then a loud voice saying, ". . . the guy that shot Hamilton Carver"; and then jumbled cries of "Carver . . . Janice . . . Alma . . . Billy . . . right out of the courtroom."

Janice looked up briefly, then looked across the street where bystanders were watching from the curb, and then straight ahead, walking a few steps behind the guard and the handcuffed prisoner. With his free hand, the guard carried the backpack. Soon they had reached the far wing and were circling around to the sheriff's office, mounting a short flight of wooden steps. The door stood open.

Maneuvering the prisoner through the doorway, the guard steered him to the left into a small room used for booking. A step behind, Janice called, "I'd like a deputy, please."

The booking room was of modest size, perhaps ten feet by twelve. There was a single window, its lower half barred, and before the window stood a massive desk. Bolted to the desk was one end of a chain. From the other end dangled a handcuff. Opposite the desk there was a partition of heavy-gauge mesh. Before the partition stretched a long bench on which lawyers sat while conferring with prisoners.

In the next room a few uniformed deputies were gathered. The door was open and one had hurried forward even as Janice called out her request. "Book him please, Jud," she said.

"Do you have the warrant, Mrs. Wood?" the deputy asked.

"He's under grand jury indictment. Alma's bringing a copy. . . . I guess you can go back to court now, Billy. We'll take it from here. Thanks ever so much."

The guard departed and as the booking process began, Janice stood by. Ellis was asked to empty his pockets. A wallet and then his belt were placed upon the desk. Two photographs were taken. In one, with his cuffed hands he held to his chest a placard reading "Craddock County, Sheriff's Department" and beneath the words a seven-digit number. The other photograph was taken without the placard. Again Janice found herself moved by the look on the prisoner's face. As he stared into the camera, his eyes looked like those of a man who had dwelt in the pit of hell, had never left. Her brain clicked ahead to the faces of a jury beholding this man, beholding his eyes.

"Thanks, Alma. Good work." Janice took the copy of the indictment from her secretary and handed it to the deputy, who read it and then, uncuffing the prisoner, asked him to sign it. Bent over the desk, he signed with a swift scrawl, the scrawl of a man whose name no longer meant anything to him, a man reducing his name to a jagged line.

"You may as well have him sign a presentment waiver too, Jud, just. . . ." Janice's voice faded. Technically, the waiver she mentioned was unnecessary. It had to do with a bond hearing before the district court commissioner, but bond here was not at issue and it was a case over which the district court had no jurisdiction. A grand jury panel, because the assailant was so long a fugitive, had issued an indictment *in absentia*, automatically placing the case under the jurisdiction of the circuit court. Because of the charge —murder—and because it was a circuit court case, the prisoner would be held without bail. The case had originally been handled by the Maryland State Police, and it was for this reason that Janice had asked her secretary to summon a state police detective to take the confession.

She watched as the prisoner was fingerprinted. With a written form before him, the deputy then seated himself at the desk and began the questioning, filling in the form as the prisoner answered.

"What is your full name, please?"

"Charles Ellis."

"Address?"

"Number One, University Place, New York City."

"Place of birth?"

"Kilmarnock, Virginia."

"Spell it please."

"K-i-l-m-a-r-n-o-c-k."

"Any marks or scars or tattoos on your body?"

"No. None."

The deputy looked up as a balding, florid man in a leather windbreaker walked in. "Afternoon, sergeant."

"Got him, huh?" asked Detective Sergeant Clark Adams.

"He walked right into my office," Janice said.

"God damn," said Adams.

"Occupation?" the deputy asked.

"Photographer," the prisoner said.

"Is there any nickname or alias you are known by?"

"None."

"Age?"

"Thirty-four."

"Height?"

"Six-one."

"Weight?"

The prisoner shrugged. "One-seventy."

"Color of eyes?" The deputy looked at him and answered for himself. "Blue. Month born?"

"March."

"Religion?"

The prisoner paused. "None."

"Married?"

Again the prisoner paused. "Widower."

"Social security number?"

It was given.

"Okay. In the event we need to contact somebody, whose name do you give?"

The prisoner was looking at the floor. "William E. Ellis, Kilmarnock."

"Relationship?"

"My brother."

The deputy put down his ballpoint pen. "Okay, sergeant, he's yours."

As the deputy left the room, the sergeant took his place at the desk. From his wallet he now extracted a small card known as a "Miranda card" after the Miranda case. "I'm about to read you your constitutional rights," the sergeant said. "Please listen carefully. Do you understand me?"

The prisoner nodded.

"Okay, first, you have the absolute right to remain silent.

"Second, if you choose to answer, your answers can be used against you in court.

"Third, you have the right to a lawyer. If you want a lawyer and cannot afford one, one will be provided for you.

"Fourth, you have the right to talk privately with your lawyer before answering any questions and to have him with you during the questioning.

"Fifth, if you elect to answer questions without having a lawyer present, you have a right to stop at any time and obtain the services of a lawyer."

The sergeant looked up. "Do you understand your rights as explained?"

The prisoner nodded.

"Please answer yes or no. Do you understand your rights as explained?"

"Yes."

"Do you knowingly waive these rights?"

"Yes."

Wearily the prisoner ran his hand through his hair. For a moment his eyes met Janice's, held for a moment, and then he looked away.

"On the reverse of this card," the sergeant said, "there is a waiver, which you may or may not elect to sign. It reads as follows: First, have you read or had read to you the warning as to your rights?"

"Yes," the prisoner said.

"There is no need to answer orally. These questions you will answer in writing as you see fit." The sergeant paused and went on. "Second, do you understand these rights? Third, do you wish to answer any questions? Fourth, are you willing to answer questions without having an attorney present?"

The sergeant extended the card and a pen. The prisoner bent over the desk and began to fill in the answers. When he had finished, the sergeant said, "You may now sign it, if such is your intention."

Once again the prisoner swiftly scrawled his signature, then looked up questioningly.

"The rest I will fill in," the sergeant said. "Time . . ." He glanced at his watch. "Three-thirty-seven. Date—March twenty-seventh. Okay . . ."

After signing the card, the sergeant offered it to Janice. "Would you sign as witness, Mrs. Wood?"

Janice signed below the sergeant's signature and stepped back. As she did so, the sergeant left the room, returning a moment later with a typewriter, paper, and carbon. These he placed on the desk and then, seated once more, he pulled a pad from his pocket and riffled the pages. Finding the place he wanted, he looked up, then back at the pad, and finally at the prisoner. "On or about September fifteenth, last year, one Hamilton Carver was shot and killed with a handgun at the residence of his daughter in Craddock County, Maryland. . . ."

"Yes," the prisoner said, "I did it."

"You so voluntarily confess?"

"I do. I shot him."

Another man had entered the room. He was unknown to Janice and for a few moments ignored by the sergeant. Then, rolling paper and carbon into the typewriter, the sergeant said, "Get his prints and a couple of mug shots, Henry."

As the sergeant began to type, the prisoner was finger-printed and photographed as before. These, Janice knew, were for the files of the state police and would enable Adams to close his investigation. "Thanks, Henry, that's all I need. Thanks very much."

The man left. By now the sergeant had extracted the carbon sheets and assembled the original and copies. "Here is your written confession," he said. "You may sign here if you still so wish."

The prisoner signed. The sergeant expelled a deep breath, then turned and looked briefly through the window. Rising, he picked up the backpack that still lay where the guard had dropped it. "Is this yours?" he asked.

"Yes," the prisoner replied.

Opening the backpack, the sergeant rummaged through its contents. He pulled out a framed photograph that Janice had not noticed when Billy checked the backpack an hour and a half earlier.

The photograph was of a young woman, doubtless, Janice thought, the most beautiful woman she had ever seen.

The sergeant stuffed it back in its place and fastened the straps. Rising, he said, "Okay, my lady, many thanks."

"You're welcome," Janice said.

"I'm leaving," the sergeant said. "I'll get you a deputy."

"Jud . . ." Janice called.

The same deputy appeared.

"We're finished for now," Janice said.

"See ya," the sergeant said, and was gone.

To the prisoner, Janice said, "The next step will be your arraignment in circuit court. There's no time limit, but it could take place as early as tomorrow or the next day. Meanwhile you will be detained here in the holding tank—"Janice checked herself"—in the overnight detention cell. You will undoubtedly want to summon a lawyer. If so, it can be arranged."

The prisoner shook his head.

"If not," Janice went on, "the question of defense counsel will be decided at your arraignment. Is there someone you would like notified?"

"No. No thanks." The prisoner was looking at his backpack.

"That will be kept for you," Janice said. "Are there any questions you'd like to ask?"

"No."

"Well, in that case . . ." Janice nodded to the deputy. A barred door adjoined the mesh partition. Unlocking it, the deputy motioned the prisoner to enter. Janice advanced as far as the threshold. To the left, a short flight of stone steps led to the detention cell. To the right, another flight of steps led to a small cell block that contained what the sheriff described as the "general population." In the cell block, from where Janice stood, four cells were visible. In each, faces were pressed to the bars. Her appearance set off an uproar. She heard obscene threats, obscene invitations, all of which by now she was inured to. She turned away in time to see the deputy unlock the detention cell. Inside there were three interior cells, all unlocked. Two young men stood watching curiously as their new cellmate entered. "How ya doin'?" one asked. Ellis shrugged. With a glance at his surroundings, he entered one of the cells and sat on the edge of a cot. The deputy locked the door of the detention cell. Janice withdrew. A few moments later the deputy stood at her side. "Will that be all, Mrs. Wood?"

"Yes, Jud, that's all. Thank you very much."

Returning to her office, Janice Wood picked up the telephone, dialed her husband, and asked him to buy her a drink.

Twenty-three

In the state of maryland, for each county (or in rural areas for a group of counties) there is a public defender with a full-time staff of ten lawyers. The public defender's office is assigned by the court to defend the indigent. Supplementing the public defender and his staff are other lawyers, members of a panel who conduct an independent practice but who volunteer to make themselves available when called upon. Each of these may handle two or three cases a year, almost invariably at a financial loss since they are paid by the state and the state has a schedule of maximum fees well below the going rate for defense work. Thus, of a fee of $2,000, the state might pay as little as $1,250.

Lawyers volunteer for the public defender's panel then not for the sake of the money but because of the exposure, the opportunity to enlarge their reputations, for the variety and challenge of criminal work. Many of course also do so out of conviction, from a desire to help the needy, for the public good, *pro bono*. At lowered fees they offer their services to those who, for lack of funds, might otherwise receive heavier sentences than they deserved, or heavier sentences than an expert lawyer might be able to obtain for them.

Shortly past nine on the morning after he gave himself up, Charlie Ellis was removed by a deputy from the detention cell and led into the booking room. Here, seated at the desk, was a man who introduced himself as Fred Sewell, a lean man in a rumpled gray suit. His white shirt was unbuttoned at the throat, and the knot of his black knit tie was jerked halfway down his shirtfront. "I'd like a word with you," he said. "Have a seat."

A straight chair stood next to the desk. Ellis sat down. Lifting the chain, the deputy attached the handcuff to Ellis's wrist and withdrew.

Sewell said he had heard of the confession on television the night before and had come to volunteer his services as defense counsel. If necessary, he would take the case as a member of the public defender's panel, which meant, he explained, that his fee would be taken care of by the state.

"Has the public defender been in touch with you?"

Ellis said no.

"Do you have a lawyer in mind?"

Ellis shook his head.

"If you don't have a lawyer, one will be appointed by the court at your arraignment," Sewell said. "Probably a member of the public defender's office. What is your financial condition?"

Ellis replied that he had a modest bank account as well as certain items of furniture, clothing, and photographic equipment contained in an apartment in New York City.

"The court may very well rule that you're entitled to defense as an indigent," Sewell said.

Ellis started to interrupt and was himself interrupted. "Listen," Sewell said, "you should know something right off the bat in case you don't know it already. You're in big trouble, very big trouble. I'm here to offer my help. I'm willing to defend you on an indigency basis, assuming the court rules you indigent. In either event I'm offering to take the case."

Ellis nodded as if he understood, but his eyes had a faraway look. Sewell peered at him closely. In the white jeans and blue shirt, Ellis looked slim to the point of gauntness. His eyes had a look of intelligence. He seemed stunned, and everything about him seemed to indicate that he had no great interest in what might be in store for him.

In Sewell's mind the thought of an insanity plea had been present from the start. It was reinforced by what he had observed. He now suggested an insanity plea as a possible defense.

"I'm not insane," Ellis said.

Sewell began to explain certain aspects of what constituted legal insanity.

Ellis interrupted him. "By any definition, I'm not insane," he said.

Sewell lowered his voice. "Look, I'm not asking you to cop a plea or beat a rap. I'm not asking you to pull a Hinckley. I'm merely talking about an effective defense. I'm talking about submitting yourself to psychiatric evaluation. It's next to impossible to get a qualified big-city psychiatrist to come talk to you in your jail cell, so what happens is that you're sent off to a state institution for evaluation. You might be there three days or you might be there as long as a month, or even longer. Whatever defense is decided upon, the psychiatrist's opinion will be useful. And the judge is sure to allow it, probably even order it at your arraignment."

Ellis did not reply.

"Look," Sewell said. "We're talking about murder. The sentence could be life imprisonment. We're talking about where you'll be spending the rest of your life. Do you want it to be in prison?"

"I'm expecting it to be," Ellis replied.

Sewell watched him in silence. Finally he shrugged. "Maybe this is all premature. How do I know that you even want me to represent you?"

"Why should you want to?" Ellis asked.

Sewell nodded. "That's a good question, of course." Until now he had been facing the prisoner across a corner of the desk, a corner carved with initials, triangles, heavily pitted near the edge, as if someone had stabbed it repeatedly with a pointed object, perhaps an ice pick. Sewell got to his feet, turned his back, and stood for a moment gazing from the window. He faced the brick face of the building. Looking to the left, he saw cars moving slowly by, watched a woman put a coin into a parking meter. There had been a light snow overnight, but the day was already warming and the streets were filled with slush that gleamed with tire marks.

"I can't give you a good answer." Sewell turned. "Let's just say that I'm for underdogs, and you're an underdog if I ever saw one. Boy, are you an underdog!"

A deputy looked through the open doorway and then stepped from sight.

"There are some things you should know about me," Sewell said. He was seated once more at the desk. "I'm not the most popular guy in this county. People think of me as being sympathetic to criminals. The state's attorney sits on his white horse and charges out after evil, and I'm a dragon standing in his path. It may be hard to pick twelve jurors who don't think I'm a son of a bitch."

Sewell, on his feet again, glanced through the window

and turned, looked briefly at the prisoner's handcuffed wrist. "So what good am I to you? Why, for that matter, do I want to represent you? A lot of things go into the answer, but what's important for you to know is that for a lot of years now I've made it a practice to defend underdogs and I've done pretty well at it. I'm the poor man's F. Lee Bailey." Sewell smiled faintly. "It also happens that I hate Hamilton Carver's guts, hate everything he's ever done, and hate everything he stands for—*why did you kill him?*"

The question was abrupt. Ellis seemed to be studying it, looking down at the desk, then at the handcuff, finally into Sewell's eyes. When he did not reply, Sewell pounded the desk. "For almost a whole summer you worked for Warren Donaldson. You set up his nephew. You picked Donaldson because his house is directly across the cove from the house where Carver stashed his daughter. For a whole summer you waited, getting chummy with the daughter, and when you got the chance you killed the son of a bitch. *Why?*"

For the first time since he walked into the room, Ellis showed emotion. His eyes smoldered with hatred. Raising his handcuffed wrist, he brought the handcuff down hard against the edge of the desk. His face was red. Cords stood out in his neck. His voice trembled. *"Because he killed my wife!"*

"Ah!" Sewell smiled. "Okay, so tell me about it."

Two days later, on the morning of March 30, with Sewell and a representative of the state's attorney's office present, the prisoner was arraigned before circuit court judge Mark Gladding, who read to him the multiple charges contained in the grand jury indictment. Among other counts, he was charged with first degree murder, unlawful flight, and the use of a handgun in the commission of a felony. On behalf of the prisoner, Sewell entered a plea of not guilty on each count. He entered a companion plea of not guilty by reason of insanity and requested psychiatric evaluation for a period of thirty days.

In Maryland there had been for many years only two

psychiatric detention centers, Spring Grove in Baltimore and Perkins at Jessup. A third had recently been completed at Annsville. Spring Grove and Perkins were badly overcrowded and there was, as Judge Gladding noted, a long waiting list at both. Sewell said it was his understanding that there were vacancies at Annsville and requested that the prisoner be sent there. After conferring with the state's attorney's representative, Judge Gladding agreed to honor Sewell's request.

Under Maryland law, a trial must take place within 180 days of arraignment. Judge Gladding deferred setting a date for trial. He ordered that meanwhile the prisoner be remanded to Annsville forthwith.

Part V

For the Defense

Twenty-four

FREDERICK SEWELL lived in what had been a caretaker's cottage set well back from the shoreline of a secluded creek and a good quarter mile from the manor house dominating the estate of which the caretaker's cottage once had been part. Here in the cottage he lived alone, his only companion an Irish setter named Red, a puppy when Sewell bought the cottage and now nine years old.

Once Sewell had been a puppet husband, a kept country squire known around the county as Freddie. In those far-off days, indolence, ease and an atrocious marriage had all but wiped out a promising legal career.

As an impoverished undergraduate at the University of Pittsburgh, Freddie Sewell was an A student, and in law school he graduated near the top of his class. With offers from all over the state, he chose the most prestigious law firm in Pittsburgh and here he stayed for five good years. At twenty-eight, he married Mary Claire Merriman. A year later, following the death of her father, they left Pittsburgh and moved to the county. After that, for a long while, Freddie wasn't much good at anything.

Mary Claire was the only child of Henry L. Merriman, who had made a fortune in pig iron and who, at the time of his death, was chairman of the board of one of the three major American foundries. Mary Claire had already inherited money from her mother, and when her father died she inherited a great deal more, some said as much as seven million.

For three hundred thousand dollars, a bargain even then, they bought one of the showplaces of the county, an estate with an old house of mellowed brick and more than a mile of shoreline. The house, with its steep gables and stout chimneys, stood on a neck of land between a river and a creek, and the property was so spacious, so secluded, and its outbuildings so many and varied that it gave the impression of a medieval manor, a domain all to itself. A farm manager was hired. The land was planted in wheat and corn. Sheep grazed over the broad lawns. In deep summer, cattle strayed from the shaded shoreline and stood motionless in the cool shallows of the creek. It was a place marvelously endowed by nature, a place of grandeur, a Constable painting, and to Freddie, whose boyhood had been spent in a rundown neighborhood in a row house of tapestry brick and who had helped himself through school by working in one of Henry Merriman's pig iron foundries, it was a place that seemed fit for a nobleman.

Law, he told himself, could be practiced anywhere and on whatever level one chose. With a sense that he was making the right choice, he now chose the role of a small-town lawyer, a country lawyer, and it was but a small step to see himself as a country squire as well. He set up practice in a restored colonial building near the courthouse, fitting it out with antique furniture of polished pine, covering the paneled walls with fine prints of ducks and geese on the wing.

Because of Mary Claire's wealth and distinguished father, and because they lived in the county's principal showplace, she and Freddie went to the best parties, mingled socially at what were considered the highest levels. Freddie found his new life very much to his liking. He dressed in tweeds, corduroys, and plaids. He lunched with other lawyers and with men who, before their retirement, had been executives in prominent corporations all over the United States. No sailor, he learned to sail. No hunter, he learned to shoot ducks and geese. On winter mornings he and his new friends sat together in a blind, warming themselves with bourbon and oyster stew while they waited for the birds to fly in against the rising sun.

Mary Claire, too, embraced the ways of the county. She patronized Esther's Salon of Beauty on Tuesday and Saturday mornings. On Tuesday afternoons she played duplicate bridge, while on Saturday evening there was nearly always a cocktail party or dinner invitation. For perhaps twenty-four hours after a visit to the beauty parlor, her dark hair had a congealed, waxen appearance, and the way it was arranged gave her a top-heavy look as she walked unsteadily on the high heels she never gave up wearing, even when they were out of fashion. She had thick calves and a plain face and something of her father's brain. She quickly established a reputation as one of the top bridge players in the county.

In Pittsburgh, Freddie had dealt as much as possible with criminal cases. Now he found his practice restricted for the most part to drawing up deeds of trust, searching titles, preparing wills and estate plans. As time went on, he found that lunch with his newly found peer group had become the high point of his day.

At cocktail parties he was a familiar sight, ruddy, cherubic, beginning to lose his hair, dressed in bright jackets and trousers, always ready to sing around the piano, kissing the ladies hello and goodbye. By some he was regarded as a clown, cheerfully drifting his life away. Some said he might yet find himself. Others felt he had no desire to—that he had found all he ever wanted to find when he found a rich wife. A few contended that he played the clown only to hide the disappointment over his career. After all, they said, it was no bargain being the husband of an heiress.

If he had married Mary Claire for her money, he was not conscious of it; yet from the day they were married he was insulated, protected. The high walls of wealth surrounded him. Inside he wandered about, confused and aimless, a young man grown pudgy and balding, less interested in the law than in the social pursuits he found so to his liking, the parties, the sailing and hunting, the good life. If a man was going to be an occupational failure, it was nicer to be one in a pleasant environment.

By the early seventies, with his law practice occupying so little of his time and attention, he had become a dabbler. In 1970, using Mary Claire's money, he opened a book and record shop that quickly failed. In 1971, again with her money, he bought an ancient movie house, one of the first ever built in all the United States, a domed, wood-shingle structure that he had found still standing intact in a remote Chesapeake hamlet. His idea was to move it on a flatbed truck, set it up as one of the outbuildings on his estate, and show old movies, but before he could have it moved it burned to the ground. He had neglected to insure it, and around the county Freddie and his movie house became the butt of jokes. Mary Claire overheard them at parties and at her duplicate bridge club. It was not the first time she had known the pain of being the wife of an unadmired man.

The affair of the movie house had a chastening effect on Freddie. For a time he turned to buying books he felt might be good for him, and occasionally he got ideas from his reading. He read that for every character trait a man possesses, it is quite certain that within the same man there is an opposite trait of equal strength. From this he reasoned that for all his apparent laziness, somewhere ambition raged, and that for all his steadily waning need to make something of his life, there was an opposite desire to spend his days drifting downhill toward middle age. For all the bright-hued trousers and jackets he wore, there was an equal desire to wear sack cloth and ashes, or to wear a tin can on his head and call himself Boob McNutt.

One night in a cold driving rain, Freddie walked slowly up and down his long driveway. He was thirty-seven years old with no assets of his own, none that could be liquefied without the consent of his wife. With shame for his life he walked bareheaded in the rain, asking himself what had happened. How could he have spent his life as he had spent it? If there was always an opposite truth, then perhaps from the very start he had not wanted to pursue a law career but had instead coveted the security and comfort of a rich woman's money.

This was during the week between Christmas and New Year's Day. Because of the energy shortage, Richard Nixon ordained that year that daylight saving time begin on January 6. The afternoons and evenings had the light of spring, and the weather by a remarkable coincidence became suitably mild. Never had the county known such a January. Day after day the temperature was in the sixties, and by the end of the month dandelions and bluets were popping up in the lawns. Trees twigged out. Camellias bloomed. A yellow haze covered the willows. The rivers and creeks had the soft blue look of spring and summer.

In early February the false spring ended. Although with daylight saving time there was now light in the sky until seven o'clock, the weather was bleak and cold. Sky and water were the same dull gray, separated by bands of dead marsh grass and strips of pineland.

When the cold weather returned, Freddie's back began to bother him. In the evenings he seemed content to lie on a heating pad and watch television. In a small downstairs room he would switch on his color TV and stretch out on a large daybed, head propped with pillows, heating pad beneath the lower right side of his back, where the pain was focused. He favored shows with cops and private eyes.

There was a smaller television set in the kitchen, and here Mary Claire watched weekly episodes of "War and Peace," wishing she were Natasha and that someone who resembled her father were Prince Andrei.

On other nights she imagined herself in eighteenth-century England, riding in the Dover-to-Calais coach in company with a mysterious traveler who wore an ankle-length black cloak and whose dark eyes burned into hers from the seat opposite.

Meanwhile in the darkened room at the far end of the house, Freddie was Kojak, he was Barnaby Jones, he was Mannix. On Wednesday nights he was a fat man named Cannon and on Thursdays a fleshy-nosed detective named Stone who patroled the streets of San Francisco.

Of them all he liked Kojak best. Kojak was a very tough cop with a tough name, a man who enjoyed his work and his life, one whose hatred of villains was equaled only by his compassion for victims. He leered, sneered, postured, licked

lollipops, spoke of dollars as balloons. His self-esteem had
no limit.

Mary Claire watched her husband grow fat, watched
him sit frozen before a picture window and stare at the
river, watched him asleep in the television room with the
set blaring, a plate with cake crumbs on the floor beside
him. At five in the morning she would wake to find him
quietly smoking in bed, staring at nothing.

There was a party where she watched him slop gin
down the front of his brand-new size forty-eight red plaid
jacket. Very fat and very drunk, he was sitting on the floor
telling dirty jokes in a loud voice. The women didn't seem
to think he was cute any more. The men egged him on,
calling him "ole Freddie," "ole stud," "ole son of a bitch."

That night he awoke in the television room to find himself staring at a blank screen, a programmed emptiness
suited to the audiences of deep night. He closed his eyes and
a second later heard a footstep. Mary Claire stood in the
doorway, looking down at him. It seemed important to him
not to let her know he was awake. When he opened his eyes
a slit, she was just standing there, looking at him, her face
bathed with dull lavender light from the television screen.
"Fat pig," she whispered. "Worthless fat pig." A second
later she was gone and he heard her going upstairs.

He stared at the empty, silent screen and found neither
true emptiness nor true silence. The screen was filled with
tiny slashes, suggestive of a driving lavender rain. From the
set came a muted roar, the sound of a distant waterfall.

Lying on the couch in the dark, hearing his wife call him
a worthless fat pig, knowing it was true, listening to the
silence that followed—these moments he would always regard as the rock bottom of his life. He would go no lower.

Lurching to his feet, he turned off the television set,
silenced its distant roar, blacked out its grotesquely striated,
pointillistic lavender blankness. For a few moments he
stood facing the dark screen, then climbed the stairway and
told his wife he was leaving. "Thank God," she said. Within
half an hour he was gone. For a week he slept in a motel,

then moved into a one-room apartment, furnishing it with a bed and a table and two chairs that he bought at a used-furniture barn. Never again did he have access to a penny of his wife's money. Under the terms of the divorce settlement, he voluntarily ceded away all conjugal rights to their home, the cars, and all the stocks and bonds and certificates of deposit that they had held jointly. As completely as possible, he had now returned to what he had been on the day he was married.

Around the county for long weeks Freddie's walkout was big news, good mostly for laughs. In the eyes of the county he remained a buffoon. A few might have applauded, but most thought him merely a silly man, one who had made a silly melodramatic gesture, a gesture that would cost him dearly in friends and status and one he would regret. In spite of the divorce, many predicted that he soon would be at Mary Claire's doorstep, asking her to take him back. This did not happen, nor was it something he ever considered. For her part, Mary Claire had very quickly selected someone to take his place. The county was filled with wealthy, less than comely women who bought husbands to adorn their estates, adorn their yachts, escort them to parties, and fill their beds. Within weeks, Mary Claire was being seen with a jovial, at best marginally successful man named Tark Brubaker, a boat broker in his early fifties who would divorce his wife when Mary Claire gave the word.

During all his years in the county, most of Freddie's friendships had been based upon the comradeship wrought by wealth and leisure. Stripped of his entrée, he dropped from the ranks of the socially elite. His invitations quickly dwindled, and those he received he turned down. Soon there were none. He felt no regret, felt no loss. He was living now less with people than with memories. His memories were of his father and the grimy exhaustion of his face when he returned from his day's work in the blast furnace; of his mother's frugality and endurance, of her frail body; of the people in the tapestry brick row houses of his neighborhood, some getting by on the solace provided by churches, on the diversion offered by beer and bowling and the Pittsburgh Pirates and Steelers, others finding solace nowhere and becoming drunkards, drug addicts, wife beaters, child abusers. He had come from the poor people of the earth and now once more was one of them.

As part of his third-year curriculum he had worked with indigents. All are equal in the eyes of the law; yet very early he realized that some are more equal than others. Injustice was rampant, and almost invariably those unjustly convicted had one thing in common—poverty. These were his feelings when he was a law student and these his convictions when, as a young lawyer during his five years in Pittsburgh, he had handled all the criminal cases his firm would give him.

How easily his idealism had been eroded by wealth and association with the wealthy. As a puppet country squire he had frequently encountered or heard of cases in which the miscarriages of justice had been flagrant, cases in which the law was tilted against the poor, but his friends had seemed unperturbed and he himself had taken no stand. No judicial system was perfect. To be concerned was to be considered a knee-jerk, bleeding-heart liberal. Fees, fees, gigantic fees were what it was all about. Any lawyer who made less than two hundred thousand dollars was a washout, but if one was going to be a washout, it was quite bearable to be a washout in a pleasant environment, living a life of ease, even though it was made possible by his wife's money.

Day by day he found himself feeling ever greater distaste for those in his erstwhile set. He had begun to see his former friends for what he now, in an excess of scorn, considered them to be—wealthy people who, if they went to enough parties, went often enough to Florida or the Caribbean, maintained enough houses around the world, drank enough liquor, bought enough cars, told enough amusing anecdotes, passed on enough racial jokes, committed enough adultery—could somehow manage to blot out the rest of the world.

As his clientele changed, he found himself representing people whose existence he had sensed only dimly. They had been out there all along.

Soon after leaving Mary Claire, he had volunteered for public defender work and among the poor his name became quickly known. On their behalf he enjoyed nothing better than going head-to-head with the state's attorney, plea bargaining at times and when plea bargaining was refused him, or when it seemed not to serve his client, winning cases far more often than not. He became a savage cross-examiner, fiery, eloquent, scornful, a man possessed by demons. For his success he was more hated in the community than admired. He was looked upon as at best a renegade, at worst as an enemy, if not of the people then surely of the system —an enemy flagrantly hostile to established notions of law and order. As he passed people in the street, he was often ignored. Few spoke and to these he returned an amused smile, a superior smile, pleased with what he had become, pleased to be scorned, even hated, and hating them in return for their condescension, for their memories of Fat Freddie Sewell, the kept husband. He was no longer Freddie. He was Frederick L. Sewell, honed and hardened in mind, body, and spirit. He had become a new man.

Sewell's outlook was calmer now. The fever, the anger, the hatred and shame were long since spent. When he thought of himself as he had been in the years after leaving Mary Claire, an embittered, humiliated, still young man, venting his scorn and hatred, he now felt amused. There were good and bad among the rich and good and bad among the poor. His excesses had been a reflection of his own self-disgust. Yet self-disgust had accomplished a worthy purpose. It had catapulted him from a marriage he hated, propelled him back into the work he had always felt destined for.

Mary Claire had long since remarried, and her husband was living the sort of life Freddie Sewell had lived, running his brokerage business as a facade behind which he performed the duties of consort. Sewell himself had never remarried. He dated occasionally, traveled a great deal, often on legal business, at times for pleasure. For exercise he played golf. Now and then he had lunch with some of his former friends. The animosities had been patched over. He was regarded now not so much as a renegade as an eccentric, a man without family or close friends, a loner whose life was his work.

That night in late March, Frederick Sewell, now forty-eight, lounged in a chair. A fire danced in the fireplace. The dog lay coiled at his feet, its russet coat touched by firelight. Sewell was thinking of Charlie Ellis and his story, his long quest for revenge upon the man he considered responsible for his wife's death. He found Ellis a young man to be pitied, but beyond this he hated Hamilton Carver with a very special hatred. It would be the greatest pleasure of his life to defend a case in which Hamilton Carver was the victim. Sewell's eyes were on the dog, on the flames, but his thoughts were far away. He was already planning the case.

Twenty-five

WINNING AND LOSING, Sewell had read, was not the proper way to regard a trial. A trial should instead be regarded as a quest for truth. Yet to him the law was undeniably a game. Each new case, each trial, was a game to be played and he played to win.

This time the game would have very special meaning. Rage and revenge were involved. Hamilton Carver was not on trial. He was dead, beyond revenge but not beyond defamation, and Sewell could admit to himself that although his interest lay in defending Charles Ellis, it lay no less and perhaps even more in the conviction of a dead man. Ten years ago, Frederick Sewell had met Carver face-to-face and for Sewell the experience had been crushing.

At social occasions around the county, pretty much the same old faces showed up week after week. Occasionally a rapacious hostess was fortunate enough to garnish her party with a visiting celebrity, most often someone high in government, down from Washington for the weekend. In 1971 Hamilton Carver spent the last week of November shooting ducks and geese as the guest of a local millionaire who was chairman of the board of a corporation Carver was engaged in taking over. It was a coup indeed for the covetous hostess when he was persuaded to make an appearance at her Saturday evening party. Sewell had been there an hour before he was introduced. This was during the days when he was playing the buffoon, quickly drunk, quickly loudmouthed, inanely genial. He apparently had caught Carver's notice, and when the introduction was performed, Carver stood looking him in the eye with cold hauteur, clearly less amused than disgusted, while for long moments Sewell's pudgy hand hovered before him, waiting for the handshake that never came. Face flaming, he withdrew his hand and turned away, and as he did so he heard Carver's question: "Who's *that* silly ass?" Feeling humiliation deep enough to penetrate even his protective fog of drunkenness, he staggered off to the bathroom where, as he relieved himself, he stared at his eyes in the mirror, eyes filled with tears of shame and hatred. For a long while he stayed in the bathroom, befuddled, seething, impuissant, finally dashing cold water on his face and stalking unsteadily back down the hall, determined to ask Carver to step outside. He was ashamed at the relief he felt to find that Carver was gone.

Ever since that evening, Sewell had been a close student of Hamilton Carver. He hated him for the insult, and as the years passed and he learned more about the man, he hated him for his senseless appetite for power, his seeming compulsion to desecrate the land. The land, the waters, the ocean, especially the ocean, had been created by the Almighty to be used for one man's profit. Carver had shifted the sands to his liking. On sand he had built skyscraper condominiums all up and down the coast, edifices that would be wiped out by the next hurricane. From barrier islands he had wrested enormous profit. The man was mad with a special strange madness. From the shopkeeper, the farmer, the homesteader whose aim was to do enough work to house and shelter wife and children and keep them from harm, it was a long evolutionary leap to Hamilton Carver. To be worth ten million was nothing to him. For another ten and then another he had an insatiable need. He had made the capitalist system his special tool, his toy, and was doing his best to destroy it, just as surely as if he had been Karl Marx himself.

Although to Sewell an insanity plea still seemed the best bet, and although a dead man could not be placed on trial, part of his defense would be based upon the character of Carver. To the extent that the presiding judge would permit, he would do all in his power to let the jury and the world know what manner of man was involved, a man who so casually, so offhandedly, so carelessly and callously had stolen a young wife from a young, guileless, deeply caring husband and had added her name and body to a long roster of women with whom he had whiled away his years. Women and money, more and more women, more and more money—all he had lived for; these and the feeling of power they brought him, the relief from ennui they had brought him, using them to fill a spiritual vacuum that was astonishing and profound.

Within three days of the arraignment, Sewell was in New York City, headed for the Waldorf Astoria Hotel. Although investigators were at his disposal through the public defender's office, he was determined to do the pretrial investigation on his own. In his attaché case was a copy of the April 14 edition of the *New York Daily News*, folded to page three. On that page appeared a headline:

For the Defense

WOMAN EDITOR KILLED
BY SUBWAY EXPRESS

Beneath the headline was the following news item:
A woman identified by police as Anne Myatt Ellis, 32,
of 1 University Place, Manhattan, was killed last night
when she jumped or fell in front of a Lexington Avenue express train near Grand Central Station. Police
ruled the death an apparent suicide.

A *cum laude* graduate of Sarah Lawrence College, the
victim was a senior editor at Castle Press, Manhattan,
where she had been employed for several years.

Witnesses said that she jumped from the platform and
entered the tunnel, running toward the oncoming
train a few seconds before its arrival. The train operator said that although the train was losing speed for
its station-stop, it was still traveling at close to 40
miles an hour at the moment of impact.

The victim is survived by her husband, Charles Ellis,
of the University Place address, and by her parents,
Mr. and Mrs. James Myatt of Mamaroneck.

Occupying considerably more space than the news account
was a large photograph, captioned, "Anne M. Ellis."

For several years before his death, Carver had maintained a forty-second-floor suite in the luxurious Waldorf
Towers. From an assistant manager, Sewell determined the
location and from the housekeeping staff he ascertained the
identity of the chambermaid who had been responsible for
Carver's suite. He found her on the forty-second floor and,
as he had with the others, introduced himself as a lawyer
involved in the Carver murder and told her he had the
hotel's permission to ask her some questions.

The chambermaid was a young Puerto Rican with
crimped hair and a beautiful complexion, trim and neat in
black uniform with white collar and cuffs. She said her
name was Juanita. Spreading the newspaper, Sewell
showed her Anne's picture. "*Sí, sí* . . ." Her eyes were filled
with sadness. "Very terrible . . . very sad . . ."

189

She remembered Anne, knew of her suicide, knew of Carver's murder. Within the hotel, among the staff, it of course had been of enormous interest. Anne, she said, had lived there with Carver for two, perhaps three weeks. What had she observed? Observed? "Very beautiful, very nice." Had Carver kicked her out or had she left of her own accord? She had no way of knowing. There were many, many, so many she could not keep track of them, but Anne was special because she had been so nice, had asked about her children, asked to see snapshots of them, admired the snapshots, talked with her about Mexico, occasionally speaking with her in Spanish. She had not known Anne was married until the story appeared in the newspapers, had thought her to be one of a neverending procession of unattached young women who came and went. Had she ever heard anything between Anne and Carver, an argument perhaps? No, none. Carver had never spoken to the chambermaid—he had ignored her existence—and when he was present she never expected conversation with Anne. Perhaps an exchange of smiles, nothing more.

"Did you ever at any time have the feeling that she was being held here against her will?" Sewell asked.

"No. She went out and came back, went out and came back, just as she wished."

Was there anything to indicate that Anne was thinking of suicide? When had she last seen her? How had she acted?

"She left at night. I saw her that same afternoon. She was in bed."

During the final week she was very often in bed, asking the chambermaid to come back later to do the room. That afternoon, when the chambermaid returned at four o'clock, she was still in bed, the covers pulled up under her chin. She seemed cold. She apologized and got up, and while the bedding was being changed she sat at the window, saying little or nothing. The chambermaid let it go at that. The help was not encouraged to make small talk unless the guest seemed responsive. As she went about her job she noticed Anne looking moodily through the window with its lofty, magnificent view of the city. *"Buenas tardes, señorita,"* the chambermaid said as she left. Anne smiled and replied, *"Buenas tardes."* She got to her feet and offered her hand. "Goodbye, Juanita, and good luck."

"When she say 'goodbye' that way, I think to myself she is leaving, but I did not ask. That was the last time I saw her."

Sewell nodded. He shook her hand and thanked her.

"De nada. So sad, so nice a girl. So sad for her poor husband. In his position, my husband too might have killed."

That night Sewell drove back down the New Jersey Turnpike, reviewing his next move. Under the law, the state's attorney was required to supply him with a list of the witnesses who would be called to testify for the prosecution. The list would not be delivered until a trial date was set, but he could pretty well judge in advance the names it would include.

Back in the days when he was a member of the cocktail party set, he had met Martha and Warren Donaldson and found them both decent people with a marriage that not only had lasted—unusual in itself—but one marked with what seemed to be genuine affection. He knew that Warren and probably Martha as well would be called by the prosecution, but as he drove up their lane the following night, a misty night in early April, he hoped they might be of value to the defense as well.

They received him off the kitchen in a room resembling an Early American tavern, in some respects a blacksmith shop, with its black pots, dark beams, and stark white walls. A fireplace, built with deliberate crudity, stood against the wall on an angle, like a corner cupboard. The hearth was knee-high and Warren Donaldson had started a small fire. A deeply stained railroad tie served as a mantel, and hanging above it was an expensive Christmas wreath festooned with waxed fruit and mistletoe.

"It's been a long time," Donaldson said. In his white

turtleneck and blue blazer and with his silver hair, he looked, Sewell thought, very much like a retired diplomat.

"It's good to see you both," Sewell said.

Martha was slim in a dark green sweater and slacks, a woman well preserved, her hair still dark. "Freddie, what can we get you?"

He winced at the name but made nothing of it. "Not a thing, thanks, not a thing." He looked from one to the other. Both seemed ill at ease. "As I told you on the phone, there may be something you can help me with. Some questions I'd like to ask. Whether you care to answer them is entirely up to you."

By now all three were seated. Donaldson sat in a leather chair, his legs stretched before him. He was looking at the tips of his highly polished cordovan loafers. "You're defending the young man in the Carver case, I understand."

"Yes," Sewell said. "Now as I understand it, he spent the summer with you after setting up Martha's nephew."

"To our sorrow, yes," Donaldson replied.

"And your house is directly across the cove from the place where Carver kept his daughter."

"Yes."

Sewell nodded. "As you probably know, the prosecution will be calling you. The state's attorney will put you on the stand to help show premeditation."

"He's already talked to us," Donaldson said. "Several times."

Sewell addressed himself to Martha. "You wanted somebody here, as I understand it, to look after Warren while you were in Europe."

"I wanted to go to Europe, and I wanted to go with a clear conscience, and the only way I could do that was to know that somebody was here with Warren. I arranged with my sister to have my nephew come. I should have known better. But I thought he was okay."

"Your nephew?"

"No. The boy. Mark."

"Charles Ellis," Sewell said.

"Yes. Charles Ellis."

"You saw him before you left for Europe?"

"Yes, I picked him up at the bus stop the night before, and I saw him again the next morning before I left. He seemed nice. I felt Warren would like him. After I got to Europe and Warren's letters indicated nothing to the contrary, I assumed there was nothing to worry about."

On the wall hung a Tide Clock. Abruptly it made a whirring noise. Sewell looked up. The hand pointed to Half Tide Rising.

"I also did something that was utterly stupid," Martha was saying. "In the spring I had a phone call asking if we needed help for the summer. I said we already had somebody and then proceeded to give him Eliot's name and where he lived. It must have been Ellis; in fact, now I'm sure it was. I handed him the whole thing on a silver platter. Stupidly. Warren says I always say more than I need to say. In this case he was certainly right."

Donaldson looked at Sewell. "Martha was housebound. She'd been waiting on me hand and foot for six months. She needed to get away and I wanted her to have the trip."

Sewell glanced at the window. It was raining hard now, slashing against the panes. He looked from one to the other. "You shouldn't be so hard on yourselves," he said. "Nobody's accusing you of complicity."

"Around this county you never know," Martha said.

"Not complicity, but certainly gullibility," Donaldson said.

Sewell nodded. "I can understand how you feel, but that's not exactly what I came to talk about."

"Sorry," Donaldson said. "I guess we're still pretty badly churned up about the whole thing." Rising, he poked the fire, put on some more wood, and returned to his chair. "What would you like to know, Freddie?"

"Something about Ellis," Sewell said. "How you felt about him."

"You want an honest answer?"

"Please."

"I liked him."

"You liked him?"

"Very much. At least for a long while I did. He was quiet, intelligent, considerate. I was very pleased. I guess I should have had enough sense to realize that nobody that nice could have been a friend of Eliot's, but. . . ." Donaldson shrugged. "I guess I just thanked God for small favors. I took it as it came. I was looking forward to a calm, restful summer and that's exactly what I got. I was happy about the whole thing."

"Did he ever at any time strike you as somebody who was plotting cold-blooded murder?"

"Not at all. Never. Even today I find it hard to believe."

"Did anything strike you as unusual about his behavior?"

Donaldson took a deep breath. "For a while I felt that maybe he was—acting a part."

Sewell frowned. "A part?"

"I felt he was an incurable romantic and that he was acting out a fantasy about the girl across the cove. Daisy. For a long while I thought he was acting the role of Jay Gatsby in Fitzgerald's novel."

"Okay . . ." Sewell waited.

"I didn't find anything—insidious about it. I simply found it amusing for a while because of the romanticism. It was clear right from the first that he yearned for Daisy, just as the man in the novel did."

"How did he show all this?"

"He spent a lot of time down by the shoreline, looking across the cove, sort of moonstruck. He watched her when she was out in her sailboat. It seemed clear that he was in love with her, that he wanted very badly to strike up a relationship with her and didn't quite know how to go about it."

"But he managed . . ."

"Yes. By using me. He asked me to pay a visit to Daisy. He asked me in other words to act as his intermediary, just as Gatsby asks Daisy's cousin Nick in the book. It got so that by looking through the novel I could almost anticipate his next move." Donaldson shook his head. "The ending turned out to be quite different."

Sewell waited.

"One night he even called me 'old sport,' which was Gatsby's favorite phrase, but of course he could have gotten that from one of the old movies he kept watching. The whole thing was probably my imagination."

"But you got them together . . ."

"Yes, I went over and introduced myself to Daisy, asked her to drop by and so forth. I established contact. And then the next time she was out in her sailboat she sailed right up to the dock. And Mark—the person I knew as Mark—went helling over the lawn to help her dock the boat. After that they were together almost constantly."

"Did he seem to be in love with her?"

"At first, very much so. At least it seemed so. I say 'at first.' Actually it went on much longer than that. I didn't really notice any change in his attitude toward her until right at the very end. The night we took her out for her birthday."

"Which would have been a week or so before Carver was shot."

"Yes."

"What was different?"

"He seemed cool to her at dinner. Now that we know what we know, I suppose we can say that she had served her purpose and he no longer needed her. I felt sorry about it. I felt sorry for Daisy and disappointed in him."

"Poor Daisy," Martha said.

"Poor Daisy," Donaldson agreed.

"She's still there, I understand," Sewell said.

"Yes. We've been over to see her a couple of times."

Sewell nodded.

"He had me badly fooled," Donaldson said. "I must say, he had me badly fooled. He was sensitive, intelligent, observant, highly responsive, extremely responsible, at least for most of the summer. But there was also a deep sadness about him. In retrospect, I can say that he was a young man who had very grave doubts about what he was doing and what he planned to do. Maybe I'm just saying that because I want to believe it. But I *do* believe it."

"In other words," Sewell said, "once again—he did not strike you as a young man who was planning cold-blooded murder?"

"Good God, no. He was too gentle. Hell, he fed the ducks; he kept seed in the bird feeder. He loved birds. He loved nature, and until right up to the end he showed genuine tenderness toward Daisy. He did not seem like a man who would cold-bloodedly use her and discard her. It's something I couldn't believe about him. I still find it hard to believe—yet, I guess that's exactly what he did."

Sewell was on his feet. "I may call you myself, Warren."

"As a defense witness? Can a person be both?"

"Yes. It's legal."

"Whatever you decide," Donaldson said. "Whatever I can do. I couldn't feel worse about all this. In a way I feel responsible for the death of two people. Carver and Ellis. Whatever sentence he gets his life is over. And also for Daisy because he broke her heart."

"Warren still has a soft spot in his heart for him," Martha said.

"Yes, I guess I do," Donaldson said.

"He committed murder," Martha said.

Donaldson was looking at the floor. "Yes, I realize that."

Twenty-six

HAMILTON CARVER'S ESTATE after taxes was valued at just under fifty million dollars. The list of beneficiaries was very long. Among those handsomely remembered were key officers of his company, who received amounts ranging from one million to five. There were lesser bequests for company employees, for caretakers of his various residences, and for the custodial couple whom he had entrusted with raising his grandchild. The list also included a number of women, identified only by name and address, all presumed to have been his mistresses at one time or another. Among these was Noreen Albright, Daisy's companion, who had received fifty thousand dollars and promptly taken off for the south of France.

Daisy herself received five million, all of it to be held in trust. She could touch none of the principal but would live on the interest for the rest of her life. Upon her death, the remainder would be placed in trust for her daughter.

John Sloan, the young man known as Turk, received nothing, and after the will was probated he packed his bags and left.

Of the trio, only the caretaker, the man known as the Huntsman, seemed perturbed by Carver's death. An ex-convict named Harley, fanatically loyal to Carver, he had been left twenty thousand dollars. Furious at his failure to bring Ellis down with his high-powered rifle, he had vowed to atone. For a while he continued to live on in his cottage somewhere among the loblollies, but eventually he too gave up and left. Thus, as Frederick Sewell knew, Daisy had been living alone for almost three months.

It had been raining now for a solid week. As Sewell approached the parking lot, the wet gravel glittered beneath bright outdoor floodlights. Daisy had seen him coming and as he climbed the steps the door swung open. "Please come in, Mr. Sewell," she called.

"What a lousy night," he said.

"Isn't it just awful?" As he closed the door behind him, she offered her hand. He grasped it, and it was the hand of a child, lost in his. "Here, let me take your raincoat."

"It's wet," he said. "Just throw it anywhere."

Instead she hung it carefully in a closet and led the way

down a long hall to a room filled with wicker furniture. A television set was on. She snapped it off. "Please sit down," she said. "Is it warm enough for you? That heater seems to do a fairly good job." An electric heater stood in a corner.

"Just fine," he said. He looked across the river. Through the rain he could barely make out the blurred lights of the Donaldson house.

She stood facing him in faded blue jeans and a navy blue V-necked sweater. Her neck was long and slender. Her light brown hair, held with barrettes and pins, was skinned back like a ballerina's.

Picking up a cup and saucer, she asked, "Could I get you some tea—or something else?"

"No thanks, nothing at all."

"If you'll excuse me, I'll get myself some more tea. Be right back."

He sat waiting for her to return. The house was silent, with no sound except the splash of rain spilling over from a clogged gutter and pattering on the ground.

On the settee a volume of poems by Emily Dickinson lay facedown. He picked it up. It was opened to a marked passage:

> There comes a warning like a spy—
> A shorter breath of day,
> A stealing that is not a stealth,
> A symptom that is not a sound,
>   And summer is away.

He replaced the book as she had left it and sat there, feeling ill at ease, an intruder in a cloister of sadness.

"Okay . . ." She had returned and was curled on the settee, cup to her lips.

"I'm sorry this is necessary," he said.

"Please don't. I understand."

"I am defending Charles Ellis. . . ." He paused. "As you may know, he's been sent to the prison hospital at Annsville for psychiatric evaluation. I don't know what the psychiatrists will conclude, but as his defense lawyer I'm compelled, of course, to do whatever I can to present the most effective defense possible."

"Of course," she said softly, looking into his eyes. She had the features, he thought, of a madonna; yet in her face there was no luminescence, no pride, only weariness, apology, penitence, an impression of waiflike fragility. Her eyes were reddened around the rims and and the lids were swollen.

"We have filed a plea of not guilty by reason of insanity," he said.

She looked at him dubiously.

"You will be called by the prosecution. You will be asked certain questions."

"Yes, I've been told. The state's attorney has talked to me about it."

Once again Sewell paused, listening to the silence. "This is very delicate for me," he said. "I wish it weren't necessary."

"It's okay. . . ." As she tucked her feet beneath her, one of her worn Topsiders fell to the floor.

He looked at the shoe and then once again raised his eyes to hers. "What makes it so difficult, of course, is—your father."

She interrupted. "Mr. Sewell, I'm not surprised that my father was killed. It was inevitable that someday someone would kill him. I just—never dreamed it would be—Charles Ellis."

She had gulped the name and now for a moment turned away. As she did so, his eyes rested on the soft wisps of hair that strayed down the back of her neck.

"Does it upset you too greatly to talk about it?" he asked gently.

Still looking away, she shook her head and then, facing him again, said, "No. I know it's necessary."

Sewell found himself drawn to her. He was finding her enormously appealing. He wanted to cross the room, hold her close, hold her head against his shoulder, stroke her head, stroke the pale cheek, kiss the swollen eyelids.

Through his mind flashed memories of Mary Claire and all the loveless years.

He took a deep breath. "What Ellis did to you was a horrible thing," he said. "I think we all agree on that."

"He did what he felt he had to do," she said. "I understand why he did it."

"And you don't hate him for it?"

Her head now was turned to one side, quivering with tension. "He was nicer to me than any man has ever been in my entire life. . . ." Her voice caught. "I know that he was acting a part for a purpose, but even so I know he genuinely liked me. At least I like to think so. It makes me feel better to think so."

Sewell was looking at the floor, at the worn, scuffed Topsider. The electric heater, responding to its thermostat, clicked on, and there was a faint whine as heat filled the elements.

"Charles Ellis is not insane," she said. "He's not any John Hinckley. He did what he did because—he felt my father deserved it. The whole thing, I'm sure, made sense to him. He was *compelled* to do it."

"Would you say that he struck you as a man in the grip of a compulsion? An obsession?"

"Now that I know everything . . . know about his wife . . . I can say yes, he was."

"But at the time . . . during the summer? . . ."

The teacup was poised before her lips. She set it down. "He seemed perfectly normal. The only thing that didn't seem normal . . . was that he should be in love with *me*. That's what constantly surprised me. Each morning . . ."— her voice caught and tears filled her eyes—"I woke up and it was like waking up in a huge sunlit room, a whole world filled with sun and air and light breezes . . . because every day I knew I would see him, and every day was beautiful. Nothing can erase those feelings. I had them; I felt them. They existed and no matter what's happened since nothing can erase what I felt. Those days, those feelings, existed.

They will always exist. Have you ever felt that way, Mr. Sewell?"

"No," he said. "I never have."

"I'm sorry," she said softly. "It gives you a feeling that life's—okay." She was smiling although the tears still shone in her eyes. "The fact that he was so deeply in love with his wife—even that doesn't change it."

"And the fact that he killed your father?"

She was looking toward the window, jaw set, and gradually Sewell was beginning to believe what he had had no inkling of, something that had been farthest from his mind, but now he wondered: She was not sorry her father was dead. She was sorry that Ellis had been the one to kill him —yet still in love with Ellis. Slowly he tried to fit it all into place.

"May I ask why you feel it was so inevitable that your father would be killed?"

"He had many enemies." The voice was firmer now. "And he in turn was the enemy of so many. There's a difference. It may sound—" She paused. "I'll say it anyway. He was—God's enemy. He hated two people mainly. He hated God and next to God he hated me."

"*You?*"

"Yes. He hated me very deeply."

"How could he possibly hate you? IIis own daughter."

"I think because—I was his *daughter.* "

Sewell frowned.

"It goes back to the time when I was eleven years old. My brother was eight. We were in Paris. My father was still young then, not rich but already making money, and he took us to Paris for a vacation. The four of us. He and my mother. My little brother and I. After we'd been there a week, we spent the weekend in a little town about forty miles from Paris. A little town called Pierrefond. The name of the hotel was—*Hôtel de l'Enfer*, which means. . . ." She paused, looking off into space. "Hotel of Hell. It's still there.

On Saturday afternoon we rented bicycles. My father and
I—and Matt . . ."

As she went on, Sewell could see it happening. The
eight-year-old boy, the bus careening over a cobbled street,
a bus filled with a wedding party, the boy in its path, his
hands uncertain on the handlebars, the front wheels wob-
bling, the look of fear, then of panic as he turned the bicycle
directly into the path of the bus.

"My father blamed me for having lived," she said. "That
night I heard him say to my mother, 'Why couldn't it have
been Daisy instead of Matt? If it had to be somebody, why
couldn't it have been *Daisy?*'"

In the adjoining room in the Hotel of Hell, her brother's
bed empty, she had listened to her father's wracking sobs,
heard his fists against the wall, heard her mother's quiet,
steady weeping, heard her father damning God, and had
finally sobbed herself to sleep. Her life, none of their lives,
would ever be the same.

For herself, she said, there were two courses. She could
have hated her father—or tried in a pitiable way to make it
up to him, to do all she could to please him, to try to be Matt
to him. She tried this for a long while but finally gave up
because it seemed only to harden his heart the more. Her
teens were spent in a series of boarding schools. After her
mother's death she ran off and married a transcontinental
truck driver who, when he found she was pregnant, rudely
dumped her in Arizona one night—stopped the truck, ordered her to get out, and when she clung to him shoved her
from the cab somewhere west of Williams, Arizona, and
sped on down the highway, California-bound, while Daisy
whimpered her way on foot back to Williams, where she
stayed until her father sent her the money to get to Al-
buquerque and thence to New York.

"He wanted me to have an abortion. He did everything
but pick me up and carry me bodily to an abortionist because he said he would have no grandchild whose veins
carried the blood of Leonard King—and mine. He called me
a bitch, he called me a slovenly whore, the blight of his life."

She escaped, ran away, had the child, and soon after-ward had the first of a series of nervous breakdowns. The child was taken from her to be raised by foster parents, subsidized by Carver.

Ever since, she had counted for nothing in her father's life. Often she had felt the bludgeon of his hatred, just as often the pain of his indifference. To him, she was a con-tinuing, neverending nuisance, a cripple, always having nervous breakdowns, always under sedation, always in the care of a psychiatrist, first one and then another. He came to visit her on holidays, on her birthday, as if he were periodically checking on one of his less-prized possessions.

Meanwhile he pursued his path of destruction, his path of vengeance, desecrating the land and the waters, leveling trees, usurping the waters for his slips and marinas, shifting the ocean sands for his condominiums. Hated by environ-mentalists and ecologists, his answer was always the same: It gives work to people. Work and money to a single genera-tion; a pocked land for all those to come later.

"There was a pattern to his destruction," Daisy said. "A very clear pattern. He deliberately picked beautiful places to destroy, and beautiful women. If God had taken from him, he would take from God. It's not surprising that he had so many enemies. That's why he lived his life in hiding. He feared assassination. He feared his enemies. I think maybe he came to fear God."

Her hand trembled as she picked up the teacup. It slipped as she set it in its saucer. Tea flowed over the cush-ion of the settee. She sat looking at it as if she had not even noticed. "I hated my father, Mr. Sewell. I'm not sorry that he's dead. I feel better now that he's dead. I feel stronger. I feel now that I can live some kind of life. I want my child. I want to raise her, love her. I want to live like a normal human being. My doctor says it's something I can look forward to very soon. I may have her by next week."

She raised her eyes to his. "Last summer I felt I was almost ready. Last summer, when—Charles Ellis seemed to be in love with me—I told my doctor that I had finally found someone who could be my child's father, someone I could trust. The first man I had ever trusted in my—whole life."

She turned her head away, looking through the window at the lights across the cove.

An hour later, Sewell sat in the cottage that he had for so long called home. Except for the light from the fire that burned on the hearth, the room was dark. The dog lay at his feet. He was thinking of Daisy and of what she had told him about her father. What was one to think? That but for the tragedy he would have lived a model life? That but for the fateful three seconds he would have been a model father? That but for those seconds the course of many lives would have been different? He could never know. All he could know for certain was that Carver had devoted his life to making the world as ugly as the world visited upon him on the day his son died. His entire life had been spent in an effort to block from his mind the horrible three seconds that it took for him to stand helplessly by, watching the wheels wobble, the handlebars jerk, the head crushed beneath the wheels.

In his eyes, a most sadistic God had been at work that day. A God who was never to be forgiven.

Living well the best revenge? Laughter the best medicine? Laughter was profane. Living well not nearly enough. Revenge then, against God and his precepts. He had spent his life transgressing the laws of God. Only a single law had he kept. He had never committed murder . . . but had himself been murdered.

Charles Ellis and Hamilton Carver. Two men moved by the same passion. The passion for blind revenge.

The dog stretched and got to its feet. Its silky head lay on his knee. Softly stroking its head, Sewell sat looking into the fire.

Part VI

Madness and Punishment

Twenty-seven

THE PRISON HOSPITAL AT ANNSVILLE WAS NEW, and although relatively small it ranked high in comfort and cleanliness and in the modern facilities it provided. A gymnasium with basketball court doubled as an auditorium where singing groups sometimes entertained the patients. Once a week there was a movie. In a small chapel, fresh flowers brightened the altar, and on a side wall hung a copy of da Vinci's *The Last Supper*. In a wing adjoining the main building, there was an occupational therapy workshop where ceramics and woodworking were taught. Private donors had stocked a small library from which patients might withdraw books and take them back to their rooms: rooms, not cells, just as the inmates were known as patients, not prisoners. Uniforms were not of the black-and-white-striped variety so cherished by cartoonists. Indeed there were no uniforms. Aside from shoelaces, belts, and ties, the patients were allowed to wear ordinary street clothing, and Charlie wore what he had worn in the Yucatán, what he had worn on the day he surrendered to the police at the Shaftesbury Courthouse.

Each ward had its dayroom and here he spent much of his time, rarely conversing with his fellow patients, many of whom sat for hours ranged about a television set, watching in silence. There was a Ping-Pong table, seldom used. The walls were hung with crudely crayoned faces, the work of deranged patients. One wall was dominated by a large cruciform poster of a black man, its caption: "Black Moses."

In his white jeans and blue shirt, Charlie sat and read at a long oak table. As he did so, he was aware of a young man, hardly more than a boy, with an extremely pale, bloodless face and long, stringy black hair. He wore a dirty, white collarless shirt and between his teeth clenched an unlit pipe. In a chair against the wall, he sat with his hand inside his trousers, masturbating, an act he performed several times a day. He seemed unaware of Charlie's presence and Charlie always ignored his. Charlie kept on reading. Scattered over the table were several magazines: *Field and Stream, Time, New Ways in Penology, Money, People, Audubon Magazine, National Geographic.* The older issues and even those reasonably current were torn, tattered, ripped, and scribbled upon. It was impossible not to find irony in the choice of some of the magazines. Confined, imprisoned, the patients were offered glimpses of foreign countries, rocks and rills, deep forests, glacial slopes. The whey-faced boy ejaculated, closed his eyes, moaned with pleasure, finally withdrew his hand, got slowly to his feet, and leafed through one of the magazines, staring dully at an article that described what it was like to take a field trip in Utah to observe and record the life cycle of the peregrine falcon. He moved away, seemed about to leave the room, then joined the group seated before the television set watching a soap opera. A heated discussion had broken out. *How can a baby talk? How come a friggin' baby comes into the world knowing how to talk? He learns it from other people, that's how it happens. No, man, a born baby knows how to talk right away. He opens his mouth and talks words.* The boy who had just finished masturbating joined in. *Jesus Christ is pure blood,* he said. *Man, I'm talking about babies. Jesus Christ is pure blood,* was the reply.

From the dayroom a corridor led back to the rooms where the patients slept and in which they were locked up at night. The corridor was lined on one side with single rooms, on the other with six-bed wards. During his first few days, Charlie had been housed in a small admissions ward for a physical workup and an initial impression of his capabilities and stability. This done, he was transferred to his present accommodation. To his relief he had been given one of the single rooms. This, although cell-like, was larger than a mere cubicle, containing a locker, a dresser, and a narrow but quite comfortable bed. In some of the single rooms, there were radios and even stereo equipment, sent in by friends from the outside. As he walked down the corridor, he could see photographs in small easel-frames, set on the dressers. His own room had none of these. The photograph of Anne he kept in an envelope beneath the mattress.

For those with a desire to use them, there were windows, barred though they were, to the outside world. The building stood at the bend of a wide river, so deep that it was available to ocean shipping. Since his arrival, the weather had alternated between false spring and a reprise of fierce winter. Plying its way back and forth across the river was a small ferryboat, which he watched by the hour. Ignoring the jibber-jabber of his fellow patients, he stood at the window and followed it with his eyes as it crossed the river, growing steadily smaller, a toy boat, a white oval with a tiny cabin and a single stack, faintly visible against the far bank. On the soft mild days, the broad river was placid, and the ferryboat's passage was a swift glide over smooth blue water. But when the weather changed and the northwest wind poured out from Dinwiddie, the water was the color of steel, and heavy foaming seas marched across to pound the Annsville shore. Standing at the window, watching the ferry's careful approach to the dock, he smiled with admiration as the captain skillfully backed the boat down, balancing the reverse power of the engine against the force of the following wind until the craft drifted gently and miraculously into its curved nest of pilings. He admired the captain, envied the nimble way he scurried about to secure the lines and hold the ferryboat fast against the waves that tossed its stern, envied his involvement with the tides and the currents and the wind.

In the fall, in this part of the country, wild geese flew in by the thousands, slung out in long, high wavering Vs, filling the autumn sky with delicate tracery. After the harvest, when the moon was bright, they fed all night long, and Warren Donaldson had told of awaking to hear them chattering out in the cornfields. Now in April most of them had gone back north to Canada, but one night Charlie awakened to hear the sound of their honking as they flew overhead. He got out of bed and stood by the window, awed by the soft beauty of the night. The ferryboat was in its slip, and in the light of the descending moon he could make out the silhouette of its cabin and stack. The deck was skimmed with silver; the wind was still. On the river nothing moved. As he sat gazing at the ferry, a phrase entered his mind. The other side . . . a crossing . . . a passage . . . the far shore, dimly seen. Merely to think the words brought a sense of excitement and mystification, a strength that seemed to spring from a deep layer of instinct, where others had dwelt before him.

At such times he felt no sense of confinement or imprisonment, except insofar as everyone was imprisoned by the dumfounding circumstances of environment, with windows that afforded occasional glimpses of unspeakable beauty.

During his second week he was interviewed twice by a psychiatrist named Dr. Randicott.

At the first meeting, Randicott held up a rubber ball and asked him to describe its shape—round or square?

"Round," Charlie replied.

"Good. What are the colors of the American flag?"

Charlie frowned. "Red, white, and blue."

"Can you name four presidents of the United States who held office after 1900?"

"Wilson, Coolidge . . . Nixon . . ." He shrugged. "Ronald Reagan."

During the remainder of the session, he was given an IQ test and a Rorschach test in which he viewed a series of cards, each containing an inkblot, and was asked to tell what each inkblot represented to him.

Now, at the second meeting, Randicott asked him once again to offer an interpretation of ink blots, this time a different series.

When Charlie hesitated, Randicott asked, "Do you find this trivial, Mr. Ellis?"

"I don't see the point of it," Charlie said.

"You'll have to let us be the judge of that," Randicott said.

"It seems like a waste of time. There's no question about my sanity. I'm sane."

Randicott sat, elbows on his desk, staring into Charlie's eyes. The room was silent; the door locked. There was a single window covered with a lowered venetian blind. The walls were white; the floor of mosaic tile. On a shelf behind Randicott's desk rested a telephone. When he felt himself physically threatened by a dangerous patient, he had only to tip the receiver from its cradle and armed guards would come swiftly..

He wore large glasses with very thick lenses, and his bulging eyes swam like indolent fish behind the glass wall of an aquarium. At times the glasses slid down and he peered over the panes, resembling then, in the dim light, nothing so much as an inquisitorial bullfrog gazing out from a lily pad. In one of the inkblots, Charlie had seen him in just this way.

Randicott was removing a card from his wallet. "Let me read this to you, Mr. Ellis. This is known as the Model Penal Code. It applies in Maryland and twenty-one other states. It reads as follows: 'A person is not guilty of criminal conduct if, at the time of such conduct, as a result of mental disorder or defect, he lacked substantial capacity either to appreciate the criminality of his conduct or to conform his conduct to the requirements of the law.' "

Slipping the card back into his wallet, Randicott said. "Do you understand the meaning of what I just read?"

"Of course. Mr. Sewell has already read it to me. I know that what he hopes to show is that my need to kill Carver was based on such a fierce need for revenge that my judgment was impaired. This may be true, but it was cold and calculated revenge, planned with great patience. Who could possibly think otherwise?"

Randicott was staring at him across the desk in his censorious way. "That's what we are here to determine," he said.

"You were sent here by Judge Gladding for evaluation."

"There's nothing to evaluate. You can give me all the tests you want, but what I did was the very essence of murder in the first degree. Cold-blooded, coldly calculated. Nothing could have been more coldly calculated."

Randicott was staring at him again from the lily pad. "If ice can burn," he said, "then pain can turn at times into an agony of exquisite pleasure."

"I don't know what the hell you're talking about," Charlie said.

"The coldness you speak of. The cold calculation . . ." Randicott tapped his pencil on his notepad. "No matter— what you did was quite ingenious, by the way. Do you agree?"

"Not at all. It was simply the only way I thought it might work—because to look for Carver, to actually find him, encounter him, was an impossibility. It was just as if he didn't exist."

Randicott sat back in his chair. He was looking now at the ceiling. "Who shall know Hamilton Carver? Neither you nor I; yet he exists everywhere and nowhere. Everywhere he touches our lives. . . ."

Charlie frowned. "I knew there would come a day when he would or at least was very likely to show up at a certain place on a certain day."

"The corporeal Carver . . ." Randicott said softly.

"*What?*"

Randicott shrugged. "Are they treating you well, Mr. Ellis?"

"Yes," Charlie said.

"Good. We'll talk again."

There were nights when he awoke and listened to a silence that seemed always metallic, a silence filled with the perseverations of clanging echoes born of clanging doors— echoes long since died away but never dying away, still reverberating somehow in the silence. His ear had already become so attuned to the sound of metal striking metal, steel against steel, that he felt the echo was always but a moment away, a moment just past. He lay and listened to the seamless metallic silence, knowing that it would be the sound he would be hearing for the rest of his life, lay listening until the silence was broken by the sound of men howling in anguish in the deep of night.

Sleep when it came was fitful. He was always awake long before dawn and he had become aware of the birds. He had come to listen intently for the first bird of morning. It gave him pleasure to detect the first notes, to hear its precise start. The bird was always the same—a song sparrow, he thought, so modest in appearance but liquid to hear. He knew that on the eastern horizon the bird had seen the first glimmer of light, perhaps no more than a suggestion of light. It was light that he could not see, but the bird had seen it and had begun to sing. He lay awake listening, knowing the bird had seen it. And then gradually the gray light filled his room, his cell.

Twenty-eight

ABOUT HIS DOOM he felt strangely calm, perhaps because doom seemed so inevitable.

Twice a week he was visited by Frederick Sewell, who seldom failed to show his irritation at having a client so stoic, so unwilling to help himself. "I talked to your friend Tex Poffenberger," Sewell said one morning. "He says to tell you how sorry he is. He says you should have come with him to California and made dirty movies."

Charlie nodded. "Maybe I'd have been better off."

"He said to tell you he kept Eliot there as long as he could. He gave him a couple of walk-ons. He said he was too ugly to play a stud."

Almost daily he talked with Dr. Randicott and each interview seemed more fruitless than the one before. He found the questions increasingly pointless and his resentment began to show.

"Do you find something funny in all this, Mr. Ellis?" Randicott asked one day.

"Funny?"

"I detect a twinkle in your eye."

"Maybe it's only a reflection of the twinkle in your own," Charlie said, meaaning it only as a commentary on the man's never-ending solemnity.

"I assure you there is no twinkle in my eye," Randicott said.

"And I can assure you that I agree," Charlie replied.

Randicott sighed with barely concealed exasperation. "I had been given to understand that you were an extremely earnest young man," he said.

"I am," Charlie said. "I suppose I was looking for a light moment, doctor. With what's facing me, is it wrong to look for a light moment?"

"I'm pleased to know that I am able to provide you with light moments," Randicott said.

Sometimes he had the feeling that Dr. Randicott would have been pleased if he had come to his office trembling and gibbering, alternately sucking his thumb and masturbating.

Daily he felt more numb. Amid the cacophony and gibberish of the ward room, amid his demented companions, he moved through the days, finding feeling only in memories.

It pleased him at times to recall his days with Warren Donaldson, an eminently decent man, a man who cast such an aura of courtliness, of sheer kindliness that he felt occasionally warmed, genuinely liked, and it did indeed seem genuine, even though the poor man had no idea of the person he thought he was liking. Yet undeniably there were moments: when they had breakfast together on the porch, with the sun pouring in and Donaldson drowning as always in Vivaldi, drowning as always in his morning newspaper; and just as often at supper, when the sheer class and refinement and quietude of their life got to him. There were moments when he could almost forget why he was there. But only moments, for he always knew that the man was in essence a tool, an instrument serving his purpose.

Yet even now he thought of Donaldson's life with envy. He had the impression of a man who seldom if ever questioned his life, or life itself. From glimpses of his wife, the one short trip from the darkened bus stop, during which he had driven her splendid old Lincoln convertible down the darkened road, and a moment or two the following morning, he felt the same about her as he did about Donaldson. He had an impression of a very happy couple.

He had seen himself and Anne grown as old as they, living the life of grace they lived; he had asked, why them and not us? Yet could he and Anne ever have? It would have taken a certain kind of man, which he might or might not have been; and a certain kind of woman, which Anne could never have been.

At times he took her picture from its hiding place. She was smiling, and sometimes it was the smile she had given him as she looked up from her manuscript pages when he walked in at night from the photo lab, the wonderful smile of welcome.

At other times, when he looked into her eyes, he saw a waif, tortured, confused, vulnerable, begging for help, in danger of destruction. This was the woman whose death he had been driven to avenge.

At still other times, although it was the same photograph, the same smile, it seemed to be mocking him for his innocence, for a view of life that she must always have felt to be naive.

He had a letter from her father, offering sympathy, offering help, expressing sorrow, a model father-in-law, just as he had been the model father.

It set him wondering, just as he had so often wondered, about her father's effect upon her. There was nothing new of course in the awareness that a woman's life is affected forever by her relationship with her father; yet each case was endlessly new, endless in its variations and shadings. Anne was loved by her father and she loved him in return, perhaps too greatly. He was a man virtually without fault, perhaps so good, so faultless, that she had despaired.

To be the daughter of a god was not easy. Could it turn one toward evil? Judging herself far beneath her father's lofty level, perhaps Anne had felt she had no recourse but to find a level where she could feel more at ease. This was a strand that must have run all through her life—her attempt to find in her father human failings, to find him less than a god, to bring him down from his pedestal. Finding it impossible, she chose a lesser god, gave herself to him, sacrificed herself. To which god, the good or the evil? In the drama she was acting out, Charlie knew that his own role was not a major one, for he was neither sufficiently good nor sufficiently evil.

He wondered what she would think of him now.

Poor Daisy's problem seemed far less complex. For a father she had a tyrannosaurus. When he was around, anywhere in the house or hovering near it, she took refuge in sleep. Only when she knew he had gone did she come out of hiding. Small wonder that she was prey to the first man who came along. Thinking perhaps that she had chosen someone who differed from her father, she had instead merely chosen yet another reptilian, with different scales and different carapace, but a reptilian with blood just as cold and one who just as quickly engendered fear.

Daisy lived by fear. By this very fear, by her vulnerability, did she evoke cruelty? At first she had even seemed fearful of him, of Charlie, as in the end she had every reason to be, for he had made her his tool, just as surely as he made Warren Donaldson his tool all through that false, beautiful summer. He had been aware of its falsity every step of the way, calculatedly willing to take advantage of her soft, damaged self. How false it all was, as they slid through the water, idled in the bright sunlight, let the sails luff, listening to their gentle rustling, she trailing her hand in the water, smiling a dreamy smile, and soon a trusting smile. God! Sometimes he felt that his crime was more surely against Daisy than against her father.

It tormented him to think this. He felt anguish and then, alone at night in his room when all was quiet, he questioned the importance of his anguish and then its validity. Stoic until now, he felt panic, wondering if he was being affected by his association with the demented and by the numbing solitariness of his days.

He tried to explain his feelings to Dr. Randicott.

"Is this another of your light moments, Mr. Ellis?" Randicott asked.

"Just the opposite," Charlie said.

"You're not trying to be funny?"

"Not at all. Never mind. Forget I mentioned it."

"That's not so easy to do," Randicott said. "Are you trying to tell me that you question the existence of human emotion?"

"I don't know."

"Its validity? Its substance?"

Charlie remained silent.

"Or that you are finding yourself incapable of feeling emotion?"

"I feel it," Charlie said. "It's just that last night . . ." His voice trailed off. Abruptly he had been pierced by the memory of the question Anne once had asked him: *How do we know if something is beautiful?* He sat there, shaken.

For a long while Randicott stared at him in silence, and he wondered if it was occurring to Randicott that he was making an attempt to feign insanity.

After he had been escorted back to his ward, he lay in bed, clinging to something, he didn't know what, yet to cling seemed vitally important. He remembered the way he had felt the night he sat looking at the silvered deck of the ferryboat, and then of his thoughts about man's inability to fathom beauty. He felt close to Anne in a way that was unwelcome and even frightening.

That night he prayed. Before falling asleep he recalled his first and only trip to the Grand Canyon, where, at age twenty-five, he had gone with his camera. It was an astonishing experience. He found himself unable to look at the canyon's splendor head-on, and his inability to do so had nothing to do with vertigo. It was more a matter of being overpowered, a matter of being unable, as a human being, to comprehend. In order to comprehend, he could only turn his head and view the canyon from the corner of his eye, let it enter along the periphery of his vision. He had arrived toward sunset on a day in late May, driving up from Flagstaff and getting out of the car at the first outlook point. There was no one else around. He stood alone on a bluff. Down in the canyon and along its walls the falling sun was creating tricks of magic, contouring and recontouring, painting and shadowing in a way that made his senses spin and fail. It was beyond his sensory powers.

The thought occurred that in other lighting the canyon might have been something different. Under the light of the sun at high noon, for example, the magic might not have been present. Yet he treasured his own view, treasured it even as he was unable to comprehend it, even look at it. It was like looking full into the eyes of God. Another thought occurred. He linked it with man's fall at the Garden of Eden. Perhaps there and then man had been deprived of his ability to comprehend such breathtaking beauty. As he stood there on the high ridge alone, with shadows stealing along the canyon floor and mounting the russet bluffs and columns, he had a sense of before-birth experience, as though at one time, eons earlier, he had gazed upon such beauty as this with full senses, with senses intact, but now he had only a dim memory and all that remained was the comprehension that came from looking at it from the corner of his eye. It was as if a sense, once present, had been removed. On an impulse he lowered his head as far as he could, so that now he was looking at it upside down. As he did so it became not a gorge but a cathedral.

Twenty-nine

Sunday was a beautiful early spring day, warm
and bright. In the prison yard some of the patients basked
in the sun. The yard included a baseball diamond and a few
were playing catch, but Charlie's interest that morning was
in the outside world, the world beyond his window. All
week it had rained and now, in the mild, hazy sunlight,
there was a feeling of reward, of a village blessed by the day.
The village was crowded with people. Some rode bicycles.
Others, cameras in hand, strolled past his window or stood
watching the river traffic. Still others gathered along the
banks of a small cove near the ferryboat slip, where ducks
floated just offshore on the lookout for tourists who fed
them bread and corn.

The ferryboat drifted into its slip, and as it did so the
captain skillfully looped a line over a piling, and when the
boat was made fast he raised the gate and motioned the
drivers forward. People threw bits of bread to the ducks,
and now the swans came flying in for their share, huge
white birds with webbed claws thrust out to hold back the
water as they landed.

A gun sounded. A sailboat race was underway. The
breeze was mild and the surface of the blue water was
lightly rippled. From his window he watched as the small
boats began to move slowly about their triangular course,
as slowly as the white puffs of cloud that drifted through the
deep blue sky.

It was just past noon. Off in the village church bells
pealed, and he was reminded of the rolling, reverberating
chimes of Mérida on that Sunday morning that now seemed
so far away.

A road passed before his window. Beyond the road was

a steep incline, a grassy slope, which, as it descended, gave way to a stone revetment and thence to the shallows, and beyond these the broad expanse of the river itself, stretching to the distant Dinwiddie shore. As he sat there idly watching the sailboats, a girl passed, and for a moment his heart stopped. He asked himself if it could be Daisy.

She was walking just off the road, along the ridge of the grass embankment, a slim girl in blue jeans flared so wide that the cuffs brushed the ground, all but covering her white canvas shoes. She wore a matching blue-denim jacket, swinging open, and her hair was pulled back and tied with a black ribbon. With her lowered head and sagging shoulders, she had the look of someone in mourning.

He wondered if it was truly Daisy, yet knew that it could not be. She walked on, angling away after a time to run lightly down the grassy slope. He strained his eyes, trying to keep her in sight, but with the crowds gathered along the bank it was difficult. For a time he saw her standing there, watching as people fed the ducks, and then she disappeared. He could not decide whether he was regretful or grateful, but he was deeply stirred. Memories of the summer returned in a flood of sadness and grief, of remorse and longing.

It was midafternoon and the day had changed. The sky and the river beneath it had turned from blue to gray. The sailboat race had ended and the crowds had thinned out. Soon only a few people remained. Across the river, the Dinwiddie shore had the forlorn look he had come to associate with it. Along its distant bank the pines were bleak and shaggy, and it had the look of a desolate land.

The gospel singers had arrived. They came each Sunday afternoon, a dozen or so in all, and from the dayroom he could hear them in the gymnasium, their voices full and beautiful, a lyric soprano, a contralto, sometimes carrying the melody, at other times moving off on their own, one voice playing against another, and underlying them a deep vibrant bass voice, all singing of the way to salvation, their way, or the way they had been taught was the way; or perhaps, with belief set aside, simply singing for the thrill of singing, for the joy they found in their ability to create swelling sound, filling the prison with their voices.

On the first Sunday of his confinement he had gone with the rest to hear them and was impressed by these very things—their ability to lose themselves in the rich sound of their own joyous making and the pride they took, each dressed for Sunday, dressed for gospel singing, each dressed all in white. He was impressed too by other aspects of their appearance: the roly-poly woman whose ordinary face seemed so at odds with the beauty of her contralto voice; the scrawny lyric soprano who sang like a bird; the stooped man whose bass voice was so true and powerful. Very soon that evening he had stopped hearing the words, caught up in the sound and distracted as well by the varying reactions of those who had come to listen. He was distracted by the slack mouths, the glazed eyes, glazed with pleasure perhaps in the case of a few and others by dumfoundment at the chasm that lay between what they were being offered and the reality of their confined, blighted lives; others openly resentful, sardonic, feeling demeaned perhaps by the message of salvation and redemption, feeling contempt for prison authorities, for a system that would presume to offer them something that they had no choice but to ridicule.

. . . there is a green hill far away, outside a city wall . . .

Now from the dayroom he heard them again, but as he listened his thoughts wandered to Daisy and from Daisy back to the men in the gymnasium listening to the singers. Some of those men were mad; some on the borderline of madness; a few were hardened criminals. *Men are so necessarily mad that not to be mad would amount to another form of madness.* What created this madness, Pascal said, was man's realization that his life had no meaning, that he came from nothing and went back to nothing, came from a void and returned to a void. To the extent that he was able to forget his fate, distract himself from his nothingness—to that extent he remained sane; yet Pascal would have said, insane nonetheless.

> . . . *the night is dark and I am far from home*. . .

Once again he was aware of the singers and thought once again of the men listening. The truly ill perceived little but sound. Others perceived more. If distractions helped men forget themselves, they were indeed distracted—not so much by the singers, but more perhaps by the very fact of their confinement. Their fate had been taken from them, removed from their hands. They had a scapegoat. But for their confinement, they felt, they would be happy. For now they did not have to look beyond the fact of their confinement. It was enough to absorb their resentment and futility and hatred. Release would mean freedom and freedom would bring happiness, but if one believed with Pascal, then cure and release would mean merely that they were free once more to stand among the ranks of the mad-at-large.

> . . . . *casting down their golden crowns around the glassy sea* . . .

And Daisy . . .

If Pascal was right, then the best that one might do was to stand always in the vast army of those who were honorably and quite justifiably mad.

But there were those debarred even from this. First they must be "cured." With what hope and comfort poor Daisy looked forward to the days when her psychiatrist drove down from Washington. Crippled by life, crippled beyond the norm, she felt that visit by visit she was ridding herself of her affliction.

Her reward? To join the ranks of the unafflicted mad.

Anne perhaps had seen it this way and sought a way out, a way that led swiftly to the void from which she had come. She sought a way to leave the ranks.

Daisy sought a way to rejoin them.

. . . through the crowded streets of life we catch a vision . . .

He would later think with astonishment of the timing; yet as the words soared he saw a distant figure moving toward him, walking along the ridge of the embankment, and as she drew nearer he could see that it was the girl he had noticed earlier. The clouds had thickened and the day was ending, the river the shade of metal. She was standing now just beneath his window, looking up, and it was indeed Daisy, her face stricken, eyes hollow, just as he remembered them on the day she first sailed up to the dock—the look that had gradually been replaced by hope and joy as the summer moved toward its end.

He waved but the bars intervened. She did not wave back, yet he felt she saw him, felt she had come to visit and had changed her mind, or perhaps merely to catch a glimpse of him. In a moment she turned and moved away, disappearing around a corner, gone from his life once more.

The singers had left, but he could still hear them, still singing as they left the prison. A snatch of song, a fragment, a reprise, the throaty contralto, the bass that shook the ground. Off they went to their cars and they could not stop singing.

Thirty

April 22

My dear Daisy,

I hope you will receive this. We are allowed to send letters. The social workers mail them for us. Whether they are opened and read before being mailed, I have no way of knowing. It's possible that mine, this one to you, will be examined for some phrase, some nuance, that casts light upon my sanity or lack thereof. As I'm sure you know, that is why I was sent here, to determine whether I'm fit to stand trial for the murder of your father and whether I was sane when I killed him. I am sane and was sane at the time, but the decision is not mine to make. It will be handed down by a panel of psychiatrists, psychologists, and social workers after a period of evaluation as long or as short as they care to make it.

But I'm not writing to talk of them. I am writing because I want you to know that yesterday, when I saw you outside the window, I felt deep emotion for the first time in many weeks—deep remorse and deep yearning. Even though it was from a distance and even though through bars, I looked into your eyes at that moment and I felt myself crumble. I hate what I did to you; I suffer because of the look in your eyes, the look of your face. I was quite willing at that moment to die, and yet coupled with this is a deep yearning to be with you once again, a deep yearning for it still to be August, a deep yearning to move in the dark around the bend of the cove, my head in your lap, looking up at the stars, the phosphorescent light streaming out behind with the wake of the boat.

How can you believe what I am saying when for so long now you surely must have judged that everything I did and said was filled with deceit? I hope that your contempt is greater than your hurt; or perhaps that somehow your hurt is absorbed in your contempt, overwhelmed by it. I lie awake at night sometimes, hoping that your hatred of me is very strong and powerful, because, just as one pain drives out another, so, I think, an emotion may surrender to a stronger emotion. Thus I hope that for these many weeks you have hated me.

Yet, perversely, even as I ask you to hate me, I have

an enormous and doubtless destructive desire to tell you
that even though what I did was within the framework
of deceit, there were many times, more and more as the
days passed, when my emotions and feelings contained
no deceit whatever, because I grew to love the person I
was so fraudulently using. I realize it's impossible for
you to believe this, and I don't really want you to
believe it because it may be harmful to you to believe it.
Yet, selfishly, I want very much to say it. There were
often times when I could forget what you were—my tool
—and forget who you were—the daughter of the man I
loathed and whom I had every intention of killing. Yet,
forgetting, I could hold your hand and even as I held
your hand, touched your lips, pressed my body to yours,
I could, always against my will and always caught
unawares, feel enormous love for you. Pity undeniably,
but it went beyond pity into something totally
unexpected. Was it partly because of the knowledge of
what I knew I was going to do? Was the love that I felt
a sort of before-the-fact act of contrition? Something of
this, but I did love you.

I think of all the unexpected and God knows
undeserved moments of beauty, the stabs of joy sneaking
up on me. I remember an afternoon when we anchored
just offshore on your side of the cove, close enough to
shore to be covered by the shade of an enormous willow
oak. It seemed unusual and somehow very beautiful to
be in a boat, on the water, and yet to be covered with
natural shade. It's a beautiful memory.

As the summer was ending and the day approaching,
I know you felt a change in me. How could you not? It
was deliberate and it took effort. There were moments,
many of them, when simply because of my feeling for
you I felt tempted to turn away from my plan, my
scheme. I felt that I could not do it, felt that you, my
tool, had turned into an impediment, enough so that I
was all but diverted. I had not foreseen loving you, only
using you, so that as I felt you become an obstacle I had

no choice. It was as though before killing your father I had to in a way kill you, or kill your love, for I could not let you stand in my way. I was loving and making love to a girl whose father I planned to murder. I felt like something hardly of this earth—yet when the two feelings collided, the other prevailed, had to prevail, because the hatred I felt for him was too strong, the most intense feeling of my life. I won't dwell upon it. To tell you of its intensity is hardly appropriate. Yet it was there, unconquerable.

My dear Daisy, how feeble, almost cretinous, to say I hope you are well. Instead I will say that I hope you are not too deeply damaged, not too severely set back, for I love you, care for you, and for these very reasons I hope you have grown to hate me with all your heart.

Charlie Ellis

Thirty-one

"YOUR LETTER WAS MAILED this morning, Mr. Ellis. Will you be expecting an answer? . . . No? Why is that?"

"I just don't expect one."

Her hands glided swiftly over her desk. Her hands were always busy, rearranging stacks of paper, picking up paper clips and dropping them into a tray, straightening the alignment of sharpened yellow pencils. She gave an impression of efficiency at once crisp and aimless. Her eyes darted from him to the pencils to the door and back to him.

"Will you tell me my name, Mr. Ellis?"

"Miss Ross."

All the social workers were women and their presence was considered good for the patients. The sight of women, the company of women, was considered a comforting and stabilizing influence.

Miss Ross was small and her dark hair was cut short. Two months earlier one of the patients had attempted to rape her. He was there to be interviewed, and as she let him in he grabbed the keys from her and locked the door. When she reached for the phone, he grabbed her hand, pinned her body, beat her badly, and then tried to rape her. Unbeknownst to them both, another social worker was in one of the back offices. She alerted a guard who came in time to forestall the rape but not the beating.

Charlie looked at her. She had nothing to fear from him.

Her dark eyes looked briefly into his. Still pursuing the letter, she asked, "Would you like to tell me who this young lady is? Is she a special friend?"

It seemed surprising that Daisy's name was not familiar to her. Perhaps it was, and she was testing him.

"Would you care to talk about it?" she asked.

"No."

Her lips were compressed. She was restraining her frustration. His eyes were on the pocket of the man's white madras shirt she wore. Two pastel pens were clipped to the pocket.

"It would be much easier," she said gently, "if you could manage to be more cooperative, Mr. Ellis. Easier for us, easier for you."

He shook his head. "There's nothing to talk about. I'm here to have my sanity tested. I've said that I'm sane and I *am* sane. I'm totally convinced that I'm sane, and I feel there's nothing left to talk about."

Again her lips were tight. "Do you feel like talking about your life? What would you say were the high points of your life? Could we talk about those?"

The province of the social worker differed from that of the psychiatrists and psychologists. Her job was to approach the patient in terms of everyday problems. When he was first admitted, she had asked if there was any personal business she could handle for him: the payment of debts, the

collection of money that might be owed him, the handling
of his bank account? He had given his brother Ike power of
attorney, for which she had handled the necessary paper-
work. She was also charged with digging into his family
background and helping him communicate with friends
and relatives.

"What highlights would you list?" she asked. "Give me
three. Can you do that for me?"

He shrugged. "My marriage."

"Yes?"

"And killing Hamilton Carver. That's two."

"How about your childhood? Were there highlights in
your childhood?"

"It was happy. It had a lot of highlights."

"No—traumatic episodes?"

"None of any importance."

"You attended New York University. Did you like it?"

"Yes."

"Why?"

"I liked being in New York and I liked what I was
studying."

"Meaning—film? . . ."

"Yes."

"How about high school? Grade school?"

"Uneventful."

"Would you say you were popular?"

"I always got along with people."

"Were you gregarious?"

"At times."

"And at other times? . . ."

"I liked being by myself."

"And what did you do when you were by yourself?"

"Read a lot. Walked a lot. Went to a lot of movies."

She leafed through his file, stopped at a page, and studied it briefly. "Your brother Ike is much older than you
are."

"Fifteen years."

Looking up from the folder, she smiled. "You'll be

pleased to know that he's coming to visit you tomorrow afternoon."

"Ike?"

"Yes. Are you pleased?"

He nodded. "I'll be glad to see him."

"Is there anyone else you'd like to see?"

"Not particularly."

"How about friends from your school days, from your hometown? Have you kept in touch with them?"

"Not for quite a few years."

She looked thoughtfully into his eyes. "Would you describe yourself as a loner, Mr. Ellis?"

"To some extent, yes."

Again she was leafing through the contents of the file folder. "What we think would be very nice . . ." Her voice trailed off and she began anew. "As you may be aware, Dr. Randicott considers you something of a problem."

"I'm afraid I feel the same way about him."

"He is eminent in his field."

"Doubtless. I begrudge him nothing."

"Why do you find it so difficult to cooperate with him? Can you tell me?"

"I don't consider myself uncooperative. I told him I was sane and ready to stand trial. What more is there?"

"He must decide that for himself, he and others of us here. He—I think I can say without breaching professional ethics that you confuse him. We talk about these things, you must realize. We meet regularly to discuss the patients and compare notes. He feels you resent his methods. Is there anything you particularly object to?"

"Some of his questions seem foolish. A waste of time."

"For example?"

"Is a ball round or square?" Charlie shrugged. "My God."

"And the colors of the American flag?"

"That was another great one."

"Let me explain. Those questions are asked for a purpose. Some of the men brought here make an attempt to feign insanity. Hence they go overboard. They try to give all their answers an—insane consistency. They go to absurd lengths. A patient who contends that a ball is square is immediately suspect, and the psychiatrist will know straight off that someone is trying to put something over on him. Do you see?"

Charlie shrugged.

"It's very hard to deceive a trained psychiatrist. If a patient clams up, for example, or gives silly answers, he is closely watched, around the clock, by the nurses and other attendants, to see how he reacts in social intercourse, to see in other words whether he is putting on one face for the psychiatrist and another for his fellow patients. With you, we have observed a high degree of consistency. We find that you have virtually no contact with the other patients. So far as possible, you ignore them. We find no evidence of deception."

"I'm not trying to deceive anybody. Randicott or anybody else."

"He doesn't think that you're trying to feign insanity."

"I shouldn't think so."

"He's frustrated by certain aspects of your personality. He is frustrated by your unwillingness to talk. And when you do talk he is confused by some of the things you say. He seems to feel that you *want* to be punished."

"Is that a sign of insanity?"

"Pardon?"

"To be punished for a criminal act. Why should I be an exception?"

She looked mystified.

"The greatest punishment one can administer is to withhold punishment."

"Is that a quotation, Mr. Ellis?"

"A paraphrase."

"From what source?"

"Hegel and Socrates, for starters."

"You are speaking of men who saw the world from the viewpoint of earlier centuries."

"Science advances. Does thought?"

"You don't feel that it does?"

"It changes but doesn't necessarily advance. God!"

"Yes?"

"What's Randicott expect out of me? Gibberish?"

Her eyes were grave. "You do him an injustice." She paused and presently went on. "As civilization advances, a nation reviews its shortcomings. It looks more minutely at its legal and social and economic complexities and problems. It engages in national soul-searching. It seeks to improve itself in many areas, and one of these is the area of penology."

His eyes were once again on the pocket of her shirt.

"There are so many aspects. . . ." Her voice was somber. "If a man is born with a certain set of genes, with a certain brain, what control does he have? There he lies in his crib, an infant, and within him already resides his combination of genes. In him is his brain. His life begins, and for a long while he remains powerless, obedient to the forces that the outside world imposes upon him as he staggers, crawls, toddles, responds, obeys, and sometimes is brutalized by his parents or callously ignored. Where, at this point, is the guilt? If it be the guilt of his parents, can it be his—when his ability to control his environment is negligible if not nonexistent?"

Again she paused. Her eyes were soft, luminous. "We must approach crime in a spirit of compassion. We must be wise in our compassion and compassionate in our wisdom. If such a huge part of a human being's identity is predetermined in the womb, and in the very early years during which he has utterly no control—then how can we speak of a 'bad' person? Properly we may speak only of an unfortunate person."

From the pocket of her shirt she unclipped one of the pens and made a note on the face of his file folder. "Don't forget that your brother Ike will be here to see you tomorrow afternoon."

"Thanks."

She looked up. "I've enjoyed our talk today, Mr. Ellis. We'll do it again, okay? And by the way, the Lance Hanna trio will be playing in the gymnasium at three-thirty this afternoon, in case you'd like to hear them."

"Soul music?"

She smiled. "Yes. Absolutely."

Thirty-two

THE NEXT AFTERNOON he sat looking through the mesh partition, feeling an impulse to extend his hand, finding it strange that he could not grasp Ike's gnarled fingers in his own. "Thanks for coming, Ike," he said.

"How are you, old buddy?"

"Pretty good."

"Looking okay. Don't make you wear uniforms, huh?"

"No."

Ike sat down on the bench on the other side of the partition. Charlie sat on his side, moving his face close to Ike's.

"I'da come sooner," Ike said. "They told me there was a waiting period."

Ike's face, although it was still only April, was tanned and leathery, creased with wrinkles. Some of its weathered look had come from the April sun, but most from all the years past, all the days spent on the tractor, spent in the fields.

"I appreciate your coming," Charlie said.

"I took all your things down home."

"Thanks. I appreciate it."

"I've been talking to your lawyer," Ike said. "He says I should tell you to stop being a damned fool. He says you're not trying to help yourself."

"In what way?"

"He wants to get a psychiatrist who'll be on your side when they have the trial. I told him there was no question about the money. We're all of us ready to chip in. Every one of us, whatever amount it takes."

"I don't want one," Charlie said.

"Charlie, what the hell, boy . . ."

"I don't want one," Charlie repeated.

"If it helps you, it's worth it."

"I don't see any point."

"Hell, Charlie, god damn it!"

"How's Helen?"

"She sends her love. Everybody sends their love. Everybody loves you, Charlie. Everybody wants to help you."

"Thank them for me."

"I was down by the stream on Sunday. Just sitting there, like you used to do. Running pretty strong."

"It always does in the spring," Charlie said.

"You used to spend a lot of time there."

"Yeah, I did."

"Emily was asking for you. Been better off maybe if you'd married Emily."

"I didn't though."

"No, you didn't." Ike sat in silence for a moment, then said, "It sure don't seem like spring without you."

"I've been gone a lot of springs now."

"Yeah, I guess that's true. You've been gone a lot of springs."

"I appreciate your coming all this way," Charlie said. "I appreciate it."

"It's not all that far. I went west and hit 301 and came up over the Potomac River Bridge."

"Yeah, that's the best way."

"And then when I hit 50, I turned east and came on by Annapolis and then over the Chesapeake Bay Bridge."

"What did it take you? About six hours?"

"Five and a half, maybe. More like five and a half. I—" Ike's voice caught. "Why'd you want to go and *kill* a man,

233

Charlie? Great Christ a'mighty!"

Through the partition, Charlie could see tears in his brother's eyes. His shoulders were convulsed with great wracking sobs. "Come on back, Charlie," he croaked. "Come on back where you belong."

"I guess I belong here now," Charlie said.

"No you don't," Ike sobbed. "No you don't, Charlie. You belong back with your people. Don't just sit back and let them convict you. Fight!"

"Not much I can do about it if they convict me. They should, anyway."

Ike brushed away the tears with the cuff of his corduroy jacket. "Didn't mean to do that. Had no intention to."

"It's okay," Charlie said.

"What can we do for you, boy?"

"There's nothing anybody can do," Charlie said. "You've already done a lot by coming all the way up here to see me."

"Wish I could put my arms around you and hug you," Ike said.

Charlie looked down. There was a lump in his throat.

"Wish I could pick you up in my arms and carry you, like I did when you was a little boy," Ike said.

"I wish you could," Charlie murmured.

A uniformed woman attendant stood a few steps away. "Mr. Ellis," she said.

"She mean it's time for me to leave?" Ike asked.

"I'm afraid so," Charlie said.

"Guess they'll be feeding you supper soon."

"Pretty soon."

"We'll be praying for you, Charlie. Everybody will."

"Mr. Ellis . . ."

"So long, Charlie."

"So long, Ike. Thanks for coming."

"I'll be up again."

"It's too far," Charlie said.

"It's not far at all. It's not far. . . ."

Charlie watched as a guard touched a button. The steel doors slid open. Ike passed through and they closed behind him.

Thirty-three

THE INMATES ATE IN SHIFTS, a ward at a time, in a large dining hall filled with light. One wall was nearly covered by three very large paintings, identical paintings hung side-by-side. Each portrayed a wild goose in flight, piercing a cloud. Over the cloud arched a rainbow, heavy with pigment. They sat four to a table in chairs bolted to the floor. Empty, the room gave an impression of a recreation hall set up for a bridge tournament.

Of Charlie's three tablemates, two were incoherent, out of touch with all but the need to satisfy their seemingly insatiable hunger. One had been there nearly seven years for shooting his mother. Another, a farm boy from a remote area of Maryland's Eastern Shore, had killed his two brothers with a club. At each meal they lowered their heads, folded their hands, and then, after a moment, grabbed their plastic knives and forks and began to eat ravenously. One unfailingly picked up his plate and licked it clean, running his tongue even under the rim, turning the plate round and round as he licked.

The third, a man named Robert Matthews, sat facing Charlie, his back to the geese and the rainbows. Although the other two men usually were silent and at best incomprehensible, Robert Matthews talked all through the meal, railing at his fate. The others occasionally smiled but for the most part seemed not to hear.

Robert Matthews was a bitter man, perhaps a dangerous

man, one of those whose eyes shone with hatred for the gospel singers. He was so far the only man Charlie had encountered whom he felt he might have occasion to fear.

Matthews was seldom in the dayroom. He spent much of the day in the corridors, standing, slouching, watching those who passed. He wore a white zippered jacket and black trousers, and his black shoes were always polished to a high gloss, as if he worked upon them regularly for hours at a time. They were the glossiest shoes Charlie had ever seen.

The hospital population was composed chiefly of those sent there for pretrial evaluation and those who, having been judged insane, had been committed, there to stay, some for the rest of their lives. A third group, not numerous, included convicted criminals who had contrived to make their way there.

To men serving time in the penitentiary, Annsville, with its order and cleanliness, its vigilant attendants, seemed by comparison a promised land, an Eden. Some penitentiary prisoners had urgent reasons for seeking a transfer. Above all, they feared homosexual rape. Some ran up large debts for drugs and, unable to repay, feared reprisal from the lender. Some feared for their very lives. Hence it was not uncommon for a man to slash his wrists or otherwise disfigure himself in the hope that penitentiary authorities might consider him disturbed enough to be transferred to a prison hospital for treatment, preferably Annsville.

Robert Matthews was one of these. Confined in the Baltimore penitentiary, he slashed himself repeatedly. His arms and wrists were a mass of scars. He had been at Annsville now for almost six months, but it had done little to stem his hatred for the system that had made him a prisoner. In the dining room, jabbing the air with his plastic knife, he vented his bitterness day after day.

At supper, recalling what Miss Ross had said about a man being a slave to his genes and upbringing, Charlie could not help but relate it to the feeling he had about Robert Matthews, for along with fearing him he found him disgusting in his insistence upon being viewed as a victim of an uncaring society. He was the rapist of a seven-year-old girl but took no responsibility for his crime. To him the fault was the fault of society, of God, of the cosmos. The moment at which he laid hands upon a seven-year-old child, threw her to the ground, and entered her was a moment of decision for which he denied responsibility, because to him there was no moment of decision. It was merely, in his view, the moment to which all the other moments of his life had been leading him, an inevitable denouement decreed by fate. And he in his own view was merely a captive instrument. And if one asked him, Is there no such thing as freedom of choice? his answer was no, none—that the decision was made long since, that he was merely executing it.

"Was there a turning point in your life?" Charlie asked.

"Turning point? Man, no turning point! They never gave me a chance."

He went on angrily, self-pityingly, to speak of this lucky bastard and that lucky bastard, saying that but for sheer chance there would go he and but for fate there in his place would go another. Except for certain accidents of birth and circumstance over which no control was available, neither to himself nor to the "lucky bastard" in question, he would today be free, perhaps a millionaire pimp with a string of high-class girls working for him.

The man's argument was not easy to confute; yet it did not stop Charlie from feeling revulsion and hatred. He hated Matthews for fleeing so willingly to the haven offered by psychiatry and by starry-eyed social workers such as Miss Ross. He hated him for his willingness to consider himself a pawn, a victim, for his love of self-exculpation, for these things and for the shattering fact that what he had done was to throw a seven-year-old child to the ground and rape her.

"Maybe they'll send you to the pen, Ellis," Matthews said. "You're just the type they like to get over there. Pretty boy like you."

Charlie listened, meeting his angry glare. Their two

numbed tablemates, eyes glazed, looked at their empty plates.

Georg Wilhelm Friedrich Hegel, with his plain face, a face without life or luster, aged prematurely, bent over his notes and his snuffbox, coughing frequently (in a later age, Hegel might have been a chain-smoker), bent over his desk, dipping his pen, and, in his laborious eighteenth-century curlicued penmanship, writing that *man must be punished for the sake of his own dignity, because only through punishment is he honored as a rational being, and anything less is to treat him merely as a harmful animal.*

And Socrates: *He who is punished suffers justly. The criminal who goes unpunished has no deliverance from injustice.*

Try *those* on Robert Matthews, Charlie told himself. He could well imagine the reaction.

Although the hospital maintained strict security and close vigilance, some of the doctors—not only Randicott, but others—had been attacked. A patient might simply hate something about a particular doctor or feel that one was especially vulnerable—and strike, knowing that there would be no severe reprisal, for he had after all been committed to a hospital for the criminally insane and was merely acting as one might expect.

Charlie pitied Robert Matthews for the torture he must have lived, the torture and fear that each day must have brought him in the penitentiary. Nonetheless when Charlie was near him he had a feeling of wariness, even of apprehension. As Matthews took his daily stand in the corridor, there was something in his eyes to be feared. He was watching those responsible for watching *him.* It was as though he was on the lookout for a sign of weakness, on the alert for someone who had lost a step. He had the look of a predator. He was like a lion watching a zebra, watching for the slightest sign of a limp, and, having spotted a weakling, following the herd, focusing on a bloody fetlock, a lagging hoof, content to wait all day, waiting for a place in the open where, with a short stretch-run, he can take the zebra down. In much the same way, Robert Matthews stood in the corridor, watching and waiting, with the same patience, the same focus. He was content to wait.

Charlie waited too. Looking from the window, he felt the beauty of the spring days, sometimes with a burst of ecstasy, more often with a rending melancholy. Each day had its bounds and opposites—of light and dark, sunrise and sunset, sleep and waking, of birth at morning, death at evening. At sunrise the ferryboat moved and at sunset it stopped. It was on this side, then the far side, then back again, and the rhythm of its crossing had the rhythm of the days.

Thirty-four

"THE STATE'S ATTORNEY has asked the judge to hold you in contempt for your unwillingness to cooperate," Frederick Sewell said.

On a Saturday afternoon, separated by the mesh partition, they sat face-to-face, Sewell in a dark blue sweatshirt, the sleeves cut off just above the elbows. Through the partition, Charlie could see ridges of muscle standing out along his forearms. As always Sewell's eyes had a look of cynicism, a look of seasoned bitterness. It was as if these feelings gave him strength.

"What would that change?" Charlie asked.

"Nothing. It was a stupid motion. The judge denied it. But I can see their point. Randicott obviously can't get to first base with you." Sewell shook his head. "What's holding you together, Charlie? When are you going to crack?"

"I don't expect to," Charlie said.

With a look of exasperation, Sewell shoved up the jagged sleeves of the sweatshirt. "Maybe you've found a home," he said. "Maybe you like it here. That's what Randicott seems to think. Do you?"

"Most of the time I don't feel that I'm even here," Charlie said.

"Well you are, buddy. Make no mistake about it. You are."

"Has a date for the trial been set?"

"Of course not. And it won't be until the doctors make a decision. You sound like you can hardly wait—are you looking forward to your trial?"

"I'm ready for it," Charlie said.

"Your day in the spotlight, eh?" Leaning forward, Sewell crossed his arms on the shelf. The tatters of his half-sleeves were like jagged pennants resting on his biceps. "Do you realize what you're up against? Maybe you think of it as your day in the spotlight, but there are people out there who'll be doing their damnedest to see that it won't be much fun for you. Carver's white-collar thugs want your ass and they want it bad. They're leaning on everybody they can lean on. You can bet your ass that by now they've been on the phone to the governor and God knows who else. And they're ready to hire a whole battery of shrinks to testify for the prosecution if they have to."

Charlie shrugged.

Sewell looked at him with disgust. "Sometimes," he snapped, "you seem so dispassionate about it, so God-damned above it all that you might think somebody *else* was on trial. But it's you, God damn it! You! And on the day you enter that courtroom I want to have everything possible going for you."

"I don't see that there's much to go with. They can't possibly find me insane."

"I don't expect them to. But I do hope for leniency. For

one thing, I hope to show Carver up for the son of a bitch that he was. I'm digging up all the dirt on Carver I can find and I've already got a truckload. How much of it the judge will let me get away with, I have no way of knowing, but I'm sure as hell going to try. I hope to get a jury to realize that you shot him for good cause, in a fit of passion that was entirely justified."

"It wasn't a fit of passion. It was premeditated. For God's sake! I watched a morgue attendant slide out a drawer and show me the raw meat of my wife's body. Months later I pull a gun and shoot Carver. It was premeditated. It was cold blood."

"Okay, Charlie, leave that part to me. You don't have to be everything in this God-damned case—the judge, the jury, the accused, the prosecution. Sometimes I get the impression that you're on everybody's side but your own. Sometimes, for God's sake, you sound like the prosecution. Look . . ."

Sewell sat back for a moment and then brought his arm down hard on the shelf. "You're here for a good reason. I didn't enter an insanity plea because I expected them to find you insane. I did it so we could get the psychiatrists' observations into the record—background material, your state of mind, emotional stuff that may appeal to the sympathies of the jury. Under the rules of evidence, that kind of testimony is not admissible unless an insanity plea is entered, so any half-decent lawyer will enter one even though it may be half-assed as hell. As far as I'm concerned, most forensic psychiatry is a lot of bullshit, but if it's there to be used then I'm going to use it for the benefit of my client, who happens to be you. Is any of this getting through to you?"

"Yes."

"What I want you to get through your head is that your position is not as hopeless as you seem determined to make it. Look, you acted under a compulsion—"

"I sure did."

"Okay, listen to me. A guy's a good citizen. Somebody

does something to him and he develops a compulsion to get even *no matter what*. Whether it's with a car or a gun or a slingshot, he's going to *get* the other guy. So he becomes peculiar; he becomes a loner, alone with his obsession. Am I getting through to you?"

Charlie nodded.

"He's made an obsessive decision, a decision not to follow the rules. He's okay in every other way, except that he has his obsession. Sometimes he's driven by unconscious forces that he doesn't even understand. And nobody can be conscious of an unconscious obsession. The law's aware of all this."

"There was nothing unconscious about it," Charlie said.

Sewell sighed with exasperation. "Charlie, you could get the gas chamber. Hell, maybe that's what you want. So you can join your wife, wherever she is. Do you feel that way? Do you feel you have nothing left to live for now that she's dead? Did she mean *that* much to you?"

Sewell's voice carried something close to scorn and Charlie guessed that Sewell's experiences with marriage and women had not been good.

"Is she all you cared about in the whole God-damned *world?*"

Charlie remained silent.

"You're like a man standing at the edge of his own grave, waiting for a little push."

"Okay, maybe you're wasting your time with me."

"Don't think it hasn't occurred to me."

"Why bother then?"

"For a lot of reasons. For one, because I hated Carver with an almighty hatred. Second, because I guess I feel sorry for you. And third, because I enjoy defending underdogs. And fourth, for whatever reason, because I like you. I think you're a basically decent guy and so do a lot of other people."

"What's being a decent guy have to do with it? I did something that I knew damned well was legally wrong, a criminal act. I expect to be punished."

"*Want* to be punished."

"Willing to be. What's so wrong with that?"

"What's so good about it?"

"What's life all about if people know they can kill or rape and get away with it?"

"C'*mon*, Charlie, c'*mon* . . ."

"What kind of society is that?"

"Oh my God! What are you trying to do, lead a crusade? Who in the hell do you think you are? Saint Francis of Assisi? Joan of Arc?" Sewell's voice was heavy with sarcasm. "You're being so God-damned noble you make me puke."

"I'm not being noble; it's just the way I feel."

"I wonder how you'll feel five years from now, in a penitentiary filled with human scum, human animals. They'll make your life a living hell. If you don't get the gas chamber, you'll wish to God you had!"

Sewell was on his feet, leaning forward, his face close to the partition, voice trembling. "They'll knock you around and slice you up. Get you down and kick you around like a football. They'll rape you and rape you some more and keep raping you until your asshole is a bloody running sore. You'll feel like you've died and gone to hell. You'll be like one of the poor squirming bastards in Dante's *Inferno*. You'll wish you were dead, and maybe someday, when you can't stand it any longer, you'll find a way to kill your fucking self. They'll find you hanging from a bed sheet in your cell. They hate guys like you. You'll be a sitting duck. You're the enemy. Try and think about it."

"I've thought about it."

"And how do you feel when you think about it?"

"Unafraid, for some reason."

Seated again, Sewell looked at him gravely. "Has it ever occurred to you that you *are* crazy."

"I don't think I am."

Sewell sat looking at him through the screen in silence.

"If you'd like to drop the case, it's okay," Charlie said. "Cut me loose—I'd understand. I wouldn't blame you. If I have to have a lawyer, let them give me somebody from the public defender's office."

For a while longer, Sewell sat in silence, as if seriously considering it. Finally: "No! God-damn it, no!"

From his attaché case, Sewell pulled out a yellow pad, covered with scribbled lines. "I've already started working on my closing statement to the jury, for God's sake. Just to give you an idea of the direction I hope to take, if we ever get that far, listen."

Slanting the pad to the light, Sewell read:

"Hamilton Carver was far from idle in the idle-rich sense; yet one has an impression of—idleness. And idle in another sense seems a proper way to describe him. Idly pursuing. Casually amassing. Idly corrupting. Yet always with a deep-burning desire. He felt he had a God-given right to enrich himself, to fill his hours, fill his life. No duke, no earl, hardly even a French king of the Middle Ages could have had more. At his disposal was an entire company of lawyers, a battery of accountants, an army of artisans for his houses, an endless number of caretakers, all members of his realm. And along with them, women in hordes, women at the ready, in Acapulco, in Nassau, in Nîmes, in New York—and always he was adding to their ranks. If he saw a woman he took a fancy to, he clapped his hands and she was brought forth for his enjoyment. His need for women, new women, *young* women, was insatiable. Could an Arabian sheikh with his harem have asked for more?"

Sewell slid the pad back into his briefcase. "One of those women was your wife, Charlie. For God's sake help me, and help yourself!"

When Charlie returned to the ward, the attendant told him that something had come for him and that Miss Ross had placed it in his room. On his dresser he found a single rose, deep crimson, petals closed, sprinkled with water, damp in its bed of green tissue.

Thirty-five

By NOW THE ROSE was on his dresser in a glass filled with water. The petals were closed. The deep crimson had a dark sheen, as if it had been bruised; yet by afternoon it had begun to open and it seemed a perfect rose.

He had been told that it had been delivered to the hospital by a boy from the village. There was no card, and he wondered if it could be from Daisy. Perhaps not; yet he could think of no one else.

For a long while he sat watching the rose, imagining that even as he watched, the petals moved, curving imperceptibly away from the center. This seemed impossible; yet it gave him pleasure to think it.

Toward late afternoon he asked for and received permission to be escorted over to the arts-and-crafts wing, knowing, because it was Thursday, that Jonathan Hayman would be there. Except for a guard who sat reading a magazine, Mr. Hayman was alone and seemed glad to see him. He looked up from his workbench, smiled, asked how he was, and bent again, intent upon the slim hull of the model boat he was fashioning.

He was a man who seemed far removed from Blaise Pascal's army of bedeviled wretches and listening to him, sometimes merely looking at him, gave Charlie peace. He had a thick shock of white hair. His jaw and chin might have been laid out with a carpenter's square and sawed from a block of pine. His brow had the same solid, squared-off appearance; yet this solid face did not go with the mildness of the pale blue eyes, nor with the frailty of his body, which once must have been so sinewy and tough.

He had been born and raised in Annsville and had lived in the same house all his life, a house built by his father with his own hands. As a young boy he took to the water and it became his life. Even in his seventies, he was still considered one of the best sailors in the area, perhaps on the entire bay. His specialty was racing Chesapeake Bay log canoes, workboats with slim hulls, and it was a miniature of a log canoe that he was working on now. It was a boat he knew well. His earliest memories were of going out in a log canoe with his father to take a living from the bay, racing the canoes out to the dredging grounds and then, when the day's work was done, racing them home again.

"Comin' out of the mouth of the Miles River at the end of day, somebody would start up and right then and there there'd be a race to home." Charlie enjoyed hearing him tell about it. "The boats would be down in the water some because of the heavy load of oysters, you know. They'd stand up and sail, but that's about all you could say for them. They wouldn't really go none. But day in, day out, going and coming, we'd race, and then on Sundays we'd race all day long."

Now he was an old man, approaching eighty-two, and yet even now in spring and fall he got out on the water in his small workboat, trolling the broad river, letting the gulls act as his scouts, often not bothering to wet his line until the screaming, circling birds signaled the presence of a school of blues or rockfish. Three days a week he was at the hospital, a crafts therapist, an artist with wood.

"Gettin' 'er now . . ."

He used a small knife with a sharp curved blade. On the workbench lay a chisel. On the shelves rested miniature boat models in various stages of completion. One had its tiny mast already affixed and several had their bowsprits. He offered Charlie the knife. "Like to shape 'er up some?"

"No thanks. I'd rather watch you do it."

Carefully he continued to take fine shavings from the hull, flaring its bow, pausing to squint at his work. On Charlie's previous visits, with others present, the old man had always locked away the knife and chisel, letting the men work with sandpaper and steel wool to smooth out what he had rough-cut. Now he continued to use the knife and left the chisel where it lay. Charlie knew the old man was not afraid of him. He accepted the fact that Charlie was one of the patients; yet he seemed to have lost sight of it just as he seemed to have lost sight of Charlie's crime, although he knew about it.

Because of his age and frailty he was sometimes ridiculed, insulted, cursed by the less tractable patients. He acted as though he didn't hear.

Now, laying aside the knife, he took a square of fine sandpaper and rubbed gently, following the flare of the bow. He held it up and Charlie nodded. "It looks nice," he said.

"Comin' good enough, I guess. . . . How they been treatin' you?"

Charlie smiled. "Good enough, I guess."

The old man smiled in return and continued to move the sandpaper with his gnarled fingers. He seemed content. Charlie had asked him if he missed the excitement of racing boats and he shrugged in reply. "Onliest thing a man knows how to do, he wants to keep on doin' it, I guess."

"How about your carving?"

"There's nothin' can touch sailin' none."

The attendant glanced up, then continued to turn the pages of his magazine. "Slow day, huh, Mr. Jon?"

"Few here a while back."

The attendant had not heard him. He was still turning the pages. "How do you feel about Liz Taylor, Mr. Jon?"

"Never gave her much thought one way or other." He chuckled. "She me neither, I guess."

"The widow ladies are chasing him all over town," the attendant said. "Isn't that right, Mr. Jon?"

"Wouldn't do 'em much good if they caught me, I reckon."

Hayman looked at the smoothly sanded hull of the boat, placed it on the bench and stood at the window. Presently Charlie moved to his side. The afternoon was bright and chilly, and the river was dark with wind. The ferryboat was nearing its slip. He shared Charlie's fascination with the ferryboat and knew a great deal about it. As they stood side-by-side, Charlie had the feeling that the old man was, in a very mild way, passing judgment on the ferryboat captain's seamanship—or perhaps, because of his love of boats, was watching it simply because it was a boat, and on weekdays often the only boat on the river.

Now, as the sun fell toward the Dinwiddie shore, Hayman began to talk about the ferryboat and what he knew of it. The ferry, in various forms, dated back three hundred years. Records showed that as far back as 1682 a Dinwiddie planter was paid five thousand pounds of tobacco as a yearly subsidy to ferry people back and forth. As Charlie stood gazing across the river, it was not hard to imagine the earlier Dinwiddie, which could have looked not greatly different in the seventeenth century. Ferryman and passengers crossed the same river. At sunset, when the ferryman boarded his scow and set out upon the return trip, he was gazing toward the same Dinwiddie, the same marshy, scalloped shoreline, giving way to open fields and strings of pine. Never had Charlie known a vista that could stir such feelings of stark loneliness, particularly when viewed at sunset. Surely to the ferryman, as he sculled his way slowly across so long ago, it must have had the same lonely, desolate sweep, the same look of a marooned land.

The spring twilight softened the sky. Mr. Hayman still stood at the window, looking out upon the darkening river, talking now of his early life, of the fierce winters, and of the water and of wild creatures.

"A wild goose lives a short time," he said, "and so does a fish and so does a wild swan and so too, the good Lord knows, does a man, only he don't always have an easy time lookin' at it that way."

Death was on his mind. At his age the years were swift. Winter and summer blinked on and off. Time was plundering his life. With deep longing he gazed at the dark river, and Charlie could sense his yearning to watch the years continue to pass, even though they might be only miniatures of the long years he had once known.

The mind of the attendant was on the hour. "Way past time, Mr. Jon," he said, rising. "You better get on back to your widow ladies. Time for me to take this man to his supper."

At supper, Robert Matthews ranted and fulminated in long arcs of obscenity, and Charlie could sense that he was frustrated to think that he might have as his audience only their two mindless tablemates. He asked why Charlie was late and Charlie told him he had been over in the occupational therapy wing.

"Doin' what?"

"Talking to Mr. Hayman."

"Who's he?"

"The old man who runs the woodworking shop."

"Talkin' about what?"

"Nothing very much."

Matthews ranted against occupational therapy and moved on from this to the customary targets of his hatred. Charlie managed to block out his voice.

Back in his room, he saw that the rose had opened. Its aroma filled the air. Again he wondered if it had been sent by Daisy, perhaps as an answer to his letter. Almost against his will, he found himself hoping that it had.

To think of Daisy, to think of Frederick Sewell's long harangue, was disturbing. He didn't want to think about them, and before he fell asleep he took pleasure in thinking of Jonathan Hayman. He found comfort simply in remembering the sound of the old man's voice. It was, he thought, something like the feeling one might get after being in the presence of prayer. The echoes of his voice filled the metallic silence.

He thought of the old man looking out upon the river and dreaming upon frozen winters long past, out on the ice long before dawn, traveling by horse and wagon in the moonlight, all the way out to the lighthouse, where he would cut a hole in the ice and pull up oysters until he had a wagonload.

Just before sleep, he saw him as a young man in a large, horse-drawn sleigh piled high with oysters. Charlie was with him, and they were traveling through the village, selling oysters from the sleigh and giving them away to the poor, going all around town many years ago in the fading blue light of a winter's afternoon.

Thirty-six

THROUGH THE PARTITION, Warren Donaldson's face was somber. He wore a raincoat; his head was damp; and he seemed ill at ease.

"I just wanted to say hello and see how you're making out," he said.

"That's very good of you, Mr. Donaldson," Charlie said.

"I feel rotten about the whole thing."

Charlie nodded.

"I keep feeling I might have been able to head it off," Donaldson said.

"I don't see how you could have," Charlie said.

"We might have been able to talk about it. Maybe I could have helped you."

"I wouldn't have told you anything. Believe me."

"Sometimes just one word, one key word. If I'd said the right word, you might have opened up."

"I don't think so," Charlie said.

"I spend a lot of time thinking about it. Brooding over it."

"Don't. You don't deserve it." Charlie paused. "I was

going to write you a letter and apologize for using you like that."

"You've got more important things on your mind now. There's one thing I do want to tell you, one thing you should know. Martha and I are being called by the prosecution to testify."

"I'm not surprised."

"We'll have to tell what we know."

"Of course."

"I may also be called by the defense. Freddie Sewell stopped by. He may put me on the stand to tell what I observed about you."

Charlie nodded. "He told me he might."

"It may help you. I don't know. We'll see. I'll tell what I know. When the prosecution puts me on the stand, of course, a lot of it will work against you. . . . I almost called you Mark."

"You can call me Charlie, if you feel like it."

"Habits are hard to break. . . . We had a good summer together in a lot of ways."

Charlie nodded. "Yes. We did."

"A nice peaceful summer. I have to look at it on two levels, of course. On one level you were using me for a purpose that turned out to be murder."

"I'm sorry it was you, Mr. Donaldson. You're the last person on earth I'd want to make a fool of."

"But on another level, before I knew what was going on, I was very fond of you, and I told Freddie so."

"Thanks, Mr. Donaldson. I feel the same way."

"We had some good days together."

"We did."

"I have to keep reminding myself that you shot and killed a man. It was like two different people. The one I thought I knew and the one that killed Carver."

"I understand."

"I've told Sewell that you never struck me as somebody who would ever do such a thing."

"I did though."

"Yes, you did. You did." Donaldson paused. "I have to tell you this. I hate what you did to Daisy."

"So do I."

"Did you ever honestly feel anything for her?"

"I felt a lot for her. I didn't expect to, but I did."

Donaldson nodded thoughtfully. "Well . . . you have a good lawyer."

"Yes, I think so too."

"Well . . ."

"How is the grass?"

"Already growing. With all this rain, all we'll need is a few warm sunny days and it'll be up to my kneecaps."

Charlie smiled. "How is Mrs. Donaldson?"

"Just fine."

"Will she be going to Europe again this summer?"

"As a matter of fact, we're both going. The doctor says it's okay for me to go with her. A cruise this time. It has to be early—because of your trial. We're leaving next week. The state's attorney said it would be okay so long as we're back by early June."

Charlie nodded. "If your doctor says it's okay for you to go, then that must mean you're over the worst of it."

"I think I'll be okay. As long as I keep taking my pills."

"Pronestyl . . ."

"Yes. Pronestyl. Good memory."

"I hope you have a good trip."

"Thanks . . ." Donaldson paused. "How is it here?"

"It's okay. Very clean."

"That's good." Donaldson was peering through the partition into the dayroom. "I see you have a TV."

"Yes."

"And a Ping-Pong table . . ."

"Yes . . ."

"Well . . ." In silence, Donaldson continued to peer into the dayroom. "God!"

"I'm sorry for what I put you through," Charlie said.

"I wish you luck."

"Thanks. And thanks for coming."

"Well, so long. Should I say, 'so long, old sport'?"

Charlie smiled. "I guess I was just trying to throw you off."

"You did for quite a while."

"Sorry."

"So long, Charlie . . ."

"So long, Mr. Donaldson."

Thirty-seven

ONE MORNING A NEW DOCTOR appeared at the door of his room, introducing himself as Dr. Valentine and grasping Charlie's hand in a strong grip. His dark beard was closely cropped, and his dark, glittering eyes were as deeply set as Randicott's were bulging. "It's nice to meet you, Charlie," he said. "I'd like you to come with me to my office so we can talk a little, okay?"

His office was much like Randicott's, one notable difference being an array of framed photographs that hung behind his desk. One showed a young man in the attire of a boxer, left glove thrust forth, the right protecting his jaw. Noticing Charlie's interest in the photograph, Valentine told him that as an undergraduate, he fought for his college boxing team, winning the 155-pound conference championship in both his junior and senior years. Tall, rangy, and spare, he still had the look and movements of a boxer.

Seated at his desk, he pulled open a drawer and offered Charlie a cigarette. "I don't smoke myself," he said. "I keep them here for the patients. If it helps you relax, go right ahead. No? Okay, good enough."

Replacing the pack in the drawer, he smiled. There was something about him both sympathetic and humorous, and

Charlie found that he already liked him far more than he had liked the formidable Dr. Randicott.

"Let me start off this way," he said. "What we're trying to do is learn something about the world you live in, Charlie. That's our job. Everyone lives in a different world. What's yours?"

When Charlie did not reply, he went on. "Around here it's become pretty obvious to all of us that you're here only in the flesh. Your true dwelling place is somewhere else, somewhere deep within yourself. A prison within a prison. Is that too much of an exaggeration?"

Charlie shrugged. "As I kept telling Dr. Randicott, I'm perfectly sane and always have been. To keep talking about it is just a waste of the state's time and money. There's nothing to talk about."

"Charlie, let me remind you of something. By order of a circuit court judge—Judge Gladding—the Maryland Department of Health and Mental Hygiene has been asked to determine first whether you are competent to stand trial, and second whether you were sane at the time you committed murder. That's the job assigned us, and we won't be satisfied until we feel that to the best of our ability we can offer authentic answers. You can say all you like, but the decision is ours to make, not yours."

"I understand all that," Charlie said. "It's just that I don't have anything to say."

"Yet in this inner world you inhabit, you surely say and feel a great deal. Is that a fair surmise?"

"Maybe."

"Are you simply trying to protect your privacy? Is that your objection to talking?"

"I think irrelevancy might be closer to it."

"I wish you'd let us be the judge of relevancy." Again the sympathetic smile. "Do something for me, Charlie. Starting at one hundred, count backward by sevens, okay?"

Charlie spread his hands. "A hundred . . . ninety-three . . . eighty-six . . . seventy-nine . . ." Picking up speed, he went on. "Seventy-two . . . sixty-five . . . fifty-eight . . . fifty-one . . ."

Valentine held up his hand. "Okay. Fine." Opening a drawer, he held up a rubber ball. "Tell me what shape this ball is."

"It's square."

Valentine nodded. With his index finger he pointed at the ceiling, then at the floor. "Which way is up, Charlie?"

Charlie pointed to the floor.

Valentine's eyes glittered with amusement. He began to laugh.

Charlie smiled.

"Atta boy," Valentine said. "Ask a foolish question, get a foolish answer, huh?"

"Something like that."

Valentine nodded, his eyes still showing his amusement. "Every man has his breaking point, eh, Charlie? Yours seems to be the ball."

In the two sessions that followed, Valentine talked to Charlie about his early life. Nothing important seemed to come of these discussions, although Charlie found himself liking the man more and more.

As the fourth session began, Valentine glanced for a while at a clipboard that lay on his desk, flipped a page or two, and then leaned back in his chair. "Okay, Charlie, you've had a while to think. Today let's do a little serious talking. Let's talk for a minute about Hamilton Carver, the man you killed. You killed him because you felt he was responsible for the death of your wife, right?"

"Yes."

"Okay, let's try to separate the elements a little. You saw Carver not only as the man responsible for your wife's death, but you also saw him for what he undoubtedly was —a greedy, money-mad, unprincipled ogre, not to mention a woman-chaser and satyr. Would you have killed him for these qualities alone?"

"No."

"Okay, let's take another slant. Let's suppose he'd been just an average guy, just some guy your wife fell in love with and left you for. Just a guy named Joe. Would you have killed Joe?"

"I don't know."

"I'll go on the assumption that more than one element had to be present. Is that a fair premise?"

"I don't know."

"I'm just trying to examine how single-track your motive was for killing Carver. Whether it was single-track at all. Whether it had the purity of purpose that you seem to give it." For long seconds, Valentine sat looking thoughtfully into his eyes, and then asked abruptly, "How do you like it here, Charlie?"

"It's okay."

"More than okay?"

Charlie shrugged.

"Is there any truth to the notion that maybe you like it a great deal?" Valentine's voice was gentle. "Perhaps better than you've ever liked any place in your life?"

"No truth."

"Well, perhaps better than your *recent* life?"

"What do you mean by recent?"

"That look you just gave me," Valentine said. "It was almost as if you were asking me not to say something. Not to hurt you."

He seemed ready to pursue this line of thought, then abruptly dropped it. "Listen," he said, "there's nothing so unusual about your liking it here. What the hell—we keep the place clean. The food's okay. Accommodations not bad. No need to say much. You have very little communication with anybody—aside from Old Man Hayman over in the shop. It's comfortable here. No responsibility except to listen to the questions of a bunch of damn-fool doctors and bleeding-heart social workers. The view is nice. You seem to enjoy looking out at the water."

Charlie remained silent.

"Then there's also the matter of your trial. The longer you stay here, the longer your trial is put off—and the longer your trial is put off, the longer you escape whatever punishment you face. It's nicer here than it is in the penitentiary and certainly a whole lot nicer than the gas chamber."

Valentine was up from his desk, moving lightly to the window, standing on the balls of his feet. His back was to the room, and when he spoke now it was as if he were speaking to someone else, or perhaps to himself. "Society has several reasons for sentencing a man to prison. Deterrence, which doesn't seem to work out as well as it might. Rehabilitation. Retribution. And confining a prisoner who is a menace to the community."

Still at the window, he turned. "Then there's the question of insanity. There is some argument for the belief that in the very commission of a crime, a human being is thereby and therein insane."

"Is that something you believe?" Charlie asked.

"Yes and no." He took a deep breath. "The Hinckley case stirred up the whole country. A lot of people think it was a rotten verdict. Maybe it was. Even so, we cannot ignore the possibility that at the moment a man commits a crime his judgment may be so impaired that he cannot be judged culpable. In such a case it would be a narrow act to convict him and send him off to the gas chamber. He should be confined, yes, but confined in a hospital and given remedial treatment. You may not agree with me, but at least there's more compassion in the way we go about things. In the old days you might have been strung up from the nearest tree."

He turned again to the window and with a sudden thrust raised it high. It was a mild day and some of the patients were playing baseball out in the yard. Charlie heard cheers mixed with derisive laughter. "Come on, Harry, heads up," Valentine shouted. "What's wrong with yez, yuh bum, yez!"

He stood watching for a moment longer, then, lowering

the window, turned with a smile. "Men under treatment, getting picked off first base." The smile faded. Once again he was grave. "Let's suppose that after a certain number of months a man has been treated, cured, and judged sane. Have we the right to continue his confinement? We do not. So we release him."

Charlie frowned. "So you release him and he goes right out and maims or rapes or murders somebody."

"Think about it. Let's take it in sequence. Number one, we have no right to punish a man judged to have been insane at the time of his crime. Number two, we have no right to continue to confine him after he is judged cured."

"You're for that?"

"It bothers me—but so does its alternative. It bothers you?"

"Yes."

Valentine nodded. "Okay, let me say it again. If an insane man commits a crime, we have no right to imprison him. If he is judged cured, no longer insane, many people believe that we have no legal right to hold him. How do you feel about that?"

"I hear what you're saying. The words have a flow; the sentences sound good. . . ." Charlie looked away. "I hear it with my ear and understand it with my brain, but something else tells me it's outrageous."

"I had a man who killed his mother with an ax," Valentine said. Even the other patients hated him. They'd scream at him, 'Mother-murderer, fucking mother-murderer.' They made his life miserable. I treated him for fourteen years. Last month I released him. He reports to me every day. I'm not afraid he's going to kill anybody with an ax. What I fear more is that he's going to commit suicide because of the tremendous burden of guilt he built up after he began to realize what he had done. Tell me something, Charlie. . . ."

Charlie waited.

"If you should be released, would you consider yourself a menace to society? Would you find it likely that you would go out and kill again? Maim? Rape?"

"No."

Valentine nodded. "The panel meets on your case in a week or so. The consensus seems to be that we've taken just about all the time we should take—so you'll be standing trial. There's never been any doubt about your competence to stand trial. Until the trial date is set, you'll stay right here, and that may be quite a while."

Charlie nodded.

Valentine went on. "I understand you and my colleague Dr. Randicott did a little talking about Blaise Pascal . . . how Mr. Pascal thinks we're all a bunch of walking, talking madmen, even the best of us. Who brought up Pascal? You or Dr. Randicott?"

"I guess I did."

"For any particular reason?"

"Just—in the context of insanity. Because he was talking about insanity."

"That was the only reason? Nothing more specific?"

"What do you mean?"

"Do you agree with Pascal?"

"No."

"Why was it on your mind? Can you tell me? Did you just happen to read it? Study about it in school? What? Something you'd rather not tell me?"

Charlie was looking at the floor. "My wife . . ."

"Yes?"

Charlie was still looking at the floor.

"Your wife what? Your wife believed it?"

"She may have."

"You'd rather not talk about it, right? You have the same look of pain you had a few minutes ago when I referred to your recent life. You asked what I meant by your recent life. I meant your marriage. Do you feel like telling me something about your marriage?"

"I don't see the point of talking about it."

"Is there a reason you don't want to talk about your marriage? Was it a good marriage?"

"Yes." Charlie looked up. His voice rose. "Yes!"

"Fine. I'm glad. What about your wife and Blaise Pascal?"

"What about it?"

"You look very uncomfortable, Charlie. Relax. Would you like a cigarette now?"

"No."

"What did your wife do?"

"She was an editor."

"Aside from that."

Charlie shrugged. "Ate. Drank. Slept. What do you mean?"

"Was she happy being married to you?"

"Yes, I think so."

"She loved you?"

"I think so."

"Did she like herself?"

"Not always."

"What was she unhappy about when she was unhappy?"

"I'm not sure."

"Try, Charlie."

"What's the point?"

"Who knows? Maybe none at all. Then again . . ."

Valentine moved from the window and placed his hand on Charlie's shoulder. "I'm not trying to make you uncomfortable, Charlie, but I know that I am. I'm sorry. Don't talk if you don't feel like it." He patted Charlie's shoulder and let his hand rest there.

The silence was broken by a loud cheer from the men playing baseball outside.

"She didn't think life had much meaning," Charlie said.

"Her life? Or life?"

"Life."

"She agreed then with Pascal. . . ."

"At times I think she did. But she fought it."

Valentine removed his hand. There was a bookshelf beneath the window. Stooping, he pulled out a slim volume. "Here's a little something I'd like to read you out of *Notes from the Underground.* Dostoevsky's man—Dostoevsky him-self, of course—says as follows: '. . . a man revenges himself because he sees justice in it. Therefore he has found a pri-mary cause, that is, justice. And so he is at rest on all sides, and consequently he carries out his revenge calmly and successfully, being persuaded that he is doing a just and honest thing.' "

Closing the book over his finger, Valentine said, "Would you say that has any relevance to you?"

"I don't know."

"The interesting thing," Valentine said, "is that Dosto-evsky sets that one up only to knock it down again. His man was talking about primal causes, searching for something worth doing. Early existentialism. He was searching for something that proved he was something as opposed to nothing, that man was something as opposed to nothing. You can see how it led to *Crime and Punishment.*"

He opened the book again. "Here's how he knocks it down. This comes right after what I just read to you. 'But I see no justice in it, I find no sort of virtue in it either, and consequently if I attempt to revenge myself, it is only out of spite. Spite, of course, might overcome everything, all my doubts, and so might serve quite successfully in place of a primary cause, precisely because it is not a cause. But what is to be done if I have not even spite. . . .' "

Valentine replaced the book in the shelf. "There's a certain link there to what Pascal was saying. It reminds us of Dostoevsky's man. In search of a primal cause for being . . . did you and your wife ever talk about having children?"

"She didn't want any."

Valentine was standing next to the chair. His hand trailed across Charlie's back and came to rest on his shoul-der. "Let's have another go at it tomorrow," he said.

Thirty-eight

THE NEXT MORNING Charlie was in the dayroom when Dr. Valentine appeared and led him to his office. On the way they passed Robert Matthews, lounging as usual in the corridor.

"How's it going, doc?" Matthews called out with a cheeriness that Charlie could not believe.

"Okay, Bob. How's it with you? Who's shining your shoes for you these days?"

As they passed on there was a burst of laughter from Matthews. "Shinin' them myself these days, doc. Like to have a turn?"

"Sure," Valentine called back over his shoulder. "Just leave them outside your door. I'll take it up with the hall porter."

When Charlie looked back, Matthews was still lounging against the wall, watching as they walked away.

Once inside the office, Valentine locked the door, motioned Charlie to sit down, and then himself took a seat behind his desk. "What kind of a night did you have?" he asked.

"Not too good. I didn't sleep very well."

"What were you thinking about? Would you like to talk about it?"

"Not particularly."

"Whatever you say." Valentine was studying the clipboard again. "I was just having a look at your test results. Your tests show that your IQ is very high." This, Randicott had already told him. "Your Rorschach tests show no pronounced abnormality." This, too, Randicott had indicated.

"This morning I'd like, if you don't mind, to give you another series of Rorschachs. Please bear with me. Please

262

refrain from saying that you see Dr. Randicott as a bullfrog on a lily pad."

Charlie smiled.

"Even though he may remind you of one . . ." Valentine sounded amused, as if he understood, perhaps even agreed.

A sheet of paper covered with inkblots lay on the table. Studying it for a moment, Valentine turned it facedown. "In your previous tests, you found a face in each blot," he said. "The face of a specific person. Was each of these persons known to you?"

"Yes, I think so."

"No snakes . . ." He smiled. "No hydra-headed monsters. No genitalia. No weapons; nothing suggesting menace of any kind. Would you say that your responses were deliberate? Perhaps I should say 'studied.' That is to say, were you consciously attempting to give responses that you thought might be considered normal? By your answers, were you deliberately trying to hide anything that might be construed as an indication of mental disorder, or disturbance of any kind? You're smart enough to. We both know that."

Charlie shook his head. "He told me to give spontaneous answers and that's what I gave."

Abruptly Valentine flipped the page, covering all blots but one. "Flash answers, remember. What do you see in this one?"

"The Snow Queen."

Valentine frowned with interest, studied the blot, and then looked up, still frowning. "Tell me why you see the Snow Queen. Who in your mind is the Snow Queen? And why are there tears in your eyes?"

Charlie wiped them away.

"What caused the tears?"

"I don't know."

"Then tell me who the Snow Queen is."

Charlie shook his head. "I don't know."

"It came quick as a flash. Think about it."

Charlie took a deep breath, studied the cleanly trimmed outline of Valentine's dark beard and looked away.

"Are you repressing it? Are you deliberately blocking from your memory whatever it is that caused you to look at a splotch of ink and say 'Snow Queen'?"

Charlie remained silent.

"Is it Hans Christian Andersen's Snow Queen?"

"I don't know."

"Do you know the story? Was it read to you as a child perhaps?"

"Possibly. But I don't remember it."

"Yet you gave such an immediate answer. No hesitation at all."

Charlie nodded.

"As I recall," Valentine said, "it's about a little boy who is bewitched by a woman, a beautiful woman known as the Snow Queen."

Later, in Valentine's office after lunch, the psychiatrist placed a book on his desk and riffled the pages. "This is the story of the Snow Queen," he said. "I won't read it because it's very long. I'll just skip here and there. Okay?"

Charlie nodded, feeling an uneasiness he could not explain.

"Its starting point is a huge mirror in which the world is reflected as a place of evil. The world and everyone in it —evil. Two ogres carry the mirror everywhere they go, all over the world, so that people are forced to look into it and see their faces. One day while they are carrying it through the sky, it shatters into millions of pieces. Tiny fragments fall to earth. People get bits of glass in their hearts and their hearts become like lumps of ice."

He looked up from the book. "Does it come back to you?"

Charlie shook his head.

Valentine looked down at the book again. "A little boy is watching snowflakes fall past his window. One snowflake becomes larger and larger and, before his eyes, it grows into

a woman." He touched the page with is finger and read:
" 'She was delicately lovely, but all ice—glittering, dazzling
ice. . . . Her eyes shone like two bright stars, but there was
no rest or peace in them.' "

Valentine paused. "Nothing?"

Again Charlie shook his head.

He continued: "She disappeared and not long afterward
the little boy's heart was pierced by a sliver of glass and his
heart soon turned to ice. One day while he was out sledding,
a sleigh passed through town, a huge white sleigh, and in
it, covered from head to foot with white fur, was the lady
who had waved to him from outside his window, the Snow
Queen herself. He hooked his little sled on behind the sleigh
and off they went, faster and faster, higher and higher, so
high that he was frightened, but he could not break his sled
free."

Again Dr. Valentine looked up. "Surely this was read to
you as a child," he said.

"Not that I recall."

With a look of doubt, Valentine continued: "After a
while the Snow Queen took the boy with her into the
sleigh. She wrapped him in her furs and he felt that he was
sinking into a snowdrift. By night in the sleigh they flew
high, over woods and lakes, over oceans and islands. The
cold wind whistled below them but up above, where the
sleigh flew, the moon shone close and bright. The little boy
flew through the sky all the winter night long. By day, he
slept at the feet of the Snow Queen."

Valentine paused, awaiting a reaction. When there was
none, he went on. "Finally the sleigh arrives at the Snow
Queen's palace, a vast snow palace lit by brilliant northern
lights. In it there are hundreds of rooms, each formed by
drifted snow and frozen into ice. The Snow Queen goes off
and the boy is left alone, marooned in the frozen halls of the
palace."

"Now . . ." He glanced at the book. "Back in the town
where he lives, the boy has a very close friend, a little girl.
All this time she has been searching for him. A reindeer

leads her to the palace. She finds the boy sitting in one of the icy rooms, rigid with cold. She embraces him; she sheds hot tears. The tears fall upon his breast and penetrate to his heart. The lump of ice thaws. He cries with joy. He has been rescued, and together they go back home."

Valentine snapped the book shut. "What do you see in this story?" he asked. "Why did you say 'Snow Queen'?"

Charlie sat rigid, not answering.

Doggedly, Valentine pursued it. "The obvious way of looking at it, of course," he said, "is that you were the little boy, in thrall to a woman who led you to your doom. Who was the Snow Queen?"

"My wife was not a woman of ice," Charlie said, "if that's what you're thinking."

Valentine let his reply hang in the silence and then said, "Let's turn it around a bit. Let's say that Hamilton Carver, in whatever sexual guise, is the Snow Queen and that your wife is the one bewitched, the one whose heart is pierced and turns to ice. That would make you the rescuer. The little girl."

"God!"

Valentine nodded. "It's comforting in any event to know that you're capable of a reaction. Let's say that Carver bewitched your wife and took her off to his mansion of ice. With her heart turned to ice, and with you unable to reach her, she—jumped in front of a subway train."

Charlie sat with head lowered, pulses racing.

"All of which left the Snow Queen still at large." Valentine tapped the book with his knuckles. "I would venture to say that at some time in your childhood you read, or had read to you, the story of the Snow Queen."

"Maybe, but I still can't remember it."

"Either interpretation has some relevance, I think. In both, you are a man whose heart has turned to ice. In the first version, there's a member of the triad that I can't place. Who is the little girl who melts your heart?"

"If your interpretation is correct," Charlie said, "it's still unmelted."

266

Valentine nodded. "Let me throw a few more thoughts at you. Is it possible that your wife was a woman of ice long before she ever met Carver? Was it possible that she was attracted to him because she saw in him a man even colder than herself?"

Charlie stiffened.

"Is it possible that you were married to a woman you could never thaw? Wasn't there great pain in being married to a woman of ice? Wasn't it tremendously frustrating? "You could not reach her. She was the Snow Queen."

Charlie could feel the blood rushing to his head.

"You realized that you had given your life to a woman who was incapable of love, who could never be thawed. Was Carver truly your target? Is it possible that you were trying to kill yourself? Kill the past? That you were trying to kill the whole frustrating experience of your marriage?"

"No! God-damn it! No!"

"She didn't have to go to Carver. She wasn't kidnapped. Carver didn't grow tired of her and kick her out. She left of her own accord. She killed herself because she knew she was not of this world." Valentine shrugged. "It's impossible to know all this for a fact. I'm simply speculating, simply raising questions."

Charlie sank sobbing into the chair.

"Who or what were you trying to kill, Charlie? In the process of committing murder, a man gives up his own life. Is it too much to say that he is committing suicide?"

Thirty-nine

CHARLIE HAD BEEN TAKEN BACK to his room and now sat on the edge of the bed, quivering, his body still damp with sweat. Abruptly he was on his feet, striding through the dayroom to the attendant's station, announcing that he would like to see Dr. Valentine. The attendant dialed a number, waited, hung up, dialed another number, and then another.

Charlie stood with his face against the steel bars of the dayroom, looking down the corridor, watching for the doctor, but the corridor was empty, even of Robert Matthews.

The attendant was still dialing. Charlie turned away and paced. The same men sat before the television set, watching in numbered silence. In a corner the whey-faced boy sat masturbating. Another patient stood at his side, watching with a smile and then laughing with glee as he reached his climax. Presently the whey-faced boy laughed back. They laughed together. The attendant approached. "Dr. Valentine is in a meeting," she said. "He'll be here just as soon as possible. Would you like someone else meanwhile?"

"No thanks."

He returned to his room. On the bed lay the photograph of Anne. He had taken it from beneath the mattress, folded it in half, ready to tear it, but unable to. The fold separated her nose from her mouth. Her smiling eyes met his. He remembered her as she had smiled each morning at the news vendor and strolled off to the office.

How long had he known? How long had he fought belief? He had loved her as he felt a man should love a woman, but she had lived in a world he could never know. She had lived in a dark place. She had tried virtue and found it bare. Loving her so enormously, he had tried to believe she was merely confused, moody, dissatisfied, a victim, and had tried with ordinary means to help, to discover the cause, to give comfort and wait, but its depth was far too great for him and would always remain so.

At Chichén Itzá he had felt the sadness of life—the sadness of the little men who, under the evil guidance of high priests, were willing to bear the utmost in savagery, willing even to sacrifice their children, all to appease nonexistent gods, savage, evil gods who alone were empowered to grant them immortality, all to convince themselves that they were not merely little ant-men filing up the side of a temple, men who would die and turn to dust.

Anne had felt something so entirely different. He could believe now that it was the very savagery of the place that she found appealing. She was fascinated, even filled with envy for the young girls who sat in the pagoda, breathing copal incense, waiting for the high priest to lift them high and plunge them into the sacred well. Lying on the altar slab, she had thrilled to the fantasy of her chest being sliced open and an eagle seizing her still pulsating heart. With the thrill had come a need, a desperate need to have him make love to her on the sacrificial altar while she lay back, looking up at the sky, watching the eagle with her heart in its talons.

Sex was the opiate that never failed her. He remembered the evening in the restaurant . . . her insatiable need for sex, her need to be ravished, asking him to do things to her body that he had done with no one else. Vividly he could recall the moment when, back at the apartment, having tried, he lay, his body upon hers, while she looked at him so coldly, her eyes expressing scorn for his naïveté, his insufficiency, his lack of cruelty, his inability to be the person she needed.

After she left Carver, five days passed before she threw herself in front of the train. Where had these days been spent? This was something neither her father nor he had ever learned. Obviously seeking something she still could not find. There remained only the subway train. Not the quiet death of sleeping pills or poison. She had to descend into the dark subterranean depths, enter a tunnel, and submit herself to a speeding train that in the dark would mangle her body, tear it to bits, the ultimate ravishment.

Dr. Valentine was in the doorway. Charlie stood up as he entered. Valentine noticed the photograph but said nothing. "Sit down, Charlie," he said. Valentine was looking at the all-but-nude stem of the rose. The petals by now had fallen off, and Charlie had carefully stacked them, fitting curve to curve. The little pile rested next to the glass containing the stem.

Charlie was breathing heavily. "Easy, Charlie," Valentine said. "Take your time. Don't be afraid. If we were getting somewhere close to the truth, it's far better to recognize it. Take your time. It's okay. It's okay." When Charlie still said nothing, Valentine moved to the bed, picked up the photograph, studied Anne's face, bent the photograph backward as if to remove the fold mark, then placed it carefully back on the bed. "God, what a beautiful girl!" he murmured.

"She was—" Charlie choked and could not continue.

"Cry. Let it all come out. Don't try to hold it back."

Charlie let his face fall forward, covering it with his hands.

"Easy . . ."

Down the hall somebody was playing a stereo. The sound swelled in a deafening burst of volume, then as quickly subsided.

Charlie sat up. His hand brushed the photograph.

"Okay?" Valentine asked.

Charlie nodded.

"Better?"

The trembling had stopped. His voice was under control.

"Do you have something you want to say? Something you want to tell me?"

"Only that you were right. She was a—bitch."

"How do you feel about it?"

"Sad."

"How long have you known?"

"Maybe a long, long time . . ."

"But you didn't want to believe it? . . ."

"I still don't." His voice rose and broke. "Still don't want to."

Valentine was watching him closely. "You thought that all she had was a piece of glass in her eye. But she had a lump of ice in her heart."

"How were you so sure?"

"I wasn't. I only suspected. Some of the things you said . . . cases I've known . . ."

"My God, if only I'd . . ." Charlie shook his head help-lessly.

"Don't take all the blame, Charlie. She was too much of a handful for you. It wasn't all your fault."

"Whose was it?"

"Maybe nobody's," Valentine said.

"I killed a man—and avenged nothing. God! *Nothing!*"

Valentine was holding one of the rose petals. "It's possi-ble," he said softly, "that in Carver she felt she had found the ultimate partner in depravity, and then found even him lacking." Valentine paused, "This sort of thing is not en-tirely uncommon, you know. You'd be amazed at the num-ber of love letters men in prison get from women who don't even know them, know only what they've done. Murderers, rapists, butchers seem to have a very special fascination for some women. *Mash letters.*" He shook his head. "Some strange things go on in this world, things that aren't quite comprehensible to sane guys like you and me."

Valentine patted his shoulder. "You're sane, Charlie—just as sane as I am. Good and beauty and sanity do exist. We may not be able to prove it, but they do. Something inside us knows it. Not to keep picking on Mr. Pascal, but he also said something else. 'The heart has its reasons that reason knows nothing of.' You were in over your head, Charlie. Where did the rose come from?"

"I don't know."

"Here." Valentine placed the petal in his palm. "Call me if you need me," he said.

When he was gone, Charlie sat for a long while on the bed, staring at the rose petal in his palm and at Anne's picture, not knowing what to do with it, wanting to tear it into pieces, but unable to. Finally, folding it again in half, he placed it in the envelope and slid it back under the mattress. Presently he went out to the attendant's station and received permission to be escorted to Mr. Hayman's shop.

It seemed strange to see Robert Matthews there. Mat-

thews seemed the last person in the world to take an interest
in model–ship building, but there he was at the workbench,
sanding a sliver of wood hardly thicker than a matchstick,
which would serve as a mast for the hull that lay nearby.
Mr. Hayman's eyes were on the tiny mast, watching as
Matthews moved the sandpaper slowly backward and forward, following the rounded surface of the mast. The chisel
and knife were not in evidence.

The guard looked up idly from his magazine, yawned,
said, "Hi ya doin' today, Ellis?" and with a glance at Matthews returned to his magazine.

Mr. Hayman wore a blue denim workshirt, buttoned to
the throat. His shirts were always clean, and they always
looked as if they had not been ironed. He smiled. "Treatin'
you all right, are they?"

Charlie nodded.

Matthews continued to sand the mast, at first ignoring
Charlie's presence, and then, his hand momentarily motionless, he looked at him with disinterest. Their eyes held for
a moment before he looked away and resumed sanding. "Be
gentle as you can with 'er," Mr. Hayman cautioned. "Don't
want to break 'er." Matthews scowled, perhaps merely with
concentration, but it seemed more. A large ceramic pot
filled with hot glue lay on the bench. "Little more, then
we'll glue 'er right in place. I think maybe that ought to be
just about enough."

Defiantly, Matthews continued to sand. "Like to do a
little something?" the old man asked. Charlie said he had
just come to talk a little. "Funny day," Mr. Hayman said.
Charlie stood at the window. Thick, scudding clouds over-
hung the river. "Weather got you down?" Mr. Hayman
asked.

Charlie nodded. "Maybe a little."

He heard a snapping sound and turned in time to see
Matthews toss the two halves of the fragile mast to the floor.
"Shit!" The corners of his mouth drew back as he said it and
for a moment his teeth were bared. Then all in an instant
he had circled the bench and was raining blows on Mr.

Hayman's face. The old man crumpled into a corner. With swift, shuffling movements, Matthews delivered the toe of his gleaming shoe to the old man's crotch, once, twice, then turned, picked up the pot of glue and held it high, ready to bring it down upon the old man's head.

By then Charlie stood between them. The pot crashed against his head and burst. Lights flashed in his brain. The hot glue flowed over his face, into his eyes. The old man was moaning, "Oh my Jesus God, oh my Jesus God." The guard's revolver was at Matthews' temple.

"Shoot it!" Matthews snarled. "Shoot it, you mother-fucker. God damn you, shoot it, you yellow honky son of a bitch"

In Charlie's skull the bright lights still flashed. With the gun still tight against Matthews's temple, the guard said, "Take the phone off the hook, just knock it off the hook," jerking the words from the side of his mouth, his eyes never leaving Matthews.

Still half-blinded, Charlie found the phone and knocked it from its cradle. As if by magic, a key clicked in the lock and four guards were in the room. Matthews, still snarling, kicking, trying to bite, was handcuffed. One of the guards was on the phone calling for a doctor, a stretcher, an ambulance. Another knelt at the old man's side. Within minutes the ambulance backed to the door. The old man was lifted gently to the stretcher and, surrounded by the guards, was carried to the ambulance. Matthews, still battling, was being jerked and tugged back to the main building. Charlie was forgotten.

Part VII

The Other Side of the River

Forty

THE FIRST DAY, exhausted, he lay in the daybed, listening, dozing, springing up with a start at the sound of tires on gravel. Looking through a slit between the drawn draperies, he saw a police car come to a stop in the parking lot. A uniformed patrolman glanced from the window, his eyes scanning the house. After a minute or two he drove off down the lane.

The electricity had been turned off. The refrigerator was bare and its doors stood open. The telephone too was dead, whether because service had been suspended or because of storm damage he had no way of knowing.

Thumbtacked to the kitchen bulletin board was a brochure listing the Donaldsons' itinerary. May 5, fly to Athens, thence by cruise ship to Corfu, Gibraltar, the Canary Islands, Grand Cayman, Montego Bay, Galveston. May 28, return home.

It was now May 15.

On the kitchen counter stood a portable transistor radio. He tuned in Shaftesbury's only local station and, with the volume low, heard periodically of the search of which he was the object. An all-points bulletin was out for his arrest. Householders were alerted, although police doubted that he was still in the area. The Mexican border was being watched at all points of entry.

The old man was in the local hospital's intensive care unit, in critical condition with severe internal injuries.

In the kitchen drawer, where he knew it was kept, he found a flashlight, and that evening he lay waiting for the long spring twilight to end and darkness to fall. Flashlight in hand, he was about to slip from the house when once more he heard the sound of an approaching automobile. Again it was a police car. Against the glare of its headlights he could make out the dull red glow of the dome. A searchlight swept the house, top and bottom. To reach the house he had walked twenty-five miles in the dark, arriving at two in the morning and entering through a cellar door that he knew had a faulty lock. The police had no reason to believe that this was his destination, and from the cursory inspection he was convinced that the Donaldsons had merely left a request to have the house checked periodically in their absence.

The car was backing, turning, and leaving. Its taillights grew smaller as it moved down the lane.

Waiting another half hour, he crossed the lawn, walked to the end of the dock, and looked across the cove. There were lights in the house and he could guess that Daisy, she or someone else, was still living there. Pointing the flashlight, he blinked it on and off, on and off, and waited, looking around the cove. At fifteen minute intervals he blinked the flashlight and betweentimes sat on the end of the dock, waiting. Toward midnight he returned to the house and slept fitfully, rising at dawn to wait for another day to pass.

In the long hours of silence he lay on the daybed, or moved from room to room. Sometimes he stood motionless, as if listening for the sounds that had been so familiar. Gone was the stately tick of the grandfather clock and the delicate chimes as it struck the hour. Its pendulum hung motionless. There was not even the hum of the refrigerator or the faint whine of the electric clock that hung above the sink.

In the library, spread open on a chair, lay a leather case with plush-lined slots, receptacles for cassettes. All the Vivaldi cassettes were neatly in place.

It was a house that had been filled with music, the windows always open, a house swept with air, washed with sunlight. Looking through the Dutch door that led to the porch, he could see the glass-top table where Warren Donaldson had sat with head bent over the morning paper, sipping his coffee and reading.

Shafts of morning sunlight.

The swelling sound of music.

Hardly aware of it, he had grown to love the house, just as without knowing it he had loved the summer. He stood motionless, wishing that he might relive the summer and taste the beauty he had been unable to comprehend because he had been so filled with bitterness and hatred.

Upstairs he stood at the threshold of the Donaldsons' room, looking at the four-poster bed, which was stripped of bedding and covered with a patchwork quilt.

He envied them their house, its sunlight and air and music and all their years together.

As he continued to stand there, he thought of Anne's picture, still beneath the mattress in his cell. Maybe by now it had been discovered; perhaps by now it hung from the wall of another cell. A pinup. Pinup girl. A face that one of the inmates might find as titillating as the shots of bare pink flesh surrounding it.

She had walked down the stone steps and stood motionless in the blue light, then moved in his direction, as though she had been sent by an evil hand.

The devil's pinup girl.

It was too harsh a judgment. Even now he was not ready for so harsh a judgment. He felt a stab of sadness, but it passed. She would always remain a mystery. Her secret depths he would never know.

Slowly he retraced his steps. In one of the kitchen cabinets he had found a box nearly filled with dry cereal. There were some crackers, grown stale. He was living on the crackers and on the cereal, sometimes eating it dry, sometimes pouring water over it, spooning it into a mash.

At five o'clock, listening to a local news summary, he learned that Jonathan Hayman had died during the afternoon. He drove his fist against the wall and stood for a long while, staring at nothing.

That evening, when it was dark, he moved once more to the end of the dock and blinked the flashlight. After fifteen minutes he tried again. The night was cloudy, without stars. A boat was approaching. It had turned in from the river and was well into the cove before he noticed the red eye of its bow light. Fearing that someone aboard might have spotted the blinking flashlight, he moved back along the dock, jumped off, and crouched behind the tall reeds that lined the shore.

On the third morning he was jolted awake by the roar of the tractor. A pickup truck stood in the parking lot, and a young man was backing the tractor from the garage. Killing the motor, he disappeared into the garage, returned with a can of gasoline, and filled the tank. Once again the tractor roared and, backing up to the house, began to move down the lawn, cutting the first long swath to the shoreline. Toward noon the boy left, but he was back again at one, on the job once more. In midafternoon the patrol car appeared. Watching through the draperies, he saw the patrolman get out and cross the lawn. The boy saw him and cut the motor. For a few minutes they talked, looking now and then toward the house. Finally, the patrolman turned, walked slowly back to his car, and drove off. By then the tractor was moving along the shoreline, edging the lawn where it gave way to the reeds.

After the tractor was back in the garage and the pickup truck gone, he sat slumped in Warren Donaldson's burgundy leather chair in the library, staring into an empty fireplace, scoured for summer until the bricks of the hearth gleamed. On the cruise ship and during all the weeks in the prison hospital, he had told himself that he had no choice but to accept the consequences of his crime. The revenge he had taken was hollow and the marriage he had treasured was a travesty; yet what did this change? Whatever the circumstances, he had committed murder, and murder in any civilized society demanded the ultimate punishment.

He had felt revulsion for Robert Matthews and all the countless others who had dodged justice, slipped through legal loopholes, copped insanity pleas. He had told himself that he was above them. He was not insane and not an animal. He was a human being who had known precisely what he was doing. His crime demanded punishment.

Yet now that he had tasted freedom, he was unwilling to give it up.

He remembered Frederick Sewell's words, pictured himself raped, battered, bleeding, crawling on all fours in the inferno of the penitentiary, living out his years in the anteroom of hell, and perhaps in the end slicing his wrists, as Robert Matthews had done to escape to the safe shadow world of Annsville.

He was not the hero, not the crusader that Sewell had so sarcastically painted him. He owed society a life, had a life to give. But now he yearned to keep it a while longer.

It was not until the fourth night that he saw what at first seemed an apparition, so long had he waited. Straining his eyes, he saw that it was unmistakably a sail, spread before the mild south breeze and moving in his direction. He raised the flashlight and the beam touched the sail. Soon he could hear the soft purling sound of the bow cutting the water. The sail dropped and the boat drifted straight for the dock. When it was close enough, he grabbed the headstay and pulled it gently alongside. "Is it you?" Her voice was tremulous, thrilled, frightened, all in the same breathless question.

"Yes." Quickly he stepped into the cockpit, ran up the sail, and shoved off.

"I thought I'd never see you again," she said.

"Let's get away from the dock."

Trimming the sail, she moved parallel with the shore, then tacked, and when she had reached the heart of the cove she dropped the tiller, letting the boat drift.

The sail rustled in the gentle breeze. Water lapped the hull. A late-risen moon, two nights past full but still enormous, moved in and out of the clouds, now painting the cove with brilliant light, now casting it into darkness.

"Daisy . . ." He sat next to her and her hand touched his. In its touch, incredibly, inconceivably, he felt forgiveness. Putting his arms around her, he crushed her body to his, saying, "Oh God, Daisy, I'm so sorry. My God, I'm so sorry."

In the moonlight, tears streamed down her cheeks. He folded her body close again and then placed her head gently in his lap. She was looking up at the sky, her tears glistening in the moonlight. "It seems like a dream," she said. "I thought you'd be a thousand miles away by now. Have you been at the Donaldsons' all this time?"

"Four days. Last night and the night before and the one before that, I went out to the end of the dock and blinked the flashlight, hoping you'd see it."

"I saw it last night and couldn't believe it. And then when I saw it again tonight, I thought it had to be you. Or might be."

"I had to see you before I left. Thanks for the rose. Was it from you?"

"Yes."

"I loved it."

"I have my baby now."

"That's marvelous, Daisy."

"The doctor says I'm well enough."

"Wonderful." He stroked her temple, kissed the tears that still glistened in her eyes.

"Charlie . . . ," she said softly. "It seems so strange to say it."

"I'm sure it does."

She lay quietly in his lap. The cove seemed swollen with water. Never had it seemed so beautiful. Never in all the nights of the previous summer had the surface been painted so brilliantly with moonlight. Shoals of silver. Streamers of phosphorescence, blue, green, white. The soft night air of May, the smell of honeysuckle, of earth. In one of the houses at the far end of the cove, a party was going on. Voices carried across the water. The sound of a piano, laughter, people fortunate enough to live in this most beautiful of spots, celebrating life on a night in spring.

In the cove's darkness there was beauty and light. For a fleeting second he wished that he could spend the rest of

his life in just this way, adrift in a magic cove filled with
darkness and moonlight and the soft sounds of night.

There was a faint splash as a fish broke the surface. His
eye caught a shooting star. He watched it fall and then
swiftly disappear still far above the horizon, high above the
rim of this bowl of water that seemed in the dark to be filled
to overflowing.

"What are you going to do?" she asked softly.

"Leave," he said. "Find a place somewhere . . ."

She grasped his hand. "Take me with you. Take *us* with
you."

"I can't do that, Daisy."

"Please. Why can't you?"

He sat listening then to the frail girl who lay in his arms,
her lashes still moist in the moonlight, the girl who was
telling him that she loved him even though he had murdered her father and now asking him to take her with him,
wherever it might be, asking him to let her share his shattered life, his fugitive life, asking him to help raise her child,
to be its father.

A father who had killed its grandfather.

She was trying to explain something that defied explanation.

"Daisy, my God! I killed your father! I *killed* your *father!*" He raised her head, holding it in both hands, looking
into her eyes.

"My father hated me, Charlie. I'm not sorry he's dead."

"That's got nothing to do with it. I did something insane. I thought I was doing something morally justified, but
I wasn't. It was stupid and blind. Blind evil. Pure idiot evil."

"Im not really sure it was," she said softly. "Im not sure
there's any such thing as pure evil—or pure good, for that
matter. You can say it was evil, but when you killed him you
set me free from a life of fear, a lifetime of feeling inferior
and hopeless. If he hadn't died, I'd never have been able to
have Cindy with me. If it was evil, look at the good that
flowed from it."

"But I didn't do it for that reason."

"Even so . . ."

"And what I did to you, the way I used you, was evil, God knows."

"But if you grew to love me, it couldn't have been evil. Certainly not to me. Please take me with you, Charlie. We can go anywhere you say."

"I'm afraid it wouldn't work."

"Charlie . . ."

"You'd be living with a fugitive for the rest of your life. Always running, always hiding. That's no life for your child, and no life for you."

"It's what I want."

"Im only trying to save you from a life of hell."

"I've already *had* my life of hell!"

His nails dug into his palms. Suddenly he was raging at his fate just as surely as Robert Matthews had raged at his. He loved this sad, vulnerable girl. He would like to be her husband, the father of her child, not merely for atonement but for the new start, the new life, the second life that would be so much closer to the life he had always wanted.

If only at some point he had known; if only, as Warren Donaldson had said, there had been a moment, a key word, a phrase that might have stopped him. Without his blinding, confused rage, he might have seen himself clear, seen Anne clear, and not murdered Carver, hated him but not murdered him. He would have had the vision to see Daisy for the beautifully rare human being that she was, and to see the opportunity she had given him to put a bad life behind him and live another. "I'm sorry," he said.

"Oh, Charlie! Even if we only have a year together . . . a week . . . a day. I'd rather have that than spend the rest of my life without you. *Please!*"

The breeze had picked up and the clouds were scudding, the moonlight flashing on and off.

"I only wish we could," he said.

In a panel of moonlight her eyes glistened again. "There's nothing I can do to change your mind?"

"I'm afraid not."

For another few moments she lay there in silence, then sighed. "I should be getting back to Cindy."

"I'd better be going myself. . . . Is she alone?"

"Yes. She's in her crib, fast asleep—I hope. I have her strapped in. It was the only way I could see you. Where will you go?"

"Who knows?"

"Just—run?"

"Not exactly. I'm tired of running. Just—find a place and stay put. Do what I can to live some kind of life."

"Will you let me know where you are?" She was sitting erect now and her voice was firmer.

"I can't promise. Don't count on it."

"Will you do me a favor?" She was on her feet, reaching for the halyard, raising the sail. "Will you let me show Cindy to you? It would mean a lot to me to have you see her. Do you need to go back to the Donaldsons'?"

"No. I've cleaned up my mess. Nobody will know I was there. Sure. I'd love to see Cindy."

In the stiffening breeze the boat skimmed the water, slipping in and out of the moonlight, headed for her side of the cove. "How about what's-his-name? The guy who shot me?"

"Harley? He's gone. Everybody's gone."

In another few moments, she dropped the sail and the boat glided to the dock. "Just let the sail hang over the boom," she said.

He stepped to the dock and tied the boat fast. As he helped her up she pressed his hand, and he followed her up the long slope of the lawn.

At the corner of the house he paused in the shadows. The parking lot was dark and her car stood at the front door. Looking at the house, he could see Carver tumbling down the stairway, his white shirt stained with blood. "Do you mind bringing her out?" he asked. "I'd rather not go in."

"Okay."

There was a light in the front hallway and another in the

285

room with the wicker furniture. He turned away and then a few moments later turned back as light flooded the parking lot. She was carrying the child and he moved forward to meet her. "She hadn't even stirred," Daisy said. "She's a wonderful sleeper."

In the floodlight he could see the child's almond-shaped eyes, huge, beautiful, luminescent eyes, looking at him without fear. "Cindy, this is Charlie—she's still half-asleep."

"Hi, Cindy," he whispered. "You're beautiful, Cindy." The child pressed her face against Daisy's shoulder. He reached for her tiny hand and she let him hold it. He touched it to his lips. "I love you, Cindy. And I love your mother. Very much."

"Oh, Charlie . . ."

For a moment he was in a faroff land, living in a house on a winding, cobbled street. The sea was nearby. Beyond the village stretched the soft green slope of a mountain. Happier than he had ever been in his life, he was walking through dappled sunlight and in his hand he held the hand of the child.

Then he had kissed them both and was moving away, beyond the parking lot, headed down the driveway. Her voice followed him. "*Charlie!*"

He walked slowly on down the aisle between the huge deodaras. He turned and she was still standing there, the child in her arms, motionless in the bright light.

The driveway bent and when he looked again she had disappeared.

He could see the stars clearly now. So tall and sheer were the trees and so deep the darkness that it was as if he were looking up at the stars from the bottom of a well.

He would find a hole somewhere in the world and burrow in, taking his camera into the world's dark corners. Having for so long now been one of them, he would perhaps have even deeper feeling for the dispossessed and the miserable, for those living in the gray area between life and death, good and evil, madness and sanity .

286

Inevitably he would be caught. Caught or killed. Inevitably there would come a day, sooner or later, perhaps very soon, when he would round a corner, or walk into his burrow, to find someone waiting.

The prospect no longer frightened him. To avoid death was never truly to avoid it but merely to delay it—for one more breath, one more glimpse, one more day beneath the sky, to see and hear and sense, to feel joy and misery.

He walked on down the aisle of darkness, beneath the ribbon of stars.